IF A MAN IS WORTH KILLING, HE'S WORTH KILLING WELL.

In the dentist's chair Frankie Minnick eagerly clutched his *Hustler* magazine and pored over the centerfold. The killer silently opened the office door and sneaked up behind him.

He drew back his stiletto, rose on his toes like a dancer, and riveted his eyes on a precise point at the base of Minnick's skull.

The killer struck with the full force of his weight. The knife blade described a flashing arc and disappeared into Minnick's neck like a stone dropped into the sea. The victim grunted from deep within his chest. His arms and legs shot out spasmodically on the sides of his chair. He quivered for a few moments then fell still, like an insect impaled on the pin of a cruel child.

THE ICE MAN

THE ICE MAN

WYNN L. MORGAN

A DELL BOOK

Published by
Dell Publishing Co., Inc.
1 Dag Hammarskjold Plaza
New York, New York 10017

Dell ® TM 681510, Dell Publishing Co., Inc.

ISBN: 0-440-14043-9

Printed in the United States of America
First printing—March 1979

PART I

And in death, they were not divided,
Swifter than eagles,
Stronger than lions.

—Samuel

CHAPTER ONE

The trill of a thrush rose clear above the dawn chorus. The killer woke to the new day with a toothache. He deliberately sucked in air and felt the acute discomfort from the exposed nerve endings within the molar's cavity spread throughout his entire lower jaw. After a futile search under his pillow and in the surrounding sheets for his gold filling, he decided he must have swallowed it in his sleep.

Rising naked from his bed he stepped out onto the balcony porch of his Westchester County summer home. It had been light for only a half hour but already the temperature was in the 80s. The wind chimes suspended from the porch roof hung as immobile as a pawnbroker's sign in the still air. On the lake below him water beetles skated helter-skelter across the glassy surface.

In spite of the nagging pain the killer performed his ritualistic calisthenics for a half hour before taking a cold shower, shaving, and dressing in summery sports clothes. He went downstairs to the kitchen to make his breakfast of oatmeal, three-minute eggs, toast, and tea with lemon. When he had finished he sat back in his captain's chair and gingerly ran his hand over the smooth surface of his throbbing cheek.

The killer fervently hoped the pain would diminish as the morning wore on. He had a busy day ahead of him. There was no time to waste visiting a dentist, and pain-killing drugs that might dull his senses or blunt his reflexes were out of the question.

To divert his attention from his growing distress, the killer went to his study and took down the first book he could lay hand to. It was an old favorite of his titled *Mind of the Roman.* A thin smile creased his swollen face as he gazed down on a passage he had underlined many summers ago when he had earned enough in his new profession to afford a country retreat. Its words, like entrails spread by a Delphic priestess before a fortunate supplicant, augered well for the day's mission: "A Roman was aware that there is a greater power outside himself of which he must take account. It is to this power he must submit himself. If he refuses, he invites disaster. If he subordinates himself unwillingly, he becomes a victim of superior force. If he accepts willingly, he is raised to an agent and instrument of that higher power."

The killer unsuccessfully tried to read the marginal note he had made on discovering this agreeable message. Its illegibility, he knew, derived from the fact that it had been written while he had been under the influence of amphetamines. His habit of making notes during a Dexedrine high had started in Korea twenty-three years ago when he began to explore the side effects of the tablets he used to keep alert on night patrol. At that time he had become convinced that there were valuable insights submerged in his unconscious mind, and that drugs might raise them to the surface of conscious thought like sporting dolphins exploding skyward from the ocean depths.

"Oh, bullshit," his wife had told him when he confided this theory to her one night shortly after his return from war. She was steeped in Aristotelian logic from a Catholic education that had stopped just short of a teaching sisterhood.

Before he had time to marshal his arguments, she turned and curled her warm, smooth buttocks against his loins so that their naked bodies were cradled like spoons. A suggestive wriggle by her and an exploratory thrust by him resulted in his discovery that animal desire alone had anointed her to receive him. He lost all interest in disputation as he mounted his crouching wife from behind and kneaded the taut nipples of her swaying breasts.

The killer tossed the book onto the library table. He admitted to himself that his skeptical wife had been right about the efficacy of amphetamines in promoting conscious reasoning. His indulgence in them had produced few perceptions. At best there had been embryonic ideas that might or might not have escaped more formal thought. He was not, however, an egotist. It occurred to him that the fault may not have been with his method. Perhaps his thoughts were like enfeebled dolphins, lacking the necessary strength and grace to surface.

The pain in the killer's mouth reached the point of agony on his return from a practice session in the pistol range he had installed in his soundproofed cellar. By eleven o'clock his right eye was swollen shut. He regretted that it was too late to head off the prostitute he had told to drive up from New York City. There was no trace of the sexual urgency he usually felt on such occasions. When just before noon the soft-spoken brunette arrived, he had been tempted to send her away until he remembered the value of established routine in acquiring self discipline. He had gritted his teeth as he spent his seed into an avid mouth that had unnecessarily ingested a birth-control pill with its morning's orange juice.

Left alone again the killer considered his diminished choices. He concluded that were he to carry out his mission without delay, he would be forced to gamble on submitting himself to autohypnotic techniques not yet quite mastered. There was no other way, he told himself, but to trust to the will.

The pulsating, repetitive rhythms of Ravel's *Bolero* grew louder from the killer's hi-fi. He darkened the study and took a seat in an Eames chair. Breathing deeply he pressed on the carotid artery behind his ear to inhibit the circulation of blood to his brain. Dizziness swept over him in waves. Twice he almost fainted as he halved his normal pulse rate.

The first phase was over. Suffused with joy the killer took a deep breath and closed his eyes. The throbbing music merged with his heartbeat. He pictured an image of a black dot on a white background. Soon the dot came closer; its circumference expanded outward until the rim of remaining white was like the luminous corona of a total eclipse.

The blackness conquered light. The killer's mind hung precariously by a thread above the abyss of consciousness. It began to whirl violently as if caught in the vortex of a hurricane. Suddenly all sensation of movement ceased. He was on the other side of time, merged completely into the immense stillness.

The killer's powerful hold on the arms of the chair slackened. For ten minutes he concentrated on his face. Over and over again he commanded his mind that it make the swelling subside and the pain vanish. He struck a match and turned toward a framed mirror on the wall. His cheek had resumed its normal shape. He poured a glass of ice water from a silver pitcher and washed the liquid over the tooth cavity with his tongue. There was not the slightest sense of pain.

The killer's will had triumphed. He got up calmly from the chair and drew open the drapes to allow the sunlight to flood in. All that remained was to gauge the extent of his mastery over self. Without the final test, doubt, the implacable enemy of the will, would grow and spread like a malignant tumor.

The killer sterilized the nail with another match, and placed a white towel on his desk. Placing his forearm palm up upon the absorbent material, he drove the nail into an artery. Blood spurted like a fountain onto the towel, and soaked in like seafoam on sand.

His eyes riveted on his impaled forearm, he willed his blood to cease flowing. The fountain shrunk and subsided to a bubble which he wiped away with a handkerchief. Removing the nail, he studied the puckered hole with interest. He closed it and opened it like the pupil of an eye. Then three times he turned the blood flow on and off before resealing the hole. As he carried the crimson-stained towel to the bathroom hamper, he reveled in his ecstasy. The self-induced hypnotic state was the deepest he had ever achieved.

It would not, he was certain beyond knowing, fail him in the hours to come.

At one o'clock the killer dined on a light lunch of asparagus vinaigrette, fresh fruit, and mineral water. Afterwards he dressed in the costume he had assembled item by item in shops throughout New England, then put on makeup and colored contact lenses to alter his appearance. It struck him that in the intense heat his makeup might run, so he ordered his face and neck to desist from sweating. Finally he tried on a pair of surgical gloves he had purchased to give him more sensitive control over his silencer's hair trigger.

The killer drove his blue Ford out of his garage at two o'clock. He had gone only a few hundred yards when he slammed on the brakes to avoid hitting a little girl who had chased her beach ball into the road. The girl smiled sheepishly at him, retrieved her ball, and rejoined her companions on their way to the lake.

Accelerating, the killer switched on the car radio to listen to the weather report at the end of the news. A forecaster on WNYC confidently predicted that there would be no respite from the heat spell that tormented the inhabitants of the city of New York.

CHAPTER TWO

Pete Bremner, a wonderfully fit man in his mid-30s, glanced up at the tailing motorcycle policeman in his rear-view mirror and eased off the gas pedal. All he needed, he told himself, was to be nailed by a rube cop on the Sawmill River Parkway and have to submit to a possible search.

The motorcycle policeman swept by Bremner's cream-colored Chrysler Imperial in pursuit of a driver ahead who was recklessly swerving in and out of traffic. As Bremner watched the motorcycle disappear he idly wondered how much the policeman earned shaking down motorists who had violated the law and were willing to bribe to avoid a court appearance. An ex-cop Bremner knew casually swore that he cleared fifty dollars a day when on duty on the New York State Thruway.

Bremner mopped his deeply tanned brow with the back of his hand. Wishing to look fresh on arrival at his destination, he was tempted to roll up the windows of the car and switch on its air-conditioning system. However the fear of catching a summer cold was stronger than his vanity.

Five years ago good health had become a religion to Bremner. His faith rested on the foundations of proper diet, regular exercise, and the avoidance of sudden changes in body temperature. Like the faith of all late converts, it was more deeply felt for having been missing until conversion. He had even resolved to make his new religion a part of his everyday life. When his accountant spoke to him of the need of depreciating assets to offset his investment gains, he first bought a ranch in Virginia to raise cattle, then built up a trucking company to distribute his beef and others's natural foods. So greatly had his health-food business prospered, that when the current recession ended he planned to go public and become a multimillionaire.

A quarter of an hour later Bremner turned off the Sawmill River Parkway into the long, winding driveway of the Four Winds Motel. He glided past the crowded pool area on his way to the pastel-colored bungalows behind the main building. Any worries that he might have been observed arriving at the motel were dispelled by a glance at the slumberous guests lounging around the pool. At the inflated prices they were paying for their afternoon pleasure, they were not likely to bother noticing the comings and goings of a total stranger in a pale Chrysler Imperial.

As Bremner's car passed by unobserved, the poolside guests noticed instead those things that poolside guests tend to notice. The bald insurance salesman with the hairy shoulders who was seated on a stool at the ersatz bamboo bar, for example, noticed that the bartender had put gin in his tonic when he specifically ordered vodka. The redheaded hooker with silicone breasts, who was floating face up on a rubber raft in the pool noticed the hirsute insurance salesman. She hoped the bartender wouldn't steer him to her because hairy shoulders turned her off. The solicitous husband rubbing greasy suntan lotion into the undulating folds of his ample wife's fleshy back noticed the drifting redhead. He fantasized a tempestuous scene in a snowbound ski chalet in which the auburn-haired lovely writhed in passionate abandon beneath his wildly thrusting, adulterous loins.

Bremner halted his car in front of Bungalow 11 and, before stepping out, he studied the maroon Mustang convertible parked in its carport. Although he knew it was unlikely that the maroon Mustang convertible could have been any other car than the one he expected to see, he checked out its license plates. Satisfied he straightened his beautifully cut blue blazer over his shoulder holster, fluffed up his wavy hair with his palm, strode to the bungalow door, and, without knocking, stepped noiselessly inside.

Bremner set the chain lock behind him and surveyed the empty room. Puzzled, he called out softly, "Ginny?"

The bathroom door swung open and Bremner whirled around like a cat to see the blur of white terrycloth and escaping strands of shimmering blond hair.

Ginny Jackman, a year out of her teens, tall, bigbodied, stood there framed in the doorway wearing only a smile and a towel turban. One made her look more youthful; the other more statuesque. Still wet from her shower she exuded freshness and vitality. Striding straight at Bremner she locked her arms around his neck and drank him in. "I like the way you smell," she said.

Bremner thought about that a moment and managed a grin. His arms encircled Ginny's narrow waist, and he jerked her roughly against him. She rose gracefully on her tiptoes to trap his growing erection between the inverted V of her long legs. They rocked back and forth with Ginny enjoying it even more than Bremner.

Suddenly Bremner pulled away from the young girl and glared down at his shirt and trousers. "Hey, you're getting me all wet," he complained. "Go dry off, will you."

Ginny slowly removed her turban. Her golden hair cascaded to her freckled shoulders. Blowing her irritable guest a kiss, she turned back toward the bathroom.

"Don't take forever," Bremner warned, watching her dimpled buttocks grind together as she imitated a striptease artist going off stage.

Over her shoulder Ginny assured him, "Joey's working late tonight."

"A hard worker. I like hard workers." To himself Bremner added, since Joey Jackman managed a trucking terminal of his on Charles Street in Manhattan, "Especially when they work for me."

"I already ordered our drinks," Ginny informed him when she reached the bathroom door. "I told them only fresh lime juice and no sugar in yours." She closed the door modestly behind her.

"Such concern," Bremner muttered. With his missionary zeal about good eating habits, he would have been more pleased had Ginny foregone the teeth-destroying sugar too.

Bremner turned off the room's air conditioner before undressing in front of a full-length mirror. He couldn't understand how some people were so damn careless about their health. His disapproving frown disappeared at the sight of the reflection of his hard-muscled body. Forgetting all about the hazards of overly chilled rooms, he grew full of self-approval. Humming, he flexed his pectorals, teased his nipples until they hardened, then lovingly patted his flat stomach.

A discreet knock at the front door interrupted Bremner's preening. He started toward the chair over which he had neatly draped his shoulder holster.

"Room Service," came an impatient voice from outside.

Snapping his fingers, Bremner remembered the ordered drinks. He wrapped a towel around his midriff, advanced to the door, and opened it a crack, leaving the chain lock on. He craned his head around to see who was there.

The ugly snout of a silencer was thrust through the opening against Bremner's forehead. The hand clenching the gun butt was sheathed by a surgical glove.

For a fraction of a second Bremner considered slamming the door and diving to the floor, but he knew he was beyond help. Instead the victim stared fixedly at the impassive killer who stood absolutely still in his waiter's uniform.

Bremner shut his eyes and bowed his head. At least his mourners would view an unmarked face. The last sound Bremner heard was Ginny melodiously singing a tune from *Candide* as she senuously brushed out her long golden hair.

The slug from the killer's weapon bored into Bremner's skull like a worm. The killer withdrew his weapon and slipped it in the cummerbund beneath his white jacket. Bremner sank slowly to his knees.

Inside the bathroom Ginny daubed herself with perfume and slipped into the baby-doll outfit which Bremner had bought for her. Her pale nipples jutted out from the holes cut in the bra and, glancing down, she could see her pubes protruding from the frilly, split crotch. She felt utterly ridiculous and wished she had not promised Bremner she would wear the garment for him. Like many uninhibited women, she disliked kinky sex.

Sighing deeply she rearranged her expression into a smile and marched out into the bedroom. She stopped short when she saw Bremner awkwardly kneeling against the front door.

Ginny moved hesitantly toward Bremner. Just as she reached him, he flopped onto his back. She stared at his wide, vacant eyes. The streaks of blood staining his cheeks made him look like a slain painted warrior. She opened her mouth to scream but no sound issued from her parched throat. Her face turned red with exertion. The cords stood out on her neck. Finally the scream came full blown and deafeningly loud.

By then the killer's blue Ford had slipped serenely and unobserved out of the Four Winds Motel's driveway. It entered the flow of traffic on the Sawmill River Parkway and merged smoothly with the great swarm of cars racing south to Manhattan.

CHAPTER THREE

Shimmering heat waves rising from the pavement caused a curious optical distortion for John Slade. When he shifted his weight from foot to foot, the eyes of the dummy in the clothing store window appeared to follow him, like those of Christ's on souvenir Saint Veronica handkerchiefs.

Slade stood flat-footed and blinked. The dummy's cold blank eyes assumed their fixed and lifeless stare. The craggy-faced lieutenant could concentrate on the cool, elegant, Italian silk suit the dummy wore as it stood ankle-deep in a sea of phony ice cubes. Above its head an ornate sign proclaimed:

THIS SUMMER TREAT YOURSELF
TO THAT FRESHLY CHILLED LOOK!

The copy stank, he thought. It sounded like something his bird-brained ex-brother-in-law had written before leaving the agency to become advertising manager of Brooks Brothers at twice his already swollen salary.

Still, he conceded, the silk suit was handsome. He fingered his rumpled jacket. Its unfashionable cut made his heavy frame seem even thicker, and the material was far too bulky for a New York City summer with a heat spell. He cocked his head and squinted to read the Italian job's $425.00 price tag, almost hidden in the wash of bogus ice cubes. Four hundred and twenty-five dollars plus sales tax. Glancing at his jacket again he saw the sleeves had started to fray. Mental arithmetic told him the suit he wore was seventeen months old.

Money provided more than freedom from want, he thought. It also gave freedom from *shlock*. When a financially hard-up man bought clothes, appliances, cars, food, or even investments on time, he received junk for his money. When a rich man shopped for the same items he purchased quality. In the long run the rich lived more economically than their less fortunate fellowmen by shunning shoddy goods with built-in obsolescence, horrendous side effects, and swift depreciation in value.

Frowning he continued his walk west along 8th Street. The memory of his ex-wife's successful brother and his own current inability to afford a new suit annoyed him so much that he failed to notice the dark Chevrolet which had been following him for a block. As he reached Sixth Avenue the car lurched forward toward the curb and pulled up beside him. Joe Davis, a black man with glowering eyes, sat ramrod straight behind the wheel. He leaned swiftly across the front seat and opened the door. "I've been looking for you," he said.

Slade scowled and slid into the car. Davis roared abruptly off into traffic without signaling, forcing a motorist behind to brake sharply. "I don't go on for another half hour," Slade said.

"The duty sheet says you're on at four o'clock,"

Lieutenant," Davis replied.

"Then the goddamn duty sheet is wrong."

"I read it right."

Slade glanced sideways at Davis's ebony face. It had the forceful simplicity of a woodcut—and little more animation. It was characteristic of the younger detective to insist on the correctness of his reading of the duty sheet rather than the accuracy of its contents. Others might make mistakes but Davis prided himself on being free of error. His behavior reminded Slade of his own younger son James's when the boy had studied the piano many years ago. Despite James's lack of musical ability, he had practiced obsessively simply for the pleasure of playing a piece through without a wrong note.

"What's on your mind?" Slade asked.

"We got a loud squeal. Some guy in a motel in Riverdale got plugged. Climbing into the saddle with a broad."

"What's it got to do with us?"

"Dispatch said it was Special Squad. The stiff's name was Pete Bremner."

Slade was about to inquire if the dead man was *the* Pete Bremner, but he saved his question until he met his friend Detective Howie Fine at the Four Winds Motel.

"That's right, John, Pete Bremner, fastest gun in the West Bronx," the balding, saturnine Detective Fine replied.

"Got anything on it?"

Fine shook his head and shrugged his huge shoulders. Slade had thought on meeting him that he might be a weight lifter gone to seed, but Fine had explained that he had built up his body *shlepping* carcasses around in his father's butcher shop in Queens.

Fine led Lieutenant Slade and Detective Davis toward a cordoned-off area around the murder-scene bungalow. "Opened the door and took one smack in the head, it looks like," Fine said, then, catching Slade's troubled expression out of the corner of his eye, added, "Not every day a top hammer gets taken out. Tommy Luce is going to be mighty unhappy when he hears his favorite nephew's dead."

The three police officers slowed their pace to allow a group of patrolmen to clear a path for them through some curious children from the pool area. "Eddie Cassell isn't going to be too elated either," Slade noted. "Pete was married to one of his homelier daughters. I think they had a litter going."

"So Tommy and Eddie'll sit *shivah* together," said Fine as the three detectives entered Bungalow 11.

A patrolman, with eyebrows that grew together like a bayonet guard over his hooked nose, hastily rose in embarrassment from the bed on which he had been lying with his shoes on. He hurried across the room to the color TV and switched off the Mets game.

"Who's winning?" Slade asked.

"Two to one Dodgers, bottom of the ninth," the patrolman replied sourly. He had a heavy bet on the outcome and had hoped to see the ending.

Two morgue attendants wheeled a stretcher with the covered corpse of Pete Bremner on it toward the three new arrivals. Fine stepped forward and with a flourish of his hand drew back the sheet. Everyone near stared at the corpse's wide-eyed face until Fine let the sheet flutter down.

The motel manager, dressed incongruously in

striped trousers and a cutaway coat, entered the room a moment after the attendants and their charge departed. He looked with ill humor at the dust the fingerprint expert had laid down everywhere and demanded, "When can I have this mess cleaned up? I'd like to rent this bungalow tonight."

"The former occupant has until noon tomorrow to check out," Slade said. "Officially, that is."

The manager grimaced. "The lady rented it," he said like a school teacher correcting his dullest pupil. "Under the circumstances, I hardly think she wishes to retain it until check-out time tomorrow."

Slade stared the manager down. "You can never tell. Not everyone's sentimental like you and me. She might want to entertain someone else."

The manager's eyes narrowed. "What, may I ask, are you implying?"

Slade ignored the question and asked another instead. "She rent it often?"

"A few times."

"How often is a few times?" Davis asked.

The manager turned his head toward his new interrogator. There was, he decided, something distinctly menacing about him. His razor-creased trousers, starched shirt, highly polished shoes, and military carriage contrasted sharply with the easy-going manner of the other detectives. "I don't have to answer *that* kind of question," he replied haughtily.

"Look, bright eyes," Slade snapped, "you're a witness, not a suspect. Keep pissing us off with those kind of remarks, and we'll book you downtown as an accomplice."

The manager recoiled as if he had been slapped. "You don't have to get touchy. She's been renting the premises every Thursday for the last two months. What she used it for is simply not . . ."

"Same time, same guy?" interrupted Davis.

Sagging visibly the manager nervously tugged at his fleshy earlobe and said softly, "As far as I was able to ascertain, the gentleman—the unfortunate gentleman—was her only visitor. He arrived each Thursday promptly at three o'clock."

The three detectives exchanged glances. The manager retreated for the door saying, "If you no longer require me, I've got to get back to the desk."

When the manager closed the door behind him Slade said, "Runs a tight hot-pillow joint."

Fine wagged his head and said with mock severity, "You guys should be more polite to a public citizen."

A few minutes later the three police officers emerged from Bungalow 11 into the brilliant afternoon sunlight.

"Where's the girl?" Slade asked Fine.

"At the pool with the precinct detectives. They couldn't get a straight answer out of her. You want to give it a try?"

Slade nodded. The three detectives moved slowly toward the pool. Several of the children who were still hanging around started to trail them. Fine winced when he heard one call him Kojak and wished that he had worn a hat.

Slade spotted Ginny seated at a table isolated from the other guests. She was smiling through her tears at the youthful precinct detective, Sid Goldin, while his older, less sympathetic-looking colleagues vied with him for the beautiful girl's attention. Seeing Slade approach, Goldin rose and came quickly forward to intercept the senior officer for a private word. "The girl didn't see a thing. She was in the bathroom when the shooting occurred. She's really broken up."

"Love is hell," Slade said. "What about her husband?"

"We checked. He didn't leave his office all afternoon."

While Fine and Davis hovered about the table Slade took a seat facing the distraught Ginny. Her wide-eyed, innocent smile faded as she regarded Slade suspiciously. It was obvious to both of them that neither was a fool. Nevertheless Ginny cast a look of appeal at Goldin, who smiled back at her encouragingly.

"The Four Winds your only meeting place?" Slade asked after introducing himself.

Ginny looked blank.

"To be alone?" he added.

"This was it."

"You're sure?"

"Pete had a thing about this place. He was big on personal hygiene. He liked the way they laundered the sheets and put paper wrappings on the toilet seat. An anal compulsive."

Slade suppressed a smile. The times they were a-changing. Cops spouted sociology, cons penology, witnesses psychology. Half the city of New York practiced psychiatric medicine without a license.

"Why did Pete open the door?" Slade demanded.

Ginny shrugged her shoulders helplessly. She became agitated and twisted her damp handkerchief. Then she recalled, "Room Service. I'd ordered drinks."

Slade clasped his hands, formed a steeple with his forefingers, and tapped his lips with it. He signaled

Fine with his eyes, and the big balding detective ambled off wordlessly toward the bar.

"Always have drinks first?" Slade wanted to know.

Ginny started crying. Slade, without averting his eyes, waited for the sobs to subside. Before they did, Fine returned. "She called for frozen daiquiris," he reported. "Usual order. Bremner was iced before they were."

Ginny's crying turned to hysteria. Several of the guests nearby who had been seeking an excuse to gawk at the statuesque blonde turned around and stared.

Fine, sorry for his callous remark, leaned over the table toward Ginny to tell her softly, "Easy, easy. Pete never knew what hit him."

Ginny's hysteria ceased abruptly. She said loudly, "I'm going to know what hit me when my husband finds out."

For a long while the only sound to disturb the ensuing silence was the bartender shaking a Tom Collins for an already inebriated guest. Slade got to his feet and looked from Ginny to the young Detective Goldin. Goldin stared down at his scuffed loafers, chagrinned. Slade, followed by Fine and Davis, walked out of earshot of the table.

"Snow White she isn't," said Slade, "but I'd say she's for real."

Fine scratched his head and examined his fingernails for traces of falling hair. "Maybe she didn't set him up," he conceded, "but it still doesn't make sense. The Big Four are supposed to be at peace. Besides, Pete worked for Luce and was Cassell's son-in-law, so that lets them both out. Bill Strauss doesn't go in for that kind of mayhem, and Matthew Julian doesn't have the muscle."

Davis suggested that a small outfit outside the alliance of the Big Four might be responsible for Bremner's death. "There's always the Bonellos. They're always on the outs."

"No," Slade said flatly. "Nick Bonello and his tribe have been behaving itself."

"*Themselves*," corrected Fine, who before joining the police force had toyed with the idea of becoming a high school English teacher. "If it isn't some outsiders like the Bonellos, we're left with the Big Four. And as far as we know none of them has a reason to rumble."

"Since when do they need a reason?" Slade asked.

Fine nodded in agreement. Davis, smarting from Slade's abrupt dismissal of his suspicion about the Bonellos, refused to acknowledge the question.

The three detectives were heading back toward their cars when they heard the shouting at the pool and rushed there across the lawn. As they approached they could see Detective Goldin restraining a long-haired young man in a seersucker suit as he struggled to get at Ginny Jackman. It was not difficult to figure out that the irate young man in Goldin's grip was Ginny Jackman's husband.

Slade gripped Joey Jackman by the shoulder and spun him around. "That's enough," he said.

"I'm going to break that whore's head," Joey Jackman shouted.

Slade poked a finger toward Joey Jackman's face in a gesture that was intended both to silence and intimidate him. "You touch her and you'll be in real trouble."

Joey Jackman swallowed his protest and turned to glare threateningly at his wife. Slade looked over at the girl who had not moved an inch from where she stood when the altercation began. She was obviously frightened. However, Slade had the distinct feeling Ginny Jackman was scared of far more than her bullying husband's threats.

CHAPTER FOUR

The plump receptionist sat at her desk and stared enviously at the thin, angular fashion model on the front cover of *Vogue*. The hum of the dentist's drill from the inner office seemed to float toward her from some distant world.

A shadow fell across the magazine.

The plump receptionist looked up at the killer with the nylon stocking masking his face and surgical gloves covering his hands. Frozen with fear like a mouse before a coiled snake, she caught her breath as he placed his stiletto against her right breast and laid a rubber-encased finger across her trembling lips.

"Doctor doesn't keep drugs here," she whispered around the obscenely sheathed finger.

The killer drew the needle-sharp point of his stiletto across the receptionist's breast, and the material of her uniform parted to reveal her white flesh squeezed above her pink half-bra. "Call him out here, or I'll slice it off," he said in a hoarse voice.

The plump girl belched uncontrollably. "He's got a patient inside," she managed to say.

"Tell him he's got a phone call," the killer instructed her, plucking at her bra with the blade of his stiletto.

The receptionist rose slowly and moved dumbly toward the dentist's office. She did not require the prodding of the knife point between her shoulder blades. "Dr. Silver," she called after knocking timidly. "There's a phone call."

Inside his office, Dr. Silver, a middle-aged man with a warm smile calculated to put his clientele at ease, switched off his drill. His patient, Frankie Minnick, reclining in the dentist's chair with a suction instrument in his mouth, sighed with relief at the interruption and allowed himself to relax. He was an extremely ugly man with sallow skin and cheeks like buttocks, and he had worked his way up through sheer ferocity from a waterfront union goon to a hammer in Eddie Cassell's organization. Most of his colleagues considered him a psychopath. Confirming evidence pointed both to his propensity for torturing his victims before executing them and to the insanity in his family background, particularly in his father, a Staten Island bootlegger. In 1932, Jerry Minnick, while driving a load of bathtub gin in his beloved Düsenberg, noticed federal agents closing in on him in pursuit. To prevent them from having the satisfaction of confiscating his car upon his capture, he deliberately crashed it into a wall at eighty mph and broke his neck.

"What is it, Alice?" Dr. Silver asked, trying to disguise his impatience.

"A phone call," his receptionist repeated.

"Take their number. I'll call them back."

Outside in the reception room Alice turned her head and looked pleadingly at the killer. Bringing his stiletto up under the folds of her chin, he commanded softly, "Say it's his wife and it's urgent."

"It's your wife and it's urgent," Alice echoed.

Inside Dr. Silver shook his head and lay his mouth mirror on a tray above his patient. "Tell her I'll be right there," he called out resignedly. To the man in the chair he added, "I'm sorry, Mr. Minnick. Be right back. Keep the vacuum cleaner in your mouth."

Minnick nodded curtly. He was having cosmetic surgery done on his teeth at his wife's insistence, but he wondered whether all the aggravation he was enduring was worth the effort of pleasing her, especially when he considered he was not overly given to smiling.

Dr. Silver hurried out of his office. As he closed the door behind him the killer slammed him against the wall. Then he waved his stiletto a fraction of an inch under the dentist's bulging eyes and ushered him and his receptionist toward a clothes closet.

Dr. Silver regained his power of speech at the closet entrance and tried to bargain for their safety. "There's money in my receptionist's desk. And some gold in the safe."

"The combination?"

The dentist gave it to the killer with his keys. "I won't call the police for an hour," he promised.

The killer opened the clothes closet, roughly shoved his two prisoners inside, warned them about crying out, and locked the door.

It took the killer no more than a minute and a half to take off his mask, remove the cotton wadding, which he had used to disguise his voice, from his mouth, stuff his windbreaker in a drawer of the receptionist's desk, then walk back toward the door of the dentist's office.

The killer concentrated on the room beyond until it appeared in his mind's eye with perfect clarity. So exactly alike were the proportions of the re-creation with

the original that he was able to count off the number
of feet separating the door from the dentist's chair. He
touched the doorknob and could feel the cold metal
through his rubber glove.

In the dentist's chair, Minnick grew restless. He
groped down beside him for his briefcase. Lifting it
onto his lap he shined the initials F.M. with his sleeve
and opened the lid. A copy of *Hustler* lay near a .45
automatic that had once belonged to a war-hero uncle.

Minnick clutched the magazine and snapped the
briefcase shut, then replaced the carrier on the floor at
his feet. He flipped open the *Hustler* eagerly and
pored over the centerfold. By the time his eyes had
finally come to rest on the Tampax string hanging
from the model's labia, the killer had silently opened
the office door and sneaked up behind him.

Avid for further views in poor taste, Minnick turned
the page. The killer drew back his stiletto, rose on his
toes like a dancer, and riveted his eyes on a precise
point at the base of Minnick's skull.

The killer struck with the full force of his weight.
The knife blade described a flashing arc and disappeared in Minnick's neck like a stone dropped into
the sea. The victim grunted from deep within his
chest. His arms and legs shot out spasmodically on the
sides of his chair. He quivered for a few moments then
fell still, like an insect impaled on the pin of a cruel
child.

CHAPTER FIVE

"It's funny how you can get really fond of a stiff."

Wearing a knitted wool cap and turtleneck sweater beneath his white coat, the youthful Assistant Coroner puffed out his pink cheeks and smilingly reminisced. Slade and Davis, seated across the table from him in the Cold Room of the City Morgue, listened respectfully enough for the Assistant Coroner to feel free to continue.

"Like when I was in med school," he went on jauntily. "NYU. New York University. They gave you a stiff for your very own in Anatomy." His blue eyes grew dreamy. "You got to know his every organ cutting away at him and his intimate parts. After a while you made up a biography about him, you know, how his mother dropped a pan of grease on his arm, how he was wounded in the war, how he caught clap from his fiancée who was screwing around. He became like a buddy."

Slade became queasy.

"You cut and cut, and then just when you're really getting to know him, there's hardly anything left. It kind of made you sad."

Davis shook his head understandingly. Slade turned his away to inspect the bare white walls.

"Not that there weren't a lot of laughs," the Assistant Coroner said to Slade, worried that he was losing half his audience. "Like when you were cutting into the abdomen to remove the bladder, you had to pull his ding-dong over to one side and tie it back to his shoulder by a string. Well there was this one girl in the class, enormous knockers by the way, everytime she grabs it, it slips out of her hand because of all the damn formaldehyde it's soaked in. She must have tried a dozen times to get her mitt around that *shlong*. Finally this really funny guy yells to her from the back of the room, 'Use your teeth!' "

The Assistant Coroner was choking with laughter as a lively Puerto Rican attendant wheeled in the corpse. "Cha, cha, cha," he said for no apparent reason and left.

Slade, Davis, and the Assistant Coroner gathered around. Wiping away his chuckle tears, the Assistant Coroner picked up a clipboard attached to the stretcher, scanned it, pulled back the sheet, and stood aside for his guests to regard the mortal remains of Frankie Minnick. "Could one of you guys give me a hand turning this stiff over?" the Assistant Coroner asked after estimating Minnick's dead weight.

Slade hung back. Davis stepped forward and together he and the Assistant Coroner wrestled Minnick over onto his protruding stomach. Slade leaned forward to observe the small, colorless wound at the base of the skull.

"Minnick, Frank Xaviar, etc., etc.," intoned the Assistant Coroner. "Cause of death . . ."

". . . punctured spinal cord at the posterior atlas just below the occipital bulge," concluded Slade.

The Assistant Coroner raised his eyebrows. Slade

pulled up his jacket collar for warmth. "Eighteen years and it still gives me the shivers," he said.

When Slade and Davis came out of the City Morgue into the sweltering heat and walked toward their car parked by Bellevue, the black detective asked, "Why so glum? That wasn't exactly Albert Schweitzer on that slab."

Slade did not reply. Although Davis was only recently promoted from the ranks he should have understood Minnick's murder following that of Bremner's.

"A cheap killer got what he deserved," said Davis harshly.

"He was more than just a killer," Slade felt compelled to point out. "And so was Bremner for that matter. They were two of the best in the business. Each of the firms have just a few like them, but I assure you, Joe, they're enough. They're the visible instruments of power, the real juice. They make the organizations. The decision to take them out isn't one you make lightly. The consequences have got to have been carefully calculated."

Davis refused to be impressed. "So?" he asked.

"So pretty soon Mr. Minnick and Mr. Bremner are going to have a lot of company."

"The more the merrier."

The two detectives found their car and got in. Davis drove along the congested First Avenue. Several minutes passed before Slade inquired, "When you flipped Minnick over, Joe, you get a good look at the hole in his neck?"

"What about it?"

"That kind of neck wound used to be Nick Bonello's signature."

"When I mentioned the Bonellos at the motel you

said no way it could be Bonellos versus the Big Four. Change your mind, Lieutenant?"

Smug bastard thought Slade. He pursed his lips. "Maybe," he admitted, but just to take some of the wind out of Davis's sails added, "But then again, the Big Four may not be as solid as you think."

CHAPTER SIX

It was beginning to rain when the Buick pulled up at the Avenue M and East 18th Street apartment house in the Flatbush section of Brooklyn. Harold Irving switched off the ignition and took a revolver from a tray below the dashboard to tuck into his belt. Before getting out of the car he started up the wipers again to clear the rain-soaked windows so that he could see the shiny, twilight street.

Irving had spent the day trying to keep his anxiety at bay. The deaths of Bremner and Minnick had disturbed him profoundly. He couldn't conceive of how anyone would have had the effrontery to carry out the murders. Worse it meant that he, as a hammer in Bill Strauss's organization, was no longer invulnerable to attack.

Out on the pavement Irving opened his see-through umbrella, set the theft alarm on his car, and started for the apartment house entrance. Suddenly he froze. A man, his head down and collar up, walked toward him.

Irving backed up against the wall. The man looked at him strangely but went on past him. Irving continued to glare after the man until he disappeared around a corner. Only then did Irving hurry into the building.

Leaving the elevator Irving moved down the dimly lit corridor of the fifth floor. He stopped at a door marked 5F, squared his shoulders, pressed the buzzer, and waited.

A full minute passed. Irving put his ear to the door. The door opened. A frowzy, middle-aged woman wearing mules and a scarlet housecoat stood in the doorway. She folded her arms across her ample breasts and regarded Irving without emotion. "Hello, Harold," she said tonelessly.

"Hello, Ma," her son replied, edging by her into the apartment.

No further words were exchanged for a quarter of an hour. Irving, seated at the dining room table, grew fretful as he waited for his mother to bring in their supper from the kitchen. He looked at the photos on the mantelpiece of his late brother Milt. A saint his mother always called him. Some saint. If it hadn't been for Milt he might have remained a Certified Public Accountant, might now have a family of his own, might be relaxing in his own home instead of developing heartburn over revenge or power struggles.

It was ten years ago when Milt, a prominent costume-jewelry manufacturer, proposed to his younger brother that he burn down the jewelry factory and storehouse on West Lafayette for the insurance. "Heshie," he had begged, "the army trained you to use explosives. You can make it look like the fire started from an exploding gas main."

Irving had at first refused. He gave in only when Milt swore that unless he collected the insurance he would have to send their mother to a home for the aged on Staten Island. He stared with hatred at his brother's photo. The bastard had neglected to tell him that the elderly, black night watchman would be on duty the evening of the conflagration. Had Irving made one slipup the police would have charged him with murder as well as arson.

Six months later the saintly Milt was dead from a massive coronary. After the funeral one of Milt's competitors, having correctly guessed the cause of the fire, approached Irving and threatened to expose him if he did not perform a similar incendiary feat on his failing business. For his efforts Irving received $20,000 from the competitor. From Milt's $300,000 insurance settlement he had got *bubkes*.

Irving's career as a professional arsonist might have ended then and there had not the competitor had a pressing creditor, Bill Strauss. The competitor mentioned Irving's name to the racketeer. Strauss sent for Irving and laid his cards squarely on the table in their initial meeting. He and his associates had scores of businesses either close to bankruptcy or overinsured. Irving's unique talents were in demand.

Recognizing a remarkable individual when he saw one, Strauss guided his protégé Irving into new, and even more lucrative, areas. The night watchman at Milt's factory had died accidentally. The victims on whom Strauss took out contracts did not. Irving found it fascinating. At the turn of an ignition key a car blew up. Reaching a certain altitude a private plane disintegrated and its fragments plummeted to earth. A reading light was switched on and the walls and roof of an apartment collapsed. Being able to deliver death across time and space had made Irving one of the most feared hammers in the city. Against his skills there was no protection or safety. His victims sometimes fought back with fury and determination, but they were no more a match for his technological superiority than the Stone Age Amazon natives who hurled their spears at strafing planes.

A tenement window across the courtyard from Irving's apartment creaked up. Alarmed Irving slid his chair back quickly from the table to get out of range. Then he got up, slipped his hand under his jacket to feel the reassuring hardness of his gun butt, and moved along the dining room wall to the window. He peered out.

Directly across the courtyard an old lady with a withered face leaned on her sill, staring blankly at the falling rain. Irving pulled the venetian blinds down irritably and returned to his seat at the table just as his mother appeared with their food.

"I thought a light meal would be easier for you to digest in this heat," she said, setting down a plate of cold roast chicken, potato salad, dill pickles, sliced tomatoes, and raw onions.

Irving listlessly pushed his food about his plate.

"You're not hungry, Harold?"

Irving forced himself to swallow a mouthful.

"You don't have to visit me every Friday, you know, Harold."

"I like seeing you."

"So why don't you ever talk?"

Irving relapsed into silence.

"Your job going all right, Harold?"

"Yeah."

"You look lousy."

Irving shoved his plate forward and poured himself a glass of ice tea.

"You should get out more, Harold. Meet people. Make friends."

The dining room door flew open. Irving whirled, his hand sliding under his jacket to his belt. A bird-like woman his mother's age entered without knocking.

"Hello, Herschel," the downstairs neighbor said brightly. "Visiting your Mom?"

Irving exhaled heavily and nodded slightly.

"Selma wants to know if you're playing tonight," the neighbor said to Irving's mother after receiving the same answer to the same question she had posed every Friday for the past eight years.

"I'll be down later."

"Nice seeing you, Herschel," the neighbor said, leaving the dining room.

Irving turned angrily on his mother. "I know she's old and she only sees me once a week, but do you think you could get her to understand that my name is not Herschel? And why the hell don't you lock the doors?"

"Don't curse."

"Ma, this isn't the old days. It's a very unsafe city."

Irving's mother made a face. "What does anyone want from an old lady living alone?"

"So go live with Aunt Foggie in Miami. I can afford it."

"Who'd cook your Friday meal, Harold?"

Irving got up from the table, turned on the portable color TV resting on the buffet, and sat back down. He stared morosely for awhile at Walter Cronkite then glanced over at his mother. Her watery eyes were fixed firmly on the screen. She paid no attention to her son as he said good-bye and left her apartment.

The elevator carrying Irving halted two floors below the fifth. He resisted an urge to grasp his gun for the third time in an hour as an old man with a puckered face got on backward, as if the car were full. In his arms he cradled a smelly white Terrier with advanced cataracts in its eyes.

"Hello there, Harold," the old man said over his shoulder. "Haven't seen you for ages."

Irving screwed up his face into a pained smile. One week was not "ages." The elevator stopped on the next floor. As the old man got off, he explained, "TV's busted. Going to watch on Lester's." Holding up the white dog he added, "Snowball gets lonely when I'm gone."

The door closed and the elevator began its final descent. Between the second and first floor, however, the elevator clanked to an unexpected halt throwing Irving off balance against the wall. He whipped out his gun, pressed frantically on the buttons, then pounded strenuously on the jammed door.

The ceiling panel above Irving's head slid back suddenly. Irving fired a shot through the opening at a white-gloved hand. The panel slammed shut. He held the gun barrel inches from the ceiling and cried, "I got you now, you crummy bastard."

Feverish with excitement Irving saw the panel open and fired again. A bottle fell through, brushed his cheek, and shattered at his feet. Then the panel banged shut.

Irving gaped at the wet floor of the elevator car as cynanide fumes billowed upward. He tried frantically to cover his mouth and nose with a handkerchief, but the poison gas seeped through the porous linen like water through a sieve. He made one last lunge against the door, bounced back, and fell with a heavy thud.

Atop the elevator the killer saw the wisps of deadly vapors caressing his feet. He shifted the panel to re-seal the opening but saw that the gas was continuing to escape. He had taken the precaution of reducing his heart beat before entering the elevator shaft. Now he diminished his rate of oxygen consumption as well.

It took three minutes and twenty-five seconds for the killer, holding his breath, to pry open the door to the second floor with a crowbar, then hoist himself up and out of the shaft into the corridor. He inhaled deeply and walked stiffly toward the stairs.

The sound of gunfire brought him to a halt. He realized without amusement that the shots were coming from an old movie on TV in an apartment somewhere on the floor. The voice on TV groaned, "Mother of God, is that the end of Rico?"

The killer, resuming his natural gait, descended the stairs and stepped briskly out of the apartment building onto the glistening street washed by the soft summer rain.

CHAPTER SEVEN

Slade nearly collided with the big blond as he raced up the steps of Police Headquarters on his return from viewing Irving's body in Brooklyn. It took him a few seconds to recognize Ginny Jackman behind her enormous pair of sunglasses.

"I'd just been to see you, Mr. Slade."

"You got something to tell me?"

Ginny shook her head from side to side.

"So what do you want?"

Ginny daintily slipped her sunglasses down her nose to reveal a brilliantly colored shiner around her swollen left eye. When Slade had examined it closely she pushed her glasses up again to cover it. "My husband threw a punch at me."

Slade clucked sympathetically.

"Then he tossed me out of the house."

"My fault. I should have got a peace bond taken out on him. It'd made him think twice."

"No, it's not your fault, it's mine. You tried at the motel, and that would have probably done it if I hadn't gone back to pick up my jewelry and found him there. He got sore because there was a ring Pete bought me."

"You want him charged for assault?"

"No. I really can't blame Joey." She smiled wryly. "He's all uptight and I didn't do anything to make things better. The expensive ring from Pete was the straw that broke the camel's balls."

There was an awkward silence. Finally Slade said, "I don't see what you expect me do."

"I had to leave the house in a hurry. I don't have much money. I was going to sell that goddamn ring and use what I got for it to get out of town."

"No friends?"

"I thought it might be a good idea to get lost."

Slade did not have to ask why. If she felt she was safer in the company of a police officer, he was not about to disabuse her of the notion. An hour later, after a cold beer and a hot subway ride, he ushered Ginny into the vestibule of his apartment house on Greenwich Village's Bank Street. While she waited he opened his mailbox and saw a letter from his ex-wife. He shoved it into his pocket unopened. There was no need to read it: it was, he knew, the usual letter complaining about how inflation was eating into his alimony payments and suggesting another increase might be fair and equitable.

Ginny saw his sour expression. "A bill?"

"Just a reminder."

When they entered the living room he picked up several days of newspapers from the sofa and tossed them on the floor to clear a place for Ginny. Then he went into the kitchen to fetch two beers from the refrigerator.

Settling into the sofa after a cursory examination for anything that might stain or tear her skirt, Ginny looked around the room taking in its general disorder. Rumpled clothes, broken-open packages of shirts from the Chinese laundry, and remnants of take-out meals in their grease-stained cartons, were among the more recognizable items strewn about the floor and furniture. I can really pick them, Ginny told herself good humoredly as Slade returned carrying two cans of Bud. Popping them open he handed Ginny one and sat down across the stained rug from her in a sling chair.

"Separated or divorced?" she asked.

"Divorced."

"I kind of figured you were. You don't look like the type that would go half way."

Slade let her observation hang there.

"Kids?"

"Two boys. James and Warren." He wondered why he was volunteering unasked-for information like their names.

"See much of them?"

"Not as often as I'd like. My wife moved upstate."

"She leave you for a guy with dough?"

"We just split up. There was nobody else involved. Why?"

"I don't know. I was just thinking about Joey. How it was Pete's money that made him so bitter. It's funny. Guys would rather have a girl leave them for better sex than for someone rich."

"Why do you suppose that's so?" asked Slade, who had a fondness for unprovable theories of human behavior.

"Because if a guy isn't any great shakes in bed, he'll still find some other girl who thinks he's great, someone maybe who likes it less emphatic, say, or someone who has no standard of comparison. But if a guy has no money, he's not going to find any girl who thinks he does. Right?"

"I hadn't thought about it quite that way."

They drank for a while in silence. Slade saw that his beer can was empty and rose to go back to the kitchen. "You want another?"

Ginny sloshed the beer in her almost full can. "I'm set. I'm not really much of a drinker."

He went to the refrigerator, got himself a beer, and rummaged around for something for them to eat. There was the remains of a salami and several pickles wrapped in wax paper. He rinsed off a plate to put the food on and looked for a towel to dry it. "How well did you know Pete Bremner?" he called back into the living room at Ginny as he cut a loaf of rye bread. He had avoided asking the question long enough.

"Hard to say," she called back. "We didn't have that much time together, what with both of us married. I was kind of surprised when I read the papers about him after he was killed. I mean, I knew he was into crime, but that rap sheet with all those arrests for murder, that was news to me. I thought those professional guys kept a lower profile."

Slade swore under his breath when he saw there was no clean silverware and that he would have to wash some. "Very few of them live like monks or are really loners," he said, continuing their intra-room conversation. "It's a myth. The guy who was with me at the motel, Detective Fine, the big one, I'm sure you remember, he says the image is a carry-over from the westerns where the bad guy in black rides into town alone."

Outside it began to rain again. The light drizzle turned to a downpour. Ginny got up from the sofa, went to the window, and watched the rain beat against the dirt-streaked panes. "Will you look at that," she shouted to him in the kitchen.

He came a few paces into the living room and halted as Ginny threw open the window to let the wind-driven spray rush in. Oblivious to everything, the young woman breathed deeply, put her hands on her hips, and arched her body swan-like into the swirling mist. Her damp clothes clung to her, emphasizing the contours of her lush figure. She tilted her head forward to catch the cooling moisture on her ecstatic face.

"When I was a little kid in Vermont," Ginny said, "I used to take all my clothes off and run through the summer rain. You could do that in the country."

Ginny turned from the window and smiled as Slade put down the tray of food and moved toward her. He slipped an arm around her waist and tried to ease her sunglasses off. Ginny grasped his hand to stop him. He let go of her and walked away from the window.

"Don't get upset," Ginny urged. "I know it's ridiculous, but I can't help it. The black eye's ugly as sin and I'm conceited as hell about my looks."

Slade turned back from the window and watched Ginny finish undressing. When she had stepped out of her panties and kicked them onto a chair she noticed the tray of food. "Take it with you to the bedroom," she said. "You're going to need all your strength, and I got a feeling we're going to be in there awhile."

Ginny had been right on both counts. Slade was exhausted, and it was much later in the morning when the glistening-bodied Ginny, still impaled on Slade below her, shuddered for the final time. She kissed him, raised her torso, and tossed back her luxuriant blond hair.

Slade opened his eyes and saw himself reflected in the sunglasses Ginny had refused to remove. He seemed to be floating in dark pools.

The lovers uncoupled reluctantly, rolled away, and laid there in the semidarkness and caught their breath.

Soon afterwards he fell asleep and dreamt. He awoke suddenly an hour later. His recurring nightmare had left him bathed in sweat. Ginny, her head cradled in the hollow of Slade's arm and chest, stared at him wide-eyed.

He put his hand to his breast and felt his racing heart. The nightmare had been especially vivid and, as usual, it had undergone no merciful abridgment. Unwillingly, he recalled the dream sequence and saw again the waves sweeping toward him as he sat huddled in the bow of the lifeboat. The watery walls towering above were the hue of slate, except for the tops which were of foaming white. He experienced nausea once more as he saw projected from memory, the jagged horizon narrow and widen, then dip and rise.

Slade was back again among the gray faces of the drenched children crowded in the lifeboat. Together they watched the approaching waves crash against their frail vessel and break into foam like tumbling snow. Time after time the lifeboat pranced and reared and plunged like a maddened animal. Each descent into the water-banked troughs and its subsequent ascent took longer and longer until it seemed that time itself must snap.

Shivering from the cold he sat up in bed and reached across to the night-table drawer for a pack of cigarettes. He offered Ginny one but she refused. The first drag made him cough furiously. The cigarettes had grown stale since he last smoked three weeks ago, and his throat burned.

"You okay now?" Ginny asked.

"Just a bad dream."

"What was it about?"

"I don't remember." Slade did not want to discuss the persistent fears that haunted all survivors like himself.

"Did balling bring it on?"

"No," he said, puzzled.

"That's good." Her hand trailed down his stomach and sought his testicles. She was pleased to see him smile as she parted her thighs to receive him.

CHAPTER EIGHT

The naked eight-year-old boy raced headlong down the long, sloping lawn of the palatial Long Island estate. Reaching the bottom he glanced anxiously at the deserted cabanas and pool, then darted into a cunningly designed garden maze constructed of impenetrable walls of hew hedges.

As he searched through the labyrinth the child heard the humming insects above his blond head. His face assumed the worried air of an adult. He padded forward on his bare feet. A nesting bird beat its wings and scolded him furiously.

"*Aaaaargh!*"

The boy spun around at the strangled cry, almost losing his balance. He peered back through rounded eyes along the green corridor.

Matthew Julian sprung out from a feeder lane of the maze into the child's view. His sharp-featured face with its high cheek bones and pointed nose was screwed up grotesquely and his lean body was twisted into the shape of a deformed ogre.

The child laughed delightedly and rushed into his father's outstretched arms.

Julian, elegantly dressed in white except for a turquoise-colored cravat, straightened up and easily swung his son onto his shoulders. He carried the bouncing child out of the maze.

"You promised to swim," the child cried, tugging at his father's long, straight hair like reins to turn him toward the pool.

"We'll swim later," Julian assured him, noticing a servant on the terrace signaling for his attention.

Unhurriedly Julian hoisted his son from his shoulders and set him down gently upon the lawn. He waited until an elderly English governess arrived to give his child over to her care. Then he strolled back to the mansion, crossed the flagstone terrace, and entered the sunroom.

The hammer Marty Angel, a dark compact man with a large hooked nose and eyes like tunnels, looked up over his *Newsday* at his employer Julian. "We've got visitors," he said matter-of-factly. "All three came together."

Julian grew pensive. "Well it was only a question of time," he said with a shrug. "I suppose we'd better go and greet our guests."

Inside Julian's spacious drawing room the powerfully built Eddie Cassell paced around an Op Art painting, studying it from various angles. Exuding animal vitality he radiated authority by his sheer physical presence. He shook his large head disapprovingly as Tommy Luce stepped up beside him. "What do you think?" he asked of Julian's modern work of art.

"If I look at it any longer," Luce replied, "I'm going to vomit."

The barrel-chested Luce went back to the sofa and flopped down beside Bill Strauss. The older man, his white hair neatly parted in the middle, had a retiring, elder-statesman air about him. He looked appreciatively around the tastefully furnished room.

"Where the hell is that prick?" Cassell demanded. He had never made a secret of his hatred for Matthew Julian since being forced by the National Committee to accept him into the loose alliance of organizations popularly known as the Big Four.

"Relax, Eddie, there's no hurry," Strauss said soothingly. He had philosophically acquiesced to Julian's elevation to power from the beginning. Though reluctant to argue with the hot-tempered Cassell, he had pointed out that it was hardly Julian's fault that his father, Larry Juliano, an influential Canadian bookmaker, had loaned the former head of the National Committee, Don Alvaro, $50,000 during the Depression. That was a lot of money in the days of the dons, and Juliano had neither asked what the loan was for nor when it would be repaid. There had been a $25,000 contract out on Don Alvaro's head, and Alvaro had used the loan to pay the hit man to turn his gun on his employer instead. Why shouldn't the late Don Alvaro have shown his gratitude to Juliano by advancing his benefactor's only son? In Strauss's view, Don Alvaro's sense of obligation bespoke a noble mind.

Cassell, of course, had failed to appreciate Don Alvaro's gesture. "The son-of-a-bitch Julian had it handed to him on a platter," he had protested in a rage. "Every step of the way was a gift. He worked for nothing. Slice after slice of territory." To clinch his argument he had bellowed, "Never served time, not a day! Never pulled a trigger!"

Cassell strode away from the Op Art painting to the dormer window and stared angrily at the calmly grazing horses near Julian's stable block. Strauss idly picked up a Sèvres porcelain dish on the Queen Anne table and inspected its mark like an appraiser. Cassell's deep resentment of Julian and the manner in which he expressed it amused Strauss, although they in no way altered his high opinion of the hulking figure brooding at the window. Strauss was given to rating his colleagues by how well they might have done in legitimate endeavors. He firmly believed that Cassell, for example, with his unbounding energy, quick grasp of essentials, concern for details, and love of bullying, would have become the president of a major corporation.

Luce stirred restlessly next to Strauss. He, on the other hand, thought Strauss, would have risen no higher than regional sales chief in the same corporation, despite his cunning. Before Strauss could place Julian in his mental personnel chart, the sliding doors of the drawing room opened, and their host walked in followed by Angel a half step behind. Cassell swung around to face them. His pale cheeks were mottled by suppressed wrath.

"Eddie, Tommy, Bill," Julian greeted them in turn, but on the basis of rank and power.

Cassell had to draw a deep breath before speaking. "We thought you'd want to come with us. To pay respects."

"Sure," Julian said immediately. After a pause he added, "Mind if Marty accompanies us?"

Cassell exchanged glances with Luce and Strauss. When he saw there was neither approval nor rejection, he said, "Sure."

The five men came out shortly afterwards onto the front portico of Julian's mansion overlooking the circular driveway. Julian and Angel noted the Chevrolet beside Cassell's chauffeured Fleetwood. Waiting patiently inside the smaller car were several hammers belonging to Luce and Strauss. Having taken them in, Julian and Angel directed their attention to Jimmy Croft who was a few yards beyond the cars. The rangy, thin-lipped Texan who served Cassell was squatting on the scorched lawn and playing with Julian's German shepherd. He squinted up at Angel.

Cassell hurried forward for a word with his chief hammer. "Jimmy," he asked respectfully, "would you please ride in the Chevy?"

Croft gave the dog a farewell scratch of the ears, straightened up slowly, and strolled languidly toward the designated car. The hammer seated next to the Chevrolet's driver jumped out smartly, held the door for Croft, and squeezed into the crowded back with the other passengers.

A few minutes later Cassell's Fleetwood drove off followed by the Chevrolet along the half mile of tree-lined driveway. At the gatehouse two guards struggled to open the heavy wrought-iron gate of the estate. If they were surprised to see Julian and Angel they did not show it, even though it was the first time they had glimpsed them in a car other than their own.

The two cars sped onto the Long Island Expressway. Inside the Fleetwood Cassell and Strauss sat facing Julian and Luce in the cavernous rear of the vehicle. Angel, beside the chauffeur, tilted his head back slightly to listen to the argument between Cassell and Julian.

"Nick Bonello sent us three messages so far," Cassell said, "We owe him a reply."

"I don't see Bonello nailing Pete, Frankie, and Harold," Julian replied.

"That knife job is Bonello's," Luce said emphatically.

"There's no patent on that knife job," Julian reminded him.

Cassell snorted. "Who else but Bonello is crazy enough to go up against us?" he asked. "He's a mad dog."

Julian shrugged and gazed out of the tinted window. Cassell leaned toward him, raised his beefy right hand, curled his fingers, and flicked them like snapping teeth a few inches from Julian's averted face. "Somehow, though, he never seems to bite you, Matthew."

Angel shifted around. Julian regarded Cassell calmly. "Nick Bonello and I had our differences a long time ago. We worked them out."

"You apparently have a gift for getting along with animals. I don't. I want him destroyed."

"Most of his men are blood relatives, Eddie."

"Worried about a war, Matthew? Then we take them all out."

"The National won't tolerate a bloodbath."

"Let *me* handle the National. They didn't bring us together to be sitting ducks for a publicity-hungry screwball. Or did you forget we had an agreement?"

"You don't have to remind me of my obligations," Julian said sharply.

Cassell edged his big body forward on his seat. Strauss laid a conciliatory hand on his shoulder. He smiled shrewdly and said, "There's no need for this hassle. Let's compromise. We each lost one guy. We'll double the price. Six Bonellos."

Cassell scoffed. "And if Bonello won't lie down?"

Strauss held up his palms gracefully. "We'll have no choice then."

Cassell studied his three colleagues. Finally he replied, "Six it is. But just so Bonello knows it's from all of us, we each put our best hammers up." He eyed Julian. "And we'll put your guy Marty in charge of the squad."

Julian stared evenly at Cassell. He ran his slender fingers through his hair, took a deep breath, and said, "Good choice."

As the Big Four settled back in their leather seats the Fleetwood pulled off the Long Island Expressway and joined a funeral cortege entering a cemetery. Out of the corner of his eye Julian caught a glimpse of a sea of gravestones.

CHAPTER NINE

The black children milled around the TV documentary crew. They were more interested in its sophisticated electronic equipment than in the subject of its film, Police Commissioner Alan Coombs on a walking tour through Bedford-Stuyvesant. For months they and their parents had been innundated by the media with words and images of the tall, handsome white man striding briskly along the pavement, his coatless aides trailing deferentially in his wake.

Coombs had achieved national attention during his Washington stint by being one of the select few who had not been criminally or morally implicated in the Watergate Scandal. Transferred from the Defense Department where he had served as a minor Deputy to Justice, he had shown an impartiality which infuriated both Congress and the beleaguered President. After the inauguaration of Ford he had submitted his resignation. His candor and lack of pretension had gained him widespread affection as well as fame, particularly when he refused the sop of an ambassadorship to Brazil. "I'm not rich enough to afford the position," he told *Meet the Press.* "I need a job that pays. Besides there are a lot of folks in Washington that need it more than I do. There's no extradition

treaty between our two countries." Coombs' wife
Anne, too, had provided a welcomed change from the
ordinary pol's wife. Just after her husband had been
offered the top law enforcement post in New York
City, she had been invited on *Good Morning America*.
There she admitted that she and Alan Coombs seldom
voted for the same candidate, and when asked if her
husband harbored presidential ambitions had replied,
"Of course, and New York City is an excellent
stepping-stone. Teddy Roosevelt was Police Commissioner of New York City in case you didn't know."
Smiling at her nonplussed interviewer she added,
"And Ronald Reagan was Sheriff of Tombstone."

Coombs flashed a grin at the crowd of diners who
had left the barbeque house, Adam's Ribs, to see what
all the fuss was about. He turned his head away. The
cameraman got an interesting shot of his elegant profile.

As Coombs trod on, the TV director, all in denim,
signaled the cameraman to turn his camera at the
serious-looking TV commentator who intoned sono-
rously through a beard, "Building bridges between police and public, Commissioner Alan Coombs typifies
today's new breed of law enforcement officials. A former high-level government expert, as you are all undoubtedly aware, he insists on first-rate performance
in every branch of his revitalized department."

The cameraman shook his head skeptically and hus-
tled after Coombs. A black laborer in the crowd was
trying to attract the Commissioner's attention. This
was the stuff of high TV: hostile confrontation.

"When are we gonna see more black fuzz around
here?" the laborer demanded.

Coombs halted. The TV director gesticulated wildly

for the sound technician to move in closer to the cameraman. In the event of violence, the noise would be authentic.

"When are you going to enlist?" Coombs inquired amiably. "Only one in every 166 applicants for the force is black. I find that statistic appalling in a city with a black community as large as ours."

Mike Dugan, the gray-haired police public relations officer, following behind Coombs, dug his elbow into the ribs of one of the Commissioner's aides and asked, "Is he looking for recruits or votes? Somebody ought to tell him the election's not till next year."

The aide frowned.

Dugan shook his head sorrowfully. "The electorate's like a dame who's hot under the whiskers," he continued. "You don't want to peak too early with either."

An unsmiling black, younger than the first and clad in a dashiki, stepped forward to block Coombs' path. Another of Coombs' aides, an ex-New York Giant cornerback, attempted to move protectively between the two, but the Commissioner nudged him away.

"Lots and lots of black Indians," sneered the young black. "All white chiefs."

"If you're talking about job advancement, I'm color blind," came Coombs' composed reply.

"Don't shit me, Whitey."

The crowd grew still. Coombs broke into a charming smile. "That's no shit," he said.

The brief tension evaporated. The procession moved on. The young black glared after the retreating train of white officials."

Walking along behind, the TV director beamed at Deputy Commissioner Franklin Talbot, a stylishly dressed black of thirty-five. "I sure as hell wish we could have had you field that kid's question, Deputy Talbot."

"That *man's* question," Talbot said, scanning the crowd. He spotted Slade and Davis threading their way through the onlookers toward him, and he abruptly left the embarrassed TV director to meet them.

When Talbot arrived, Slade nodded toward the TV crew and asked, "What are they shooting? Frankenstein Meets Wolf Man?"

Joining them, Dugan with his habitual deadpan replied, "That's the one they're going to do on the Mayor, John. As soon as he sobers up."

Talbot found neither man's remarks particularly amusing. Born and raised in a small town in Arizona, he felt uncomfortable with New Yorkers' wise-guy humor. "I gather you've got something important," he said to Slade in his Southwestern drawl that surprised so many people when they heard it coming from a black's mouth.

"They got Vince and Tony Bonello and a cousin Alfi last night," Slade told him. "Vince in a hotel room sleeping off two hookers, Tony taking his kid to school, Alfi cleaning up a Bonello bar in Soho. About fifteen minutes apart. Each hit went off like clockwork. The 'Morning of the Long Knives'," Slade concluded, borrowing Detective Fine's description of the triple murder.

Talbot whistled softly. "Beautiful. All we need now is a war. Coombs is addressing the Police Commissioners' Convention tonight at the Waldorf."

"They won't hear him over the cannon fire," Slade said. Talbot's concern for Coombs' career he regarded as excessive.

Talbot scowled. Dugan grinned. The PR man

strolled back to the TV director to keep him company. Talbot indicated for Slade alone to follow him and together the two men forced their way through the crowd toward Coombs. Davis pretended to ignore the slight.

When Talbot and Slade reached Coombs, Talbot whispered into his ear. Coombs patted a nearby TV executive on the shoulder familiarly, waved good-bye to some lookers-on, and had Talbot and Slade accompany him to his waiting car. Leaning on the vehicle Coombs said, "I thought a peace treaty was in effect."

"Only between the Big Four," said Slade. "The Bonellos were never a party to it."

Coombs rubbed his jaw thoughtfully. It was a gesture Slade had seen the ordinarily decisive police official use before when he was perplexed and wanted to buy time. "We can't sit on our hands and allow a full-scale war to erupt," the Commissioner said finally. "Isn't there any way to cool it?"

Slade too hesitated before replying, "I've got a line in to one of the Four. Matthew Julian."

Coombs looked questioningly at Talbot. Talbot spoke to Slade as if it were he and not the new Commissioner who required the briefing. "New boy. Only recently made it to the top. A different style from Cassell and Luce and Strauss. He's always kept a low profile. Never even been arrested."

"And you can get to him?" Coombs asked Slade.

"Not directly. But I know one of his executives. I used to work with him."

"Used to work with him?" Coombs said incredulously.

"Before your time, Commissioner," Slade told him, inwardly pleased to see his superior's momentary loss of composure. "When I joined, he was a lieutenant on the force."

"A lieutenant? Jesus!" Coombs exclaimed.

"Occupational hazard," Slade said flatly.

Talbot for the second time that afternoon failed to appreciate Slade's sense of humor. The Lieutenant refused to look contrite for his remark.

"What's this executive's name?" Talbot asked.

Coombs interrupted smoothly, "Frank, I'd rather not know. It's Slade's contact. Leave it to his discretion. You understand what I mean, don't you, John?"

Slade looked at the Commissioner expressionlessly. "Yeah. I understand exactly."

Coombs and Talbot got into the Commissioner's car. Coombs jabbed at the button of the automatic window and it whirred down. "There's a lot riding on this. I'm counting on you, John," he said before the vehicle sped away.

A few moments later Davis reappeared at Slade's elbow. Still smarting from Talbot's snub, he contented himself with noting Slade's barely suppressed rage.

"I had to open my big mouth," Slade said through clenched teeth.

CHAPTER TEN

Slade identified himself, waited until the armed guard at the entrance of the estate opened the heavy gates, then drove up the winding driveway past a gardener mowing the vast lawn with a cutter attached to a tractor.

At the house, Tony Cellini, a recently elevated hammer in Matthew Julian's organization, escorted him inside and through several long corridors to the billiard room. The young man was almost beautiful with soft, intelligent eyes and an expression of studied seriousness. It was almost as if he were unwilling to be considered frivolous as well as pretty. Ushering Slade in he closed the doors and hastened back to his station.

Marty Angel stroked his cue ball, watched it carom off a long rail into the red ball, catch two more rails, and click against the white ball for the point. Then he turned around to face Slade.

"I was in the neighborhood," Slade said. It surprised him to see how little Angel had changed in the ten years since he had seen him last.

"Help yourself to a cue, John."

"No thanks," said Slade, climbing into a high chair. "You haven't lost your touch."

"I get lots of practice."

Angel turned back to his solitary game, made another point, then rested the butt of his cue on the parquet floor. "You're putting on weight," he observed.

Slade ignored the remark and leaned forward. "Three Bonellos for Bremner, Minnick, and Irving. My front office figures you're square so that's enough. At least for the foreseeable future. I'd appreciate it if you'd pass that along."

Angel gave no indication he had heard Slade's remarks. He set up a difficult shot and studied the angles.

"You know, Marty, I don't think the Bonellos had fuck-all to do with icing Bremner and those two others. They got nobody good enough for that. Too much artistry. And who in their right mind would do it for them?"

Angel stroked fluidly for his sixth consecutive point. "That's your theory, John, and you're stuck with it."

Slade gazed through the French doors at the swimming pool and tennis courts on the sloping lawn running down to woods beyond. "Julian pays good," he observed sourly.

Angel laid his cue down on the table. "It wasn't only the money."

"What then? Job satisfaction?"

Angel stiffened then shrugged. "After all these years, you're still pissed off. Why? Because I resigned instead of standing departmental trial for shooting a junkie carrying an unloaded gun?"

"You were a good cop, Marty. There wasn't a chance in a hundred they'd have found against you."

"Who the hell were they to put me on trial? So they could have a Guinea cop up on charges to show that the Wasps were running things. Fuck them and their acquittals."

"You still didn't have to take up Julian's offer."

"Ah so that's why you're sore." Angel smiled mirthlessly. "Come on, John," he barked. "When I told you about Julian you wanted to go with me. But in the end you just didn't have the stomach for it."

"I was interested in what *you* were doing. That's not the same thing as *me* wanting."

"Double-talk. You should have been a lawyer instead of a cop."

"And what should you have been?"

"Instead of what?"

There was a sour taste in Slade's mouth. He suddenly realized that his growing sense of isolation was so great that he feared to make a final and irrevocable break with a corrupt man who had once been his friend. The word *murderer* remained unspoken. "Instead of a cop," he said at last.

"I should have been an accountant," Angel replied with a self-deprecating flick of his head. "My father, may he rest in peace, wanted me to go to commercial high school and study bookkeeping. Nice clean work, he used to say, though he made more as a bricklayer in the Depression than all the white collar guys in the neighborhood."

Slade climbed down from his chair, realizing that this conversation was a dead end. Angel said, "What's your hurry? Come on, I'll show you around."

Slade followed his one-time closest friend and then walked beside him until they reached the swimming pool. "Ever see my wife?" asked Angel, staring down at the still water.

"Not in years."

"She never understood either."

"What was there to understand?"

"That there's no good and no bad in this world. There's just what's necessary."

"Is that a fact?"

Angel chuckled. "Maybe that's why I flunked bookkeeping. The only number I could ever get interested in was on the bottom line."

Angel led his guest along a pathway. Slade stopped and looked across a beech hedge down a ridge into the neighboring estate. He was fascinated by the convoluted pattern of Julian's maze and tried to work out the exit route from its center.

"Julian saw it on a trip to England and flipped over it," Angel said. "He had it flown over and reassembled."

Slade gave up trying to find an unobstructed path out of the maze and followed Angel into a nearby greenhouse.

Inside the glass structure the air was sickly sweet with the fragrance of tropical plants. As Slade wiped the sweat from his head and neck, he saw out of the corner of his eye that Angel was impervious to the intense heat.

Angel picked up a can and watered an avocado plant. Slade said, "You got yourself a nice hobby for your old age. If you live that long with that guy out there."

Angel ignored the taunt. "This is only the beginning. Next year I'm going to buy a farm."

"And be really self-sufficient?"

"You'd better believe it, John. When those famines sweep across the world, they'll starve in those cities of yours. The hordes'll pour into the countryside looking for food. I'll have to defend my land."

"You could always call the cops," Slade said.

Angel returned slowly from the ravaged world of his apocalyptic vision and smiled crookedly. "I've got things to do," he said, terminating their meeting.

On the way out Slade walked past the impassive Cellini at the front of Angel's house and crossed the gravel driveway to his parked car. He was about to climb in when he sensed he was being watched. Turning slowly he looked at the mansion of the adjoining estate. On a front balcony stood Julian. He regarded Slade with an air of detachment. The two men's eyes locked for a moment. Slade wished he could get a closer look at the man. He was certain that just barely submerged beneath the cool surface, lurked a will unshakable and ruthless enough to desire and attain absolute power. Slade got in his car and drove away. At a bend in the road he looked back toward the mansion and saw that Angel had joined Julian on the balcony. Angel was saying something to Julian, who smiled enigmatically.

CHAPTER ELEVEN

When Slade entered the Special Squad bullpen the day after his visit with Angel, he winced at the pandemonium. Phones rang incessantly. Reports from the Morgue, hospital, Forensic, and various precincts throughout the upper West Side were still coming in on the massacre. Detectives scurried from desk to desk shouting to be heard.

Fine spotted Slade and pushed his way through a swirling crowd to reach him. "Jerry Bonello died in the ambulance," Fine said, bringing him up to date on the machine-gun attack in an uptown restaurant. "That's four Bonellos dead. They're finished for good. Your old buddy Marty Angel must've gotten your message wrong."

Slade shook his head. Yelling over the din he said, "It was a setup, damn it, from the word go. A cheap excuse to rid themselves of the Bonellos. They've been aching to get that thorn out of their flesh for years."

A ruddy-faced sergeant grabbed him by the shoulder. "Can I have a quiet word with you, Lieutenant?" he bellowed.

Slade and Fine edged through a crowd behind the sergeant to a vacant corner of the room. "We've got a witness who saw a guy in a yachting cap and blue blazer running away from the restaurant to a waiting car," the sergeant told them.

The description of the sportily dressed suspect fitted Sailor Sapinski, Luce's second-ranking hammer behind the late Pete Bremner. Slade turned back to the sergeant and asked suspiciously, "Someone actually came forward?"

"He's from out of town," the sergeant explained. "And that's not the only thing he's out of. You'd better speak to him."

Slade and Fine followed the sergeant down the corridor toward the interrogation room. Several times they were forced back flat against the grimy walls by waves of policemen hastily summoned for extra duty. As the three men came through the door, a young man with thinning hair in a mauve suit turned expectantly toward them.

The interrogating officer, a huge detective with bifocals, said, "The witness here says he got a good look at the guy going by . . ."

". . . I was just coming out from an all-night party at a friend's," the extravagantly dressed man interrupted, apparently miffed by what he considered the interrogating officer's colorless retelling of *his* story.

"And you think you could identify him again if you saw him?" Slade asked.

"As sure as God made little green apples," he replied proudly.

The police officers exchanged pained looks. Slade told the interrogating officer, "Get someone in here to take down his statement." Then he nodded farewell to the witness and headed for Commissioner Coombs' office two floors above.

Coombs was on the phone when he stepped inside the paneled and book-lined office without knocking. Talbot glanced up irritably at his intrusion. Dugan, standing to relieve the pressure on his hemorrhoids, sidled over to him. "How's business?" he whispered.

"Don't ask."

"What are you looking so worried about? You're in the only growth industry in town."

Slade snorted and eased away from Dugan so he could listen to Coombs saying into the phone, "We're doing everything humanly possible, Harry."

Coombs held his hand over the receiver and said for Slade's benefit, "His Honor, the Mayor. He's worried about the city's reputation."

"He thinks it makes the bond holders nervous," Dugan added.

"As soon as we have something, Harry, I'll let you know," Coombs promised the Mayor and hung up. After informing the switchboard operator that he was in to absolutely no one, he eyed the three men in the room bleakly. "Well, John, got any other ideas on how to cool things down?"

"The decision was already made," said Slade gruffly.

"I suppose so," Coombs agreed wearily. "What's up?"

"We have a witness who thinks he saw someone who could have been Sailor Sapinski running away from the restaurant," he replied cautiously.

"What are you waiting for?" Coombs demanded. "Bring him in."

"It's not enough to nail him."

"Bring him in anyway."

"If we do that dumb witness won't have a chance."

"Let *us* worry about the witness's safety, pal," Talbot said harshly.

It was Talbot's tone rather than his remark that made Slade lose what little patience he had left. "Who the hell are you trying to kid?" he snapped at Talbot.

Talbot uncrossed his legs and sprung from his chair in one motion. Slade, his fists clenched, moved to meet him halfway. Before the two men reached each other, Coombs rose and came around his desk to defuse the explosive situation.

"Okay, forget the witness," Coombs said. "But I'd like Sapinski arrested anyway."

Slade turned his back on the glowering Talbot and faced Coombs squarely. He waited until he got himself under control and asked the Commissioner slowly, "What good is that going to do? You'll just have to release him for insufficient evidence."

"Look, John. I've got the Mayor and everyone else on his swollen payroll calling me. I've got a roomful of reporters from the papers and TV outside hounding me for action. I've got to give them something."

Bullshit expectations, thought Slade bitterly before Dugan chimed in, "Sure, John, now that the Big Four mopped up the Bonellos, the war's over. The newspapers and TV'll sell a few copies, and in forty-eight hours it'll all be yesterday's mashed potatoes. Bonello's flunkies ain't Jimmy Hoffa in a Jersey dump."

Slade looked only at Coombs and capitulated as gracefully as he could. The Commissioner, he knew, had to make a grandstand play and nothing he could say or do would alter that fact. "All right. Sailor's out on the Island. I'll tell Suffolk County to pick him up."

Coombs' face hardened. He shook his head from side to side. "Hell, no. We're the ones catching flak. We'll make the arrest."

CHAPTER TWELVE

Sailor Sapinski's weathered A-frame house was situated twenty-five yards back from an isolated beach on Long Island Sound. From where Slade, Fine, and Davis stood on the road above, they could see his sailing sloop, its sails furled, moored to the private jetty.

"If his boat's there still, he's there," Slade said. "Joe, you stay up here on the road. Don't let anyone in or out. Howie, you better go on down the road aways and work your way along the beach back here."

He gave Fine a few minutes head start, descended the ramp to the house, and rapped on the door. When after a few moments it opened, two well-built, deeply tanned young men in fishnet shirts and tight shorts stood in the doorway.

"Police," Slade said. "Where's Sailor?"

"Australia," one replied. He tried to whip the door shut, but Slade savagely kicked it open. The two youths moved back together to block off the entrance.

"Would you mind if I had a look around?" Slade asked with exaggerated politeness.

Their spokesman mimicked him, "Would you mind showing us your warrant?"

Slade took out the folded paper and waved it under his nose. The young man snatched it, meticulously opened it, and studied it carefully. "Say, Sonny," he said to his friend, "Ever hear of a Teodor Jozef Sapinski?"

Sonny tapped his forehead and screwed up his face in thought. "Never, Freddy," he replied. "Could he by any chance be related in any way to our own Sailor Sapinski?"

Slade drove his fist into Sonny's abdomen and jammed his elbow back into Freddy's mouth. The young men reeled as he stormed past them into the house, then recovered and charged after the police officer.

"You shouldn't have gone and done a thing like that," Sonny told him as he rubbed the pit of his stomach. "It's police brutality."

Slade shoved Sonny aside and began searching the house. Room after room on the ground floor turned up no one. He started up the stairs. Sonny grabbed him by the arm, turning him around.

"You touch me again and I'll tear your head off," Slade warned.

Sonny backed off with a grin. As he did, Slade heard the three quick shots coming from the beach and rushed out through the back of the house toward the jetty. He saw Fine standing at the water's edge, his snub-nosed .38 in his hand. Beyond him was the sailing sloop under auxiliary power, already fifty yards out to sea.

Slade noticed the speedboat tied up to the jetty. Running to it he jumped down behind the wheel. The cushion beneath his leather sole shot out from under him. He felt his left ankle turn outward an instant before his full weight drove his left leg onto the exposed seat. A sharp pain shot up from his toes to his kneecap. His eyes were clouded over as he stared up at the jetty. Sonny and Freddy stood on each side of Fine.

"Looking for these?" Sonny asked, dangling a ring of keys. As Fine lunged for them Sonny threw them over his head into the water.

Slade climbed painfully back onto the jetty and advanced grim-faced on Sonny. Fine made an attempt to intercede then thought better of it. Slade drew back his right fist to his ear and measured Sonny for the blow.

Suddenly the blood drained from his face. Another agonizing stab of pain tore through his left leg. He let his cocked fist sink down to his waist and hopped on one foot past Sonny into Fine's outstretched arms to keep from falling.

"Christ, are you a mess," Ginny said to him some hours later as she removed his shirt and tossed it on the bathroom floor. She studied his swollen ankle beneath the yards of Ace bandage, shook her head wonderingly, then poured bath salts into a steaming bath she had drawn for him.

Slade fumbled with his jockey shorts for a while before Ginny came to his rescue and slid them down below his knees for him. "Service with a smile," she said.

Slade did not. He stepped out of his underwear and eased himself carefully into the tub of water. The fragrant warmth failed to alleviate the pain in his leg.

"You're supposed to take the goddamn bandage off before you get in the tub," Ginny said.

"I've got another," he muttered.

Ginny sat on the edge of the tub. She reached across

him for a bar of soap and asked, "How would you like me to do your back?"

"No."

"I'll take it easy. No waves."

"I said no."

Ginny let the soap sink into the water between his legs and watched it bob to the surface. "Christ, are you a mess," she observed a second time. "I mean, you look like a little kid who's been brawling in the schoolyard."

"Will you get the hell out of here?"

Ginny stood up. "Anything you say, Slugger." She left the bathroom slamming the door behind her.

Slade, alone at last, tried to stretch forward for the floating soap, but gave it up in exasperation. Leaning back he let his eyes travel upward to the long, jagged crack running along the flaking ceiling. It had been almost two years since he had left his ex-wife and moved into the apartment. He found it strange that he had never noticed the crack before. The impersonality of his surroundings, the futility of his work, his joyless past and bleak prospects for the future, all conspired to further darken his already black mood.

Wincing in discomfort he extricated himself from the lukewarm bath and toweled off as best he could. He put on his bathrobe and examined his elbow poking through the torn sleeve. He remembered suddenly that his ex-wife had presented the garment to him one Christmas many years ago. Then he walked out the door into the darkened living room.

Ginny struck a match and lit the tall red candles on the dining room table. She smiled wanly at him. "It isn't turning out exactly the way I planned it this morning, but what the hell? Nothing's perfect."

Slade hobbled across the living room toward the table set for two. He saw for the first time that Ginny had cleaned up the apartment and rearranged the furniture into some semblance of order. As he stood behind the chair, Ginny turned on the phonograph. A Miles Davis record she had bought for the occasion came on and they listened to the sensual response of a trumpet to the cords of a throbbing bass.

"Dinner coming right up," said Ginny, heading toward the kitchen. Her cheeriness could not quite mask her anxiety.

Slade took his seat. While Ginny put the finishing touches on their meal he uncorked the bottle of Chianti. He thought of what Ginny had said earlier in the bathroom, that his work was childish, violent, and absurd.

Quite likely she was right, he admitted to himself.

Quite likely they were all right. Davis had argued that cheap murderers were getting what they richly deserved. Dugan believed that today's headlines of outrage survived only until the following edition in the minds of readers. Coombs was willing to gamble that the apathy of the public for whom they worked was far greater than its concern for the civic good.

So what on God's earth was he upset about? Sapinski twelve miles offshore beyond the reach of the law? He'd be back on shore soon enough. That fighting crime was like fighting sin, an essentially losing struggle? He had long ago ceased to entertain any illusions about the world he lived in. Indeed, he often wondered why so few people shared his conviction that evil would inevitably triumph over good.

Bereft of both past and future he would live with great expectations for the moment. The only thing that truly mattered was that a young girl, prettier, cleverer, and more companionable than he could have reasonably hoped for had moved in with him for an indefinite stay and was preparing a special meal for their exclusive pleasure.

It would do.

Ginny brought in the food on a tray and set the sizzling steaks, baked potatoes overflowing with butter, and a tossed salad on the table. Slade realized that he was ravenously hungry. Ginny glanced at his eager face. "I'll carve," she said, drawing the meat toward her.

He picked up the bottle of wine by the neck and held it aloft. "And I'll pour, love."

CHAPTER THIRTEEN

The sailing sloop rode securely at anchor in the moonlit calm of the ocean. Outside U.S. Territorial Waters its owner Sailor Sapinski slept serenely in his berth. He had no trouble sleeping in tight quarters, having spent half his forty years in cramped jail cells for various violent crimes. Above him on deck a young seaman dozed at the wheel.

Miles away on shore the distinguished-looking criminal attorney Sanford Melville and his junior partner Larry Rothenberg worked late in an elegantly appointed law office on Wall Street. They had stayed late to decide which of three perjured alibis would best serve their client Sapinski on his return to New York City.

"Let's go with the New Jersey one," Melville said, stifling a yawn. It was almost eleven o'clock and he hoped to join his fiancée at a theater party being thrown by the wife of a United States senator from New York.

The two attorneys had just left their office building and entered a chauffeured limousine when the white-gloved killer shipped the oars of his rowboat and glided across the remaining ten yards of water that separated him from Sapinski's sloop.

Earlier, just before nightfall and alone in a fishing boat, the killer had passed the anchored sloop on its way out. Neither Sapinski nor his mate, he figured, would give more than a casual glance at his and the many other similar craft on their way to the fishing waters. Under the cover of darkness the killer had cut his engines and allowed his fishing boat to drift back on the incoming tide toward the well-lit sailing sloop. Two miles off he had thrown over his own anchor, boarded a rowboat, and began pulling toward his destination.

On arrival the killer taped the rowboat's painter to the smooth hull of the sailing sloop, then stood on tiptoes to reach the gunwale. Like a trained gymnast on a bar, he used only the strength of his powerful arms to haul himself up effortlessly on deck.

The killer stood rigid and as his eyes swept the deck he committed the layout to his photographic memory. The moon illuminated his glistening face with its cold light. When he finally started to pad barefoot toward the stern of the sloop, it was as if a figure on an ancient frieze had suddenly come to life.

The killer came up behind the young seaman. For several seconds he regarded the exposed neck of the youth as he dozed peacefully with his chin upon his narrow chest. His pale skin shone and when he breathed, his gold earring glinted in the moon beams. Only the faint creaking of the wheel and the seaman's tranquil snores disturbed the immense stillness of the night.

The killer crossed his wrists and gently dropped the looped wire over the seaman's head and around his neck. Then his crossed fists whipped apart, drawing the wire tight. Metal grated against bone.

Below deck a muffled thud brought Sapinski bolt upright in his berth. "Hank?" he hollered to the seaman.

There was no answering call. Taking a revolver from a holster hanging above him on a beam, Sapinski stealthily climbed out of his sleeping berth and stood listening intently below the hatch. Hearing only the waves lapping against the side of his ship, he called out again, "Hank," then ordered, "goddamnit, wake up."

Sapinski's order went unheeded.

Clutching his gun tightly, Sapinski walked in a circle beneath the hatch looking upward into the star-dotted sky. He saw no sign of anyone standing within three yards of the opening, but still he did not dare to go up on deck. The intruder was surely armed and waiting.

For more than five minutes Sapinski remained immobile by the ladder of the hatch trying to choose a course of action. He dismissed the possibility that there might be more than one invader on deck. Otherwise there would have been a simultaneous attack on Hank and himself. He inwardly cursed himself for having taken the young seaman along. It would have been far more prudent to have trusted only himself at sea and stood his own watches on deck. His sodomistic predilections acquired in prison had put his life at risk. "Hank," he shouted a final time without any anticipation of a reply.

A quarter of an hour passed. The intruder, Sapinski concluded, would not risk rushing him blindly. Like a chess player who had drawn white, he himself would, by the rules of the game, have to make the first move, for staying put was fraught with dangers of its own. At this very moment the intruder might be scuttling his sailing sloop.

The thought of drowning, more terrifying to a man familiar with the sea than one whose life is spent ashore, finally galvanized Sapinski into action. He picked up a copper wash basin, turned it upside down, and placed his yachting cap upon it. Then he climbed the first two rungs of the ladder up the hatchway. Everything depended, Sapinski told himself calmly as he raised the basin to the level of the deck, on determining the intruder's exact position. If he could do that he would have a chance of returning the fire, provided he survived the initial blast.

Sapinski held the upturned basin aloft so that only that hat would be visible on deck and turned it with his fingers to simulate a swerving head. He waited until the moon had gone beyond the clouds and raised it even higher.

A great wave of relief flooded through Sapinski. His sweating face was wreathed in a smile. Hank had served a purpose after all by dying in his place. The intruder had not known that there were two men aboard and had fled the sloop.

The hope Sapinski felt died when he recalled how he had cried out the seaman's name on hearing the thudding noise on deck. Despair gripped him anew. He tried to think clearly but his mind raced like a tire spinning in snow. He retreated to his bunk, desperately attempting to regain a hold on his frayed nerves. He put himself inside the intruder's brain. Had he any way of knowing his prey was alone in the cabin below? No, not with any certainty. Therefore the intruder would have to keep his distance from the hatch in case two men charged up on deck at once.

Encouraged by this line of reasoning, Sapinski again came back to the hatchway. The moon was setting. A corner of the rectangular hatch opening was shrouded in darkness. If he raised his head to eye level with the deck within the shadowed area, he could see around the ship without being seen in return.

Sapinski inched up the ladder and leaned into the darkened corner. He craned his neck, saw the vague outline of the bow, and waited until his eyes grew accustomed to the faint moonlight. The bow was empty. Ready to leap back down to safety at the slightest sound or movement, he shifted around toward the stern. His eyes narrowed then widened as he stared transfixed at the wheel.

Suspended surreally between the spokes was the severed head of the seaman Hank. The sloop lurched to starboard. The youth's decapitated body rolled to the deck.

Sapinski felt the rush of air on his flushed cheeks and instinctively tried to duck down inside the hatch. But he could not move. His head jerked upward as the wire bit into his neck and he saw the stars again in the sky. They began to revolve like a Catherine Wheel in a firework display. Lights exploded in his head, receded to a million flashing pinpricks, and sputtered out like a bed of glowing embers doused with water.

CHAPTER FOURTEEN

A high, bright sun blazed in the sky. The sound of the Atlantic swell was heavy. Slade stood next to the leathery-faced captain on the bridge of the Coast Guard cutter as it raced through the choppy sea. He was seasick and his ankle ached despite the codeine he had taken. "A lot of water out there," he observed to make conversation.

"Yup," replied the captain. "And what you see is only the top of it."

Slade grimaced at the put-on. The captain scanned the horizon through his binoculars and picked out Sapinski's sailing sloop drifting erratically under full sail. "It's inside the twelve-mile limit now," he said.

Slade looked back to shore. "How can you tell?"

"After forty years at sea you know."

The lieutenant took the proffered binoculars, found the sloop with difficulty, and asked, "What if it starts running out again?"

The captain rolled his eyes heavenward at his question. "You saw those flapping sails," he replied. "We don't have any worries about it getting away."

In spite of the rising swells the captain easily brought the cutter alongside the sailing sloop. Giving the wheel to the first mate he led Slade off the bridge, jumped across the gap between the two decks, and waited for the detective to follow him. Slade tested the deck beneath his feet and found it slippery. He cast a nervous glance at the churning water below the two bobbing ships.

"You ever been at sea before?" the captain called to him from the sloop's deck.

"I got a thing about water," Slade grumbled.

"I got a thing about waiting," the captain said, extending his arm and helping him come across. He waited while the detective drew his gun and unsteadily made his way across the deserted deck until he reached the wheel.

Slade knelt for a moment to examine the pool of congealed blood, then walked to the hatch. He peered below into the darkness and descended.

Sapinski's bunk in the empty cabin was cold to his touch. Oppressed by the eerie silence in the close quarters he hurriedly climbed back up onto the deck. "He must have abandoned ship," he shouted.

The captain, ignoring him, continued to stare up at the yardarm. He followed the seaman's gaze to the slender, tapering spar set crosswise on the mast. A sudden gust of wind blew the sails apart like a curtain.

Sailor Sapinski hung from a noose tied securely to the rigging.

Slade licked his salty lips as he watched the dangling body pirouette gracefully on pointed toes. A gull cried stridently as it circled above. Slade sniffed something foul in the air.

The captain, noticing his peculiar expression, explained, "The moment a hanged man's neck snaps, his asshole sphincter goes and the bowels and the bladder empty. That's why that fellow's pants up there are drooping."

"You're a real source of useful information."

The captain grinned and lit a cigarette in the rising wind. As he clamped down on the glowing butt Slade saw he wore dentures. "I grew up in Baltimore," the Coast Guard officer said. "They used to have hanging in Maryland right up to the end of the Second World War. Had an uncle that took me to see one when I was fifteen."

"Very educational."

"My uncle went every chance he got. Always arrived early to get a ringside seat."

"He must've had a strong stomach."

"Oh I don't know. Back in the old days when we had a hanging, it didn't seem to bother people." He meditatively rubbed the salt-and-pepper stubble on his chin. "Of course, we're a lot more sensitive nowadays, wouldn't you say?"

CHAPTER FIFTEEN

From their vantage point in the hills above, Sergeant Ralph Yeakel and the two New York State Troopers under his command, watched the approach of the four speeding cars. A Mercedes led the procession, followed by a Daimler, then two Buicks side by side like yoked horses.

The four cars racing along the country road left a trail of sun-streaked dust in their wake. When they were directly beneath the troopers they turned left up onto a private dirt road winding around the hill directly opposite the concealed lawmen. Several minutes later the four cars reached the score of other vehicles in the walled courtyard which served as the parking lot for the mock-rustic, one-story lodge at the crest of the hill.

The four cars lost no momentum as they sped through the courtyard and wheeled at breakneck speed into a flying wedge formation before finally screeching to a halt. Six armed men poured out of the Buicks on the protected sides of their cars and peered anxiously toward the lodge.

The report of a rabbit hunter's shotgun miles off rumbled through the valley like distant thunder.

From the Mercedes at the point of the wedge Marty

Angel emerged, using his car's heavy door as a shield. He studied the deserted scene before him deliberately, as if trying to fix each detail in his mind. Though he detected nothing amiss there was doubt in his eyes. He swallowed dryly then nodded almost imperceptibly toward the Daimler.

At his signal Tony Cellini slid out from behind the driver's seat and opened the door for Matthew Julian to alight. The chieftain straightened his Panama hat, started toward the lodge, and froze in his tracks. From various concealed positions throughout the walled courtyard, the surviving hammers of the other organizations stepped out of hiding. Pointing their guns at Julian were Bob Cook, a heavy-lidded black with a shaved head, and his freckle-faced sidekick Jack Kelley, both Luce's men. Cellini found himself staring into the muzzles of Cassell's Zimmermann brothers, fat Al and thin Dolph. A prematurely grey man with horn-rimmed glasses, known to all but his employer Strauss as "The Professor," covered Julian's armed guards with a sawed-off shotgun in each hand. Croft, his eyes as flat and lifeless as those on a pair of dice, aimed his .44 Magnum at Angel's head.

A breeze sprung up making the brim of Julian's hat flutter faintly. He gazed uncaring beyond the hammers at the lodge and waited.

The front door of the lodge opened. The first man to appear on the veranda was Cassell. He was joined a moment later by Luce and Strauss. The three chieftains regarded their confrere Julian with the stony impassivity of judges at the bench.

Croft, without taking his eyes off Angel, turned slightly toward Cassell awaiting his command.

"I say no!"

Cassell, Luce, and Strauss looked behind them toward the doorway of the lodge from where the imperious order had come. Standing there, arms akimbo, legs slightly apart, was Alex Merritt, a slight yet imposing man with an iron-gray crewcut. "When you contacted the National Committee," he told the three men on the veranda, "you said you wanted a meeting. I didn't haul my ass up here for a shoot-out."

Cassell pointed his finger like a pistol toward Julian who stood motionless below in the walled courtyard like a courier awaiting a royal summons. *"He* wasn't asked."

Merritt inserted a cigarette in his holder, put the holder between his lips, but left it unlit. "Maybe that's why he's here," he replied softly.

Cassell scratched his teeth with his thumbnail. "It's going to give me real pleasure seeing that bastard die."

Merritt ambled over to Cassell's side, leaned close to him, and said, "All in good time, Eddie." Then he descended the stairs of the veranda and walked over the pebble surface of the courtyard to the waiting Julian.

As the distance between Merritt and Julian narrowed, Cook and Kelley looked questioningly at Luce. The squat man shook his huge head from side to side as if winding himself up. The inquiring glance from The Professor received a similarly negative response from the courtly looking Strauss. All the hammers except Croft holstered their weapons or let them droop. The craggy faced Texan continued to point his enormous gun at Angel until Cassell shouted to him, "Jimmy, save it!" Only then did he reluctantly slip his revolver into his belt.

"You're in big trouble, Matthew," Merritt said to Julian when the two men at last stood face to face.

"I had nothing to do with all those hits," Julian replied tonelessly.

Merritt thumbed back over his shoulder toward the veranda of the lodge. "They think differently."

"And you?"

Merritt tugged at his ear before replying. "Let's face it, Matthew. They've got one pretty damn convincing argument. Four of their best guys dead and none of yours. They've all lost muscle and you haven't even been scratched."

Julian stared squarely at Merritt. "If you're holding a trial, Alex, I think I have a right to state my case. Or have we already reached a verdict?"

Merritt scratched the ground with his toe while he reflected. "All right," he conceded. "It can't hurt." He indicated Angel and added, "You'd better have him come in too. Tony also. In a way it concerns all three of you."

Julian turned toward Angel who hunched his shoulders noncommittally to show the final decision rested with his superiors.

Merritt's piercing eyes caught the nervous drumming of Julian's fingers along his trouser leg. "What are you worried about, Matthew?" Merritt asked caustically. "I invited you."

Merritt pocketed his unlit cigarette and holder, turned abruptly, and started back toward the lodge. He had gone fifteen yards before Julian waved Angel and Cellini forward to accompany him, and the three men fell into step behind the retreating Merritt.

Luce and Strauss left the veranda and went inside

the lodge before the four advancing figures reached the steps. Cassell remained a few moments longer, staring at Julian with undisguised loathing, then went to join the other chieftains.

Merritt halted at the door to allow Julian and his hammers to precede, made sure the other chieftains's hammers were bringing up the rear, and only then stepped inside to preside at the hearing requested by Julian.

The door to the lodge had just been shut when Talbot, Slade, and Fine, in their unmarked police car, arrived at the observation post on the hill across the valley bisected by the country road. Sergeant Yeakel and his two troopers came out of hiding to the car and waited for Talbot and the two detectives to climb out.

"Deputy Commissioner Talbot?" Sergeant Yeakel asked of Slade.

Slade pointed to the black man.

Talbot ignored Sergeant Yeakel's gaffe. "Right here, Sergeant. What's the latest?"

Sergeant Yeakel crossly motioned the three arrivals to follow him through some bushes to where they could have an unobstructed view of the lodge. He handed Talbot his binoculars.

Talbot readjusted the focus of the lenses and trained the glasses on Julian's six armed guards lounging in the shade of the wall near their parked Buicks.

"It's all quiet now," Sergeant Yeakel said. "Awhile ago there was a shitload of 'em out there. They almost shot each others' asses off."

"Any idea what it was all about?" Talbot asked, slightly surprised. On the long ride up from the city to the Adirondacks, he had insisted to a dubious Slade that the meeting was a war council to cooperatively discuss the identity of the unknown assassin of the four hammers.

"Beats me," Sergeant Yeakel answered. "All I can tell you is the last ones to arrive sure as hell weren't welcomed."

"You see a Daimler among them?" Slade inquired.

"Yup. Latecomer."

"That'd be Julian," said Slade. "Well, well, the un-wanted guest."

"Where are the rest of your men stationed?" Talbot asked Sergeant Yeakel.

"Could only spare us three."

Talbot tossed the binoculars back to the troopers' leader. "You reported over a dozen hoodlums," he reminded him. "All they let you have was two officers?"

Sergeant Yeakel's reply was testy. "The rest are on duty at the State Fair in Saranac Lake. Guarding the Governor. Highway Patrol's standing by, though, in case we need help."

"In case we need help," Talbot echoed.

Sergeant Yeakel hitched up his Sam Browne belt and said, "We can handle 'em."

Slade and Fine slyly exchanged glances. Fine mouthed a silent *oy vay*. Talbot surveyed the terrain while Sergeant Yeakel impatiently shifted his weight from leg to leg. Finally Talbot spoke, "Slade, Fine, you two move out to that clearing over there and cover the road up from the city. Sergeant, you and your men keep an eye on the courtyard from where we are. I'm going up to that ridge behind us. That way we'll have the whole area covered."

Fine distributed the walkie-talkies. Talbot gave a thumbs-up sign and walked away. Sergeant Yeakel ran to catch up with him. "Sir," he said almost pleadingly, "don't you think we ought to move in on 'em now? We got 'em just where we want 'em."

Talbot appraised the trooper coolly. "And what do we charge them with, Sergeant? Loitering? Not putting out their campfires? No. We're going to sit tight and see if it hots up again down there."

Sergeant Yeakel watched Talbot disappear through some dense underbrush, then returned to the others shaking his head in disgust. As he walked past Fine, the detective said, "You stay right here, trooper, and I'll cut 'em off at the pass."

Sergeant Yeakel, flashing his middle finger, frowned at the backs of Fine and Slade as they started off together. Under his breath he cursed his superior within his department for having called New York to report the gathering of the gangs in the mountain-lodge rendezvous. Those smart-assed city bastards, he told himself, would be sure to hog any glory that might accrue to their joint surveillance mission.

When Slade and Fine reached their assigned positions overlooking the mountain road, they caught their breath and looked back to where they had started out from. Above they could see Talbot climbing steadily toward a ridge on the hill adjacent to theirs. When he was out of sight in a cover of tall pines, Fine swung around and pointed to the lodge. "It must be awfully important," he mused. "Boy how I'd love to be a fly on the wall for that meeting."

Slade sat down with his back against a gnarled tree, took off his left shoe and sock, and unwound the Ace bandage. He scratched his ankle vigorously to restore the circulation.

"How do you think it'll turn out, John?" Fine

asked, mopping his perspiring face and warily regarding a hornet above his head.

"Howie, what the hell are you asking me for? I don't know. They're a bunch of fucking maniacs down there."

CHAPTER SIXTEEN

Cassell, Luce, and Strauss sat at one end of the unvarnished oak table in the main room of the lodge, Julian and Angel sat at the other. Merritt, alert but impassive, occupied a seat between the two opposing sides. All the hammers save Cellini, who reclined in a chair against the wall, were grouped around the crowded room in covered armchairs and sofas. All listened attentively as Julian began his summing up of his defense. "Frankie and Pete were iced to make it look like the Bonellos. Then Harold and Sailor to make it look like me. It's the only logical explanation. Whoever it is doesn't touch my outfit for a reason. He figures that way you'll blame me. If you move against me, though, you're playing right into his hands. You'll be doing his job for him." Julian paused to allow the main thrust of his argument to sink in before continuing. "We'll be devouring each other like wolves. And that's exactly what he wants."

Cassell shook his head disbelievingly. Luce, taking his cue from him, appeared dubious. Strauss, however, was wavering. "What you say makes some sense, Matthew," he said without conviction, "but what bothers me is the thing with the Bonellos. I mean we all shook the tree, but the fruit fell in your lap."

"Oh come on, Bill," Julian said softly, recognizing a potential ally in the older man. "Bonello's customers prefer to deal with me. That's business."

"Bullshit," snapped Luce. He had a peasant canniness to go along with his crudeness and recognized Julian's divisive tactics for what they were.

Julian carefully avoided Cassell's eyes when he replied, "Look, it wasn't me who agitated for those Bonello hits."

Cassell saw the trap that Julian was laying for him. "You really expect us to believe that some outsider's trying to tear us apart?" he shouted, hoping to put Julian back on the defensive rather than himself.

But Julian would not be drawn into overly protesting his innocence. He glanced at the tension-filled face of Angel to show he spoke for both of them and said simply, "Whoever it is, it's not me."

It was obvious to the three chieftains that Julian had concluded his final plea and would rest his case on the arguments he had already set forth. They turned to Merritt for his decision.

Merritt let his cool gaze sweep from Julian to Cassell and come back to rest on Julian. He leaned back in his chair, exhaled loudly, and closed his eyes as if to mentally reconstruct the statements, pro and con, he had heard. When he opened them he said, "From everything you all told me, there's not enough to go on. We just can't be sure—either way."

Cassell knocked over his chair getting to his feet. He glowered at Julian. "The way I run my business, if I got doubts, goddamnit, I eliminate them."

"You asked for my opinion," Merritt said unruffled. "You got it. You can take the matter to the full committee. If they'll hear you. Until then . . ." he threw up his hands ". . . you've got no authority to do anything."

Cassell's face darkened with rage at the rebuke. He opened his mouth to speak then shut it. He walked out of the room stiffly, looking neither right nor left. Croft and the Zimmermann brothers hastened after him.

For several seconds no one spoke or moved. Julian seemed to sag. He looked across to Angel who was staring thoughtfully at the empty place at the table. Luce and Strauss regarded their folded hands apprehensively. At last Merritt got to his feet. He picked up Cassell's overturned chair and slid it back under the table. "Leave it to me," he said. "I'll talk to Eddie on the ride home. He's always had a hot head. He'll cool off."

Julian and Angel did not appear particularly hopeful as Merritt left the meeting and strolled through the courtyard. Standing on the veranda they watched him as he reached the Cadillac where Cassell and his hammers were waiting sullenly, got in with them, and drove away.

As Cassell's car left the courtyard and headed down the winding dirt road, Sergeant Yeakel called Talbot on his walkie-talkie. "A caddie coming out. You want it stopped?"

Talbot replied immediately, "No. Just get the Highway Patrol to pick it up and keep it under surveillance."

Sergeant Yeakel stared wrathfully at his walkie-talkie as if it were the cause of his utter frustration rather than the message it transmitted. "Chicken shit," he muttered to himself, then slowly walked back to his own car and reached inside for his radio phone to call the Highway Patrol.

In the courtyard Angel saw Julian and Cellini go to the Daimler as he strode back to his Mercedes. His pace slowed as he saw Luce's hammer, Bob Cook, leaning on its fender. The black man, rubbing his hands together with their knuckles flattened by ten years as a professional middleweight, said cheerily, "Nice wheels, man. I really mean that."

Angel waited until Cook backed away from his car, then unlocked the door and extracted from the cramped, backseat area, a foot-long tube with a mirror shaped like a hoe blade at its end. Telescoping the tube out to its full length he inserted the mirror portion under the chassis of the Mercedes and proceeded to walk around the car examining the bottom for signs of a planted bomb.

Sneeringly Cook said, "You're a trusting bastard, Marty."

Angel, paying no attention to the hammer, continued his search. He knelt and inspected both sides of each tire in turn. Only then did he collapse the tube, put it back in his car, get in, start the motor, and pull away.

Julian instructed Cellini to follow Angel, but seeing Luce and Strauss closely tailing him in the latter's car, he countermanded the order. The Daimler halted and Julian got out and walked back toward the chieftain's car. The hammers in the cars behind looked impatient at the new delay. Luce touched the electric switch and the window hummed down.

"Tommy, Bill," said Julian soddenly. "Take your time and think over carefully what I said back there.

You'll see I'm right. We've got to stick together in this."

"We'll see, Matthew," said Strauss. "I hope we can."

Julian nodded, returned to his car, and leaned back in his seat. The Daimler rode through the gate of the courtyard.

Slade, who had shinnied up a tree for a better view of the courtyard, was seized by a cramp in his right calf. He was tempted to climb down from his perch, but the sight of Angel's Mercedes twisting in and out of view on the dirt road made him grit his teeth and remain aloft a few minutes longer.

Angel's Mercedes picked up speed as it dipped out of sight negotiating the last hairpin turn before reaching the bottom of the hill.

Suddenly there was a rumbling explosion.

Slade saw the Mercedes hurled up into the air in a great sheet of flame and billowing smoke. At first he was too stunned to move while he watched the fireball reach its zenith and ebb. It was Fine's incoherent shouting that eventually shook him into action. He leaped from the tree and began to race toward the explosion as Fine chugged behind.

Branches and underbrush tore at his face but he charged on blindly. Twice Talbot, descending from the adjacent hill, yelled to him to wait, but the sound of twigs and underbrush breaking beneath his feet drowned out the Deputy Commissioner's cries.

He raced headlong across and up the winding dirt road. When he reached the twisted Mercedes it lay blazing on its side in an enormous crater. He tried to get close but the intense heat drove him back as if he had run into a solid wall. Through the flames he saw the blackened corpse bouncing around the front seat as the fire shriveled its sinew and muscles. He slipped to his knees coughing violently from the smoke he had inhaled.

The killer, lying prone on a hill by the lodge, watched the convulsed Slade through the scope of a bolt-action 30/06 Savage. He raised the cross hairs slightly above the detective's head and squeezed off a shot with a slight pull on his rubber-encased finger.

The bullet shattered the furious Tommy Luce's forehead as he rushed toward the flaming Mercedes, flopping him backward like a discarded marionette.

Cellini, ten yards behind the fallen chieftain, stopped dead in his tracks and dove for cover behind a rock. The hammer was in midflight when the killer's second shot caught him high in the ribs and thudded him into a tree trunk, dead.

Slade ducked down into a crevice and fired three times at the concealed sniper above him. His head was throbbing and his heart hammered in his chest. He scanned the hill trying to get a fix on the unseen rifleman's position.

Suddenly he was struck on his back and shoulders with a shower of pebbles and dirt. He spun around in alarm just as Talbot slid feet first into the hollow beside him.

"Can you see him?" Talbot asked.

Slade waved his revolver in the direction of the crest of the hill above them which was studded with tree stumps and boulders. "Up there. Somewhere."

Talbot, his eyes round, his mouth slightly agape, studied the hillside. He looked awed and confused. His limbs twitched. Sweat dripped steadily from his chin. "I'm going up," he announced in a hoarse voice. "Cover me."

Slade fired his last three rounds, counting to five between each, as Talbot darted forward using the cover of rocks and deadfalls between the open spaces. As Slade fumblingly reloaded he heard other pistol shots and realized that Fine and the three troopers were laying down more covering fire in support of Talbot.

Slade picked out Talbot. His head was just visible above the ditch he was frantically burrowing into. Bullets ricocheted off stones near him and went singing off into space.

Slade waited for a lull in the shooting. A steel band seemed to tighten around his aching lungs. He stared with numb absorption at the crest of the hill. Then he jumped up and ran forward, firing as he went. He felt like he had traveled miles before he leaped head first into a ditch, rolled over, and came up less than a yard to the side of the pinned-down Talbot.

The killer opened up murderously at the two detectives.

Bullets chirruped by them like insects, or glanced off rocks and went screaming through the still air, with the tortured howl of exploding metal.

The hillside crackled with more gunfire as Fine and the troopers recommenced shooting at the crest. Talbot shouted above the din to Slade, "Let's go!"

The two detectives stumbled to their feet, fanned out from opposite sides of the ditch, and dashed up the sun-baked hill. They were less than thirty yards from the crest, running from rock to rock, sometimes climbing, sometimes traversing, when Slade saw Talbot trip over a tree root and sprawl face first onto the ground. Realizing that he was the sole remaining target, he pitched forward and covered his head with his hands to shield it from the sniper's bullets.

The firing stopped abruptly.

He was churning inside as he got dumbly to his feet and waited for Talbot to join him. Half walking, half jogging, they achieved the summit of the hill.

The white-gloved killer had fled. Silence hung like mist over the deserted landscape. They looked back down the hill. Fine, the three troopers, and several hammers in a winding file cautiously climbed the slope to reach them.

Suddenly the growing sound of a gunned car motor shattered the oppressive silence. The two men whirled around in time to see the gleaming grill of the blue Ford explode from the dense underbrush nearby. Talbot rushed at Slade, shoving him roughly just as the car's fender grazed his own hip and sent him spinning. Slade rolled and snapped off a shot at the retreating car as it bounced madly down the other side of the hill. Then he rushed to the injured Talbot writhing in the dust.

CHAPTER SEVENTEEN

While Slade waited with Talbot for the ambulance to arrive, Fine thoroughly searched the hilltop from which the sniper had shot Luce and Cellini to death. On his return he knelt beside Talbot who was resting against a tree and unfolded a handkerchief for the injured man. In it was an electronic device the size of a transistor radio. "He must have detonated the mine in the road by remote control and waited for them to come running." Fine said, "Neatly planned and well executed—no pun intended."

Sergeant Yeakel approached. "They found the blue Ford abandoned two miles from here," he said. "The plates are phony and the serial number's been filed off the motor. My guess is that it's stolen."

"That's a pretty shrewd guess," Fine said gravely.

"What about the Cadillac?" Talbot asked. His black face was ashen from pain.

"Highway Patrol missed 'em."

"Missed them?" Slade said incredulously. "We don't know now if Cassell and his guys came back to do a job."

The allusion to Croft and the Zimmermann brothers was lost on the trooper. "The Highway Patrol didn't act on my message in time," he explained sulkily.

Talbot shook his head wearily. Sergeant Yeakel smirked. The three detectives looked at him inquiringly.

"I took care of those other hoods though," Sergeant Yeakel announced proudly. Then comprehending the reason for the look of alarm on his audience's faces, went on hastily, "I only had 'em arrested."

The three detectives breathed a collective sigh of relief. "I think," said Talbot to Slade, "you'd better stay around here and keep your eye on things."

After Fine accompanied Talbot to the hospital in the ambulance, Slade supervised the removal of the three corpses and the initial forensic investigation. It was night by the time Sergeant Yeakel drove him to Lake Saranac eighteen miles away where the men arrested at the lodge were being held in the local jail.

A silver-gray sheriff, who walked with a stiff leg as the result of a hunting accident, escorted him on a tour through his jail. "We only have one cell," he told the detective as he stepped aside so that his city guest could peer through the bars. "We've never needed more until today."

Slade had no difficulty picking out Cook, Kelley, and The Professor among the nine men in the crowded cell. Like different families in the monkey cage at the zoo, the hammers and Julian's lowly regarded bodyguards had separated into two distinct groups for the night.

The Sheriff called out over Slade's shoulder to the prisoners, "We sent out for hamburgers and milkshakes."

The nine men's response to the Sheriff's hospitality was divided between indifference and repugnance.

Slade walked back with the Sheriff from the cell to his office at the other end of the corridor. A guard with an automatic shotgun lounged in his chair near the partly opened door. Through the gap Slade saw Julian and Strauss sitting on the opposite ends of an over-stuffed couch. Strauss, tieless, his hair askew, was showing signs of stress; Julian, his legs crossed and his hands folded in his lap, held himself in complete control.

The Sheriff scratched his neck beneath his collar and observed, "You couldn't tell by looking at them. Time was when crooks *looked* like crooks."

The Sheriff's further speculations on a vanished America were forestalled by a commotion in the jail's reception area. The two lawmen hurried toward it and came on the Deputy Sheriff hotly informing two pinstripe-suited men with briefcases that they sure weren't going to see the prisoners until the Sheriff gave *his* permission. Slade recognized the attorney, Sanford Melville, towering above the others. He remembered that the tall, graceful man had been an All-American basketball player at Princeton.

"How are you, John?" Melville said in a booming voice. "Meet my assistant, Larry Rothenberg."

Slade bobbed his head at Rothenberg and noted that he had paid his boss the compliment of using his tailor. Rothenberg smiled cordially, opened his briefcase, took out a stack of writs, and handed them to the Sheriff. The Sheriff glanced through them perfunctorily, counted that there were eleven in all, then told his Deputy, "Spring them all, Fred."

A few minutes later, Julian, Strauss, the hammers,

and Julian's bodyguards filed out into the reception area. Slade stepped up to Julian. "I didn't see you on the battlefield," he told him. "Maybe that's what Marty liked about you. The way you back up your men."

Julian looked at him blankly. Slade realized, seeing Julian's ravaged face, that what he had earlier taken for Julian's composure was actually stunned defeat. Julian moved like a robot around him toward the door.

Sergeant Yeakel, carrying two cartons filled with modest food and drink, came through the door just as Julian exited. He looked with bewilderment at the departing prisoners. "Hey, what do I do with all this food?"

"Shove it up your ass," the hammer Kelley said over his shoulder.

Slade was waiting outside the jail when Fine arrived in the car to drive them back to New York City. "How's Talbot?" Slade wanted to know.

"The X rays were negative. He's going to have one hell of a sore hip tomorrow when he's discharged. I never knew you could see black-and-blue marks so clearly on black skin."

"Live and learn," said Slade, closing his eyes as Fine drove away and pretending to sleep to ward off further conversation.

Fine, however, was not about to be deterred from discussing the day's events on the long drive home to Manhattan. "It's a whole new ball game, John."

"That it is, Howie, that it is."

"Today's bag brings his total to six hammers and one Tommy Luce."

"That it does, Howie, that it does."

"Where does he go from here?"

"That we'll find out, Howie, that we'll find out."

"Are you going to keep this up all the way back, John?"

"That I am, Howie, that I am."

"You give me a pain in the ass. And don't say, 'That I do, Howie, that I do.'"

Slade chuckled softly.

As the miles swept by, the residual fatigue Slade felt took hold of him. From time to time he would open his eyes. Then with his senses dimmed by a return of sleep, he would fall once more into a drowsiness in which recent sensations became confused with older memories to give double visions of himself. One moment he was baiting Julian at the jail, another he was struggling to approach the inferno of Angel's Mercedes. In his mind the acrid smell of hot metal mingled with the cooling breezes flooding in on his face through the open window of the car. He heard at once the reports of gunfire echoing through the valley below the lodge and the music drifting out of the car's playing radio.

"We're home," Fine said loudly.

Slade came awake with a start. He looked out the car window and saw the familiar entrance of his apartment house. A junkie resting on the stoop regarded the two detectives with amiable curiosity.

"What a day, what a day," he said, stretching his cramped arms and legs.

"There's a maxim by a French writer named Chamfort," Fine said stifling a yawn. "He said, and I quote the translation because the original would be lost on you, 'A man must swallow a toad every morning if he wishes to be sure of finding nothing still more disgusting before the day is over.' "

CHAPTER EIGHTEEN

Slade had no choice but to climb the eight flights of stairs to his apartment. There had been a handwritten sign on the locked elevator informing the residents that it would be out of order for the duration of the present brownout. Half way up the dimly lit stairwell he rested and tugged at his sweat-soaked sleeves to free them from his sticky armpits. He tried to recall whether it was the third or fourth heat spell to grip the city this summer.

The first thing he saw when he let himself into his apartment was Ginny. She wore only a bra and panty briefs. Her long legs dangled over the arm of a chair. Tossing her *New York* magazine to the floor she rose to greet him with a smile of relief. "Everything all right? I called your office, but they said you'd gone out of town. I was worried."

"Something came up," he replied. He stripped down to his undershirt and went to fetch a beer from the refrigerator. Returning he pulled over a chair to the open window, sat down, and waited in vain for a breath of air in the sultry night.

"Want to go out for a drink, John? The bars are still open."

He shook his head absent-mindedly without looking up. "I'm bushed."

A long silence ensued before Ginny said, "I could go get some slant food if you're hungry."

"No."

"Some deli?"

"I had a couple of hamburgers and a milkshake a few hours ago."

"Oh."

"Go downstairs and get something for yourself if you want to."

"Thanks," said Ginny flatly. She walked into the bedroom.

When Ginny reappeared in the living room ten minutes later she was carrying her suitcase. He stared at it vacantly for a moment, then up at the girl's drawn face. "You got a place to go?" he asked.

"No problem."

He nodded. The impulse to dissuade Ginny from leaving was there, but it was not strong enough to overcome the inertia that held him. He let his exhausted body sag.

"You got a nasty way of punishing someone, John."

He turned back to the window and gazed out into the night unseeing. Ginny went to the front door, opened it, then looked over her shoulder at his back.

Slade heard the door click shut.

For a long while he continued to look out the window. He edged forward to see the foreshortened figure of Ginny crossing the street. Her suitcase seemed to drag along the ground. She turned the corner and was out of sight.

Gradually he became aware of the beer can in his hand. He studied the label unable to comprehend the printed words, and he rubbed the can's cooling surface over his flushed face. So what, he told himself. The charade was over. There had been very little between them to start with and nothing in the end. No bonds of mutual need or common interests had grown in the two weeks they had lived together. The fires of pure physical attraction had peaked and waned. And that was that.

Slade hurled his empty beer can against the wall with all his might. It bounced off and clattered back across the floor to his feet. The self-serving pap he was feeding himself stuck in his throat. He and Ginny had started off with as much emotional capital as most people ever had. While she had tried against the odds to increase their shared wealth in countless ways, he had deliberately frittered it away.

He studied the long, jagged scar that ran the entire length of his forearm. He knew with utter certainty that when he finally slept that night the nightmare would return to haunt his dreams. He would huddle once more in the storm-tossed lifeboat. He would hear the terrified child with a broken arm screaming above the roaring of the inky sea. He would feel the weight of his fear in the salty darkness. He would see in brilliant relief the deck of the destroyer instantly populated with sailors carrying blankets and flasks of tea. He would hear their calm British voices trying to reassure the exhausted, shivering survivors.

Fighting back nausea, he closed his eyes on the city's flickering lights. He could taste the curious mixture of brine and sugary tea on his tongue. His eyes popped open. He looked again at the shiny, pink-white scar tissue on his forearm where the naval surgeon had operated on him as a six-year-old boy to remove the bone splinters from flesh so numbed from cold it hardly needed the local anesthetic.

It occurred to him that he should have told Ginny about his dream on that first night they had made love. He should have explained what it meant and why it had rent his sleep so many times in the past thirty years. She might have understood that he was not trying to punish her but himself.

He had lost all track of time. The smear on the black sky mushroomed into dawn. A ghostly gray pigeon fluttered down from the rooftop eave above. He watched the bird's wings dip and pivot until he disappeared from sight.

CHAPTER NINETEEN

"Could be the usual power play, only a lot sneakier," Slade speculated, sinking deeper into the leather armchair in the Commissioner's office. It was the morning two days after the triple murder at the Adirondacks. Coombs, Talbot, Fine, and two of the Commissioner's aides received this less than enlightening piece of information in silence.

"Or?" Coombs asked after awhile.

"A complete outsider. I don't discount the possibility, but getting a hit man unknown to the Big Four seems farfetched."

"Why?" one of the aides demanded.

"Well," replied Slade, "they'd just know. It's a little like the great pool player Kokomo Joe Sachs. He was written up in *Life* fifteen years ago. He used to say he'd play anyone in the world he *didn't* know. When they asked him what the hell he meant by that, he told them that he was so way up as a player that he knew the few above him who could beat him and the few below who could give him a good fight."

"What about a freak?" suggested Talbot. "There could be some self-appointed executioner out there who thinks he can save the world by cutting down a few baddies."

"There's always a black or Puerto Rican gang," Fine ventured. "We don't want to ignore our ethnics and be accused of discrimination."

Slade shook his head. "They're coming up but they've got nobody in that class—yet. No, this is a first-rate ice man."

Coombs glanced at his watch and shrugged. "This isn't helping much, gentlemen. All I can say, though, is whoever it is, he's doing us a favor."

An hour after the meeting broke up Slade was just finishing tacking up 8 × 10 photographs on a rickety bulletin board in the Special Squad bullpen. The photographs he posted were divided into two groups: the living and the dead. On one side were Cassell, Strauss, Julian, Croft, the Zimmermann brothers, Cook, Kelley, and The Professor. On the other were Bremner, Minnick, Irving, Sapinski, Angel, Cellini, and, slightly set off in recognition of his rank, Luce.

He gave the board a final inspection and turned to the crowd of Special Squad detectives assembled in the room. "That leaves three members of the board of directors." He tapped the noses in the photographs of Cassell, Strauss, and Julian. "And six key executives." He indicated the hammers. "Twenty-four-hour stake-outs on these nine men are going to keep everybody hopping for the next few weeks."

From the back of the room a pudgy, bespectacled young detective waved his hand and called out to Slade, "Sir? Aren't they going to be a little hostile if we stick to them so closely?"

Slade was unable to place the questioner's moon-shaped face. "You're Detective . . . ?"

"Weller. Sam Weller. I've been reassigned from Missing Persons."

Slade sized up the new addition to the Special Squad. "Good," he said. "You can make sure they don't get lost."

He regretted his remark the instant it was out. Weller flushed deeply at the laughter of his colleagues. Slade tried to cut short his embarrassment by shouting, "Okay, okay, you've all got your assignments, so let's get cracking."

Davis kept his seat a moment, coldly eyeing the other detectives as they noisily left the room. Fine, waiting to have a word with Slade, became intrigued at Davis's unmasked hostility. "What's eating you?" he asked.

"Why waste the taxpayers's money protecting scum?" Davis asked savagely. "Harlem's crawling with every kind of vermin from pushers to absentee slumlords and we're out keeping these turkeys from getting blown away." He got to his feet and marched out of the room.

"That guy gives me a pain in the *tush*," Fine complained to Slade. "Everytime he talks to me I feel like a defendant in a murder trial. At first I thought he was just a sorehead with a social ax to grind. But that's not it. I really believe he thinks he's the only one trying, that the rest of us are somehow goofing off." Fine snorted. "Aaah, the hell with him. I'd better call my wife and tell her I'll be working late."

The phonecall did nothing to improve Fine's disposition. "Guess what my wife told me?" he asked Slade rhetorically. "She said it was summer. And summer is the season of our sons's vacation from school. She also said our neighbor, Sid Gottleib, Forest Hill's Father of the Year, is at this very moment out in the back lawn playing catch with his sons. I said Gottleib, may they revoke his tenure, taught sociology at CCNY and didn't work during the summer. Which was the wrong thing to say."

"Cheer up, Howie."

"Cheer up, nothing. I'm not looking forward to the next few weeks. When you're not *shlepping* around on your corns, you're sitting all day on your ass in cars as hot as ovens. One of these days they're going to install air conditioning in cop cars that'll work when the motor is off as well as on."

"Five years ago you'd have welcomed a good stakeout like this."

"Five years ago I was ten years younger."

The two men turned toward the bulletin board. Fine mentally ticked off the dead men photographically represented. "You should call this side *Momento Mori.*" He shook his head as if trying to shake loose the images of the seven. "They were some mean mothers, John. The guy who sent them to the Happy Hunting Grounds must be really awful. Because they couldn't have been easy to kill."

"No, they weren't easy," Slade agreed. "They had two character traits in common. The morals of a clam. And caution."

"So how'd he manage it then?"

"He had a line on them."

Fine looked at him curiously.

"In almost every case," Slade argued, "he knew where they were going to be at a precise moment in time. With Bremner, Minnick, and Irving it was a regular pattern he'd observed. I've got a hunch that it was all in the works for a long time. Otherwise it don't make sense."

"*Doesn't*," corrected Fine pedantically. He checked

the duty roster, and added, "I see we're down for Croft."

Slade nodded. He cocked his head slightly to study the Texan's face. It reminded him vaguely of the early Marlboro Man's. "James Bateman Croft," he said. "A precision instrument. Killing machine. Christ knows how many people he's done in if he's *suspected* for twenty. It was always a toss-up between him and Angel who was best at their trade."

"Looks like Croft won the toss."

"Could be. Could be."

CHAPTER TWENTY

Slade and Fine could hardly hear Roy Orbison's rendition of an old classic on the jukebox above the clamor. The Friday-night crowd at the Prairie Oyster, a country and western bar in the Redhook section of Brooklyn, exceeded by half the number permitted by the fire department.

Two brawny customers, with rolled-up sleeves and sweat pouring down their exertion-reddened faces, arm wrestled for drinks as their partisans cheered them on. After a seesaw struggle, the smaller of the two began to get the upper hand and forced his opponent's tattooed arm down on the bar, with a resounding smack.

The detectives leaned forward so that they could see Croft at the other end of the bar, surrounded by a coterie of young, tough admirers. Croft put a freshly rolled cigarette in his mouth. One of the youths popped a lighter at him as if he had been waiting all night for the opportunity.

The sallow, pigeon-chested bartender edged toward the hammer who was dressed in a buckskin jacket. Getting his attention he whispered in his ear. Croft turned slightly and looked down along the polished bar to the two men calmly sipping their beers. The hammer's snake-like eyes narrowed to slits, then he signaled his command to the bartender.

The bartender glided down along the planked, sawdust-covered floor to where Slade and Fine sat, took away their half-filled glasses of beer from the bar, and dumped them into the sink below. "The Management says you're making too much noise," he informed them. "You're 86'd."

A hush radiated outward through the bar like ripples from a stone tossed into a pond. Roy Orbison's mournful song ended triumphantly with the singer being borne to heaven to meet His Saviour. No one put another coin in the soundless, gaudy jukebox.

Four of the toughs nodded to Croft and strolled casually out of the bar while the rest went up to Slade and Fine and leaned in close to them, pushing and crowding, as if daring them with marginal violence to go for their weapons. Some of the male customers, sensing the impending trouble, hastily escorted their dates away to more convivial watering spots in the neighborhood. As the two cops spun around slowly on their stools, they saw one of the young toughs nonchalantly rip the telephone out of the wall and, wrapping the severed cord around his forearm, hold the receiver in his fist like a club.

"I said you guys was 86'd," the bartender told them.

The two detectives ignored him. They saw through the bar's window that the four toughs outside had armed themselves with tire chains. A crowd was gathering to watch the evening's entertainment. Slade laid a restraining hand on Fine's arm. He feared Fine would try to draw his revolver and provoke an attack against which there was no defense. "Stick with me, Howie," Slade said.

They climbed down from their stools. The toughs moved with them in a tight bunch as they skirted a few customers and went up behind Croft. "Howdy," Slade greeted him.

Croft studied the two detectives over his shoulder. "Look, we didn't mean to crowd you," Slade said sheepishly. "Can't we talk about it over a drink?"

The young toughs found Slade's abject apology hilarious. A slightly gassed hooker in a low-cut white dress gazed with unfocused eyes on the two detectives within the semicircle of toughs and grinned.

"Three bourbons, Jack Daniels," Slade called to the bartender.

The bartender nervously looked to Croft for confirmation. The hammer nodded curtly. The bartender poured three drinks and set them down. Slade, Fine, and Croft lifted their brimming glasses from the bar with care. "*L'chayim*," said Croft, taking a sip and gargling it before he swallowed. "Well?"

"We're trying to do you a favor," Slade said, pushing one of the tough's hands away as it flicked out playfully toward his holster.

"Do it somewhere else, wise guys," Croft said. "You two stink of death. You draw the flies like garbage."

Slade glanced at Fine and the toughs crowded around them, then beyond to the others waiting expectantly outside. Croft took another sip of his drink. Slade shrugged, looked down at his own, and lifted it to his lips. Without raising his eyes the detective shot a short, straight, left hand at Croft's mouth, shattering the glass still inside it and sending needle-like shards exploding like bomb fragments into the hammer's lips, tongue, and throat.

Croft gagged. Blood gushed from his mouth and he clutched convulsively at his throat.

Slade and Fine drew their guns while the toughs were rooted to the spot. Slade whirled Croft around, slammed the barrel of his weapon against the base of the hammer's skull, waited until he felt Fine's back against his, then propelled his captive toward the door. The crowd of toughs, shocked beyond resistance, parted to let them through. The detectives and the hammer were at the door when the inebriated hooker noticed the scarlet stains on her white dress, and frantically tried to wipe them out as she shrieked.

Outside the bar the four toughs with chains gaped at the grim-faced detectives and their bloody prisoner as they reached the sidewalk. At first they did not see Slade's gun pressed to the back of Croft's head, and they began to converge on the three. Croft, his hand still covering his mouth to stem the flow of blood, shook his head vigorously to deter them.

But the toughs kept coming. Slade, alerted by Fine that their companions in the bar were finally pouring outside to join their comrades, fired off his revolver a fraction of an inch from Croft's head. The hammer's long, lank hair flew upward from the shock waves. In terror he yanked his red hand away from his mouth and screamed to the youths, "Get the fuck out of here!"

The crowd of toughs backed off slowly, as fearful of Croft's wrath as the detectives' guns. At the sound of an approaching police siren the retreat turned into a rout and they began to flee in all directions.

An hour later, while Fine grew ill watching, a young black nurse with a lilting West Indian accent finished bandaging Slade's left hand in the emergency ward of

Brooklyn General Hospital. "Keep it dry until the stitches they come out," she warned him.

When Slade and Fine left the hospital they met Davis on the sidewalk waiting for them. "Croft is spending the night," Slade told him. "When they dig the glass out of his throat, put a patrolman outside his room."

CHAPTER TWENTY-ONE

The maître d' at Die Meistersinger Restaurant in Yorkville was an aspiring actor. Acutely conscious of his profile, he led the obese Al and slender Dolph Zimmermann through several large dining rooms to the more intimate rathskeller at the end of the huge establishment. As they passed the bandstand musicians stuffed like wurst into lederhosen and wearing Bavarian hats played German songs in accented duple meter. Singing waitresses in Tyrolean peasant costumes barged in and out of the closely packed tables like tugboats in a crowded harbor.

Dolph beamed appreciatively at all the *gemütlichkeit*. He enjoyed the sybaritic life money bought. To a far greater degree than his colleagues, he had become first a contract killer then a hammer for the vast financial rewards involved. Al, however, was less enthusiastic about dining out. He kept his right hand in his pocket and his eyes darted nervously over the guests in the congested rooms.

The maître d' showed them to their booth and removed the Reserved card from the checkered table cloth. "Your regular table, *Herren* Zimmermann," he said, using up one third of his German vocabulary besides *bitte* and *danke*.

Dolph slid into his side of the table while his brother squeezed into his. "I'm sorry I came out tonight," Al said, anxiously scanning the rathskeller. "We're asking for trouble being out in hunting season."

Dolph made a scoffing face and studied the giant menu with keen interest. He had worked his way down to the choice thirty-eight desserts when Slade and Fine entered the room and moved toward the vacant booth to sit down next to the Zimmermanns.

Dolph glanced over his menu at the two detectives, attracted his brother's attention, and flicked his head in the direction of the two arrivals. Al leaned around the back of the booth to face the two detectives.

Slade and Fine smiled innocently at him.

"May your fucking ears drop off," he told them.

Davis appeared at the booth occupied by the two detectives a few moments after their one-sided conversation with Al Zimmermann and sat down heavily at the table. "Bad news," the black detective said. "Croft's gone. He coldcocked the patrolman on duty outside with a bedpan and snuck out of the hospital. He's vanished. No sign of him at his house, his bar, or other known haunts. Might have blown town."

"More likely licking his wounds around here," Slade said. "Even if he had a reason to run, he wouldn't."

Fine slid his menu across to Davis. "You hungry, Joe? It's on the expense account."

"I've eaten."

The three detectives observed a buxom waitress with pigtails charge through two busboys like a Valkyrie toward the Zimmermanns' table to take their order. Thin Dolph spoke first, "Dumpling soup and headcheese. To start. Two knockwurst, roast potatoes, red cabbage. Side order of the sauerbraten, skip the vegetables. Strudel with chocolate ice cream. And a stein of Löwenbrau."

The waitress kept a straight face as she scribbled on her pad, then turned to fat Al.

"Consommé and a glass of milk," he muttered.

The waitress nodded understandingly, a gesture of unsought-after commiseration that only served to enrage Al. She marched away. Al looked pleadingly at his brother and said in an agitated voice, "How can you eat at a time like this?"

"Got to keep up my strength."

"You're not worried?"

Dolph shook his head from side to side emphatically. "Like Pa said, what you can't put in your stomach or on your back isn't worth worrying about."

"Yeah. The jerk said that the night he was run over by a streetcar."

Al smiled broadly at their family joke and said, "He died because he got careless, not because he was happy-go-lucky. I eat good. I sleep good. I exercise. I fuck. And I never get careless. Nobody's going to sneak up on me. Besides," he added loudly for the benefit of the three detectives sitting in glum silence in the adjoining booth, "there's no sense worrying about U-boats. Our convoy's got a heavy escort tonight."

"I have to take a leak," Davis announced irritably.

"Be sure you wash your hands and hurry back, son," Dolph yelled after the retreating detective.

Fine, sipping his Liebfraumilch, saw Davis nearly collide with a waitress, grab onto a nearby serving hatch to keep from falling, then straighten up and march erectly with all the dignity he could retrieve to the rear of the restaurant. The band struck up a German drinking song vaguely reminiscent of the *Horst Wessel*. "I don't think music is going to sooth Al's savage breast tonight," Fine noted to Slade.

A minute later the waitress came bearing the tray with the Zimmermann brothers' choice of meals. She set them down before the two men. Before she could back away the famished Dolph was noisily slurping his dumpling soup.

Al raised his glass of milk disconsolately. "Enjoy it, ulcer, it's all you're getting."

Dolph, nibbling a dumpling, looked up happily from his shining bowl and saw his brother examining his drained glass of milk. "Sour?" he asked solicitously.

Al began to gasp for air. His face grew contorted, his agony-clouded eyes rolled in their sockets, and his head banged down on the table. He made an effort to rise, spun out of the booth onto the floor clutching the table cloth, and brought the plates of food cascading down upon himself.

Dolph scrambled to his feet in a towering rage, drew his gun, and stared down at his dead brother. A roar swelled up from his chest. He rushed toward the kitchen knocking a tray-laden busboy in the way off his feet. Slade and Fine raced past the thunderstruck diners after Dolph.

Dolph, bellowing like a savage, burst through the swinging doors into the kitchen and waved his weapon wildly at the help. Cooks, bakers, salad boys, and dishwashers cowered helplessly. An elderly pastry chef, his face covered with a fine flour dusting, broke into tears.

Suddenly the hammer staggered. He groaned, lost his balance, and fell as if poleaxed. He tried to get to his feet like a rubbery-legged drunk in a thirties movie, but rolled back in excruciating pain. Lying twisted on the floor he sucked in air which never reached his paralyzed lungs, and died.

Slade and Fine took one look at Dolph in his grotesque attitude of death, turned on their heels, and rushed back out of the kitchen. Slade shouted to Davis running toward them, "The doors! Seal the place shut!"

Davis, head down and legs pumping like a running back, dashed to the front door of the restaurant, roughly seized two fleeing customers, and flung them back into the room. He slammed the door and screamed above the pandemonium, "Police! Stay where you are!"

The police reinforcements arrived ten minutes later. They quickly set up four long lines of grumbling customers. Then as the diners filed past four tables, officers checked each identification, noted down the name and address, asked one routine question, received one routine answer, and sent the person home.

Fine shouted from the men's room for Slade to join him. "Got something," he said as Slade entered, pointing to the pushed-out screen of the wide-open window leading to an alley.

"Make a note to ask if any of the help remembers a solo diner who finished his meal just before the action started," said Slade. "They must do several hundred dinners a night, but maybe someone noticed something."

They walked through the half-cleared restaurant later and idly looked at plates of cold, unfinished food and at the deserted bandstand. "They were so scared they forgot their instruments," Fine observed, pointing to a discarded tuba.

"It's a little hard to run fast with one of those mothers," Slade said.

Davis approached them. Fine gestured with his thumb toward the men's room. "Our Mystery Chef spiced up the food with his own special flavor and then scrammed out of there when the fun and games started."

The three detectives headed for the exit of the strangely quiet restaurant. Fine snapped his fingers and said, "I'll bet he never paid his check."

"Neither did the Zimmermanns," countered Davis.

CHAPTER TWENTY-TWO

"I hought your wife moved out of the Big Apple to give the kids a better life," Fine said to Slade after pulling the car over to the curb and cutting the motor.

"Now she says the public schools up there stink."

"It's the same out in Queens. If I didn't spend a couple hours with them each night they'd grow up illiterate."

Slade got out of the car and crossed the steady traffic of Madison Avenue against the light. Fine pulled down the auto's sun vizor so that a team of passing meter maids could see the police department identification card, and watched his partner go through the revolving door of the Manhattan Trust Company.

Fine reached into the dashboard for his paperback copy of *Zen and the Art of Motorcycle Maintenance*. During the tedious hours of stakeout duty, when it was his partner's turn to be on watch, he made it a point to read books which might improve his mind rather than ones he enjoyed. Finding his dog-eared place he plunged for the third time into the section where the author defends the Kantian theory that without a priori notions of space and time, experience is impossible. Repeated readings had not made the argument any more acceptable to Fine.

He had slogged through only six pages in a half hour when he looked up from his book to see an infuriated Slade storming back to the car. A burly truck driver, forced to brake in order to avoid hitting the detective, rolled down his window and let loose with a string of vivid curses. Ignored by Slade he blew his horn in frustration, whacked the crook of his arm to make its ham-like fist fly up in the classic fuck-you sign, then drove on. Slade entered the car and slammed the door behind him.

Fine watched him rip the loan application to shreds and started up the motor. "No go, huh?"

Slade gave him a withering look. "What do you think?"

"They tell you why not?"

"They told me."

"Well, how come?"

"Because they can't get anyone to insure me for the unpaid balance of the loan, that's why."

"I guess we're in a high-risk profession."

Slade stared straight ahead.

"Of course," mused Fine, "working in a bank these days is a little dangerous too. I wonder if their own employees can get a loan. You'd think they'd have to take the spate of bank robberies into account when deciding."

"Why don't you drive back to the bank, Howie, and you can give that guy the benefit of your wisdom. I sure as hell don't need it."

They drove in silence for several blocks. Fine asked, "Did you tell him you wanted the money for your kids' schooling?"

"I told him. He was deeply touched."

Fine nodded sagely. "Look at it this way, John. You got turned down. But this way you don't owe anybody anything. You realize how few guys nowadays can make a statement like that?"

"And you know something else, Howie?"

Fine glanced at his friend suspiciously. "What?"

"You're a fucking moron."

It was past noon when they arrived at Police Headquarters. Most of the detectives not assigned to stakeout duty had gone off to lunch. Slade went directly to Forensic to get the report on the poison used on the Zimmermanns while Fine drifted down the almost empty corridors toward the Special Squad bullpen.

Fine was just about to cross the threshold of the room when he noticed Davis at the bulletin board and stopped to watch him. Humming softly to himself in the deserted room, the black detective carefully removed the photos of the Zimmermann brothers from the side of the living, shifted them to that of the dead, and meticulously tacked them up in their new positions. Then he stepped back, closed one eye, and sighted along his thumb to make sure the photos were plumb. Not satisfied with their alignment he readjusted that of Dolph by a fraction of an inch. As Fine observed his colleague he was struck by the intensity with which Davis performed his task of keeping the records up to date—and the great satisfaction he derived from it.

"Excuse me," said Detective Weller, recently assigned from Missing Persons, to Fine. "You're blocking my way into the room."

Davis spun around at Weller's voice. He stared intently at Fine. It was apparent to him that he had

been watched for some time. Turning slowly from
Fine, he asked Weller, "Anything on Croft?"

"No, sir. All our leads petered out. It's like chasing a
will-o'-the-wisp."

Weller smiled with satisfaction at his own simile
until it dawned on him that Davis was glaring at him
and Fine as if they were intruders.

CHAPTER TWENTY-THREE

The hammer Bob Cook removed a revolver tucked under his folded shirts in the large open suitcase on the bed just as Jack Kelley entered the living room of their hotel suite. Cook tossed the weapon on the pillow. "No way to get that past the box," Cook said.

Kelley looked at the gun, then at his black coworker inquiringly. "Box?"

"When they check my suitcase at the airport."

"Airport?"

"I'm splitting for Acapulco, baby. I bought me a villa there a few years ago and I didn't tell nobody. Made my reservation last night."

"Splitting?"

Cook took two tailor-made suits from the closet and carried them to the suitcase on the bed. "I'm taking a leave of absence. Until everything straightens out. I don't want to be in anybody's way. That man carries an awful big grudge. I'm gonna put space between us."

Kelley watched thoughtfully as Cook forced his stuffed suitcase shut, hoisted it effortlessly off the bed onto the floor, put another larger, empty one in its place, and began to fill it with a dozen pairs of expensive shoes. "They'll charge you overweight," Kelley said.

"That, baby, is the least of my worries."

Kelley weighed the notion of escape suggested by Cook. The idea of running away had simply not occurred to him. In the case of the five contracts he had fulfilled in the past two years on members of Luce's organization suspected of informing, flight had only temporarily postponed his victims's fate. Perhaps though, Cook was right and this situation was different. Absenting oneself might satisfy whoever was ordering the hammers' deaths. Undecided on the wisdom of Cook's decision he went to the hotel window and peered out on Fifth Avenue at the car below that had been parked there for the last eight hours. "The fuzz are still outside," he noted.

"Big deal. They can't hit a bull in the ass with a banjo. They were in the restaurant when Al and Dolph bought it."

Kelley strolled back to the bed. Cook zipped up his second suitcase. "Take me with you?" Kelley asked him.

Cook hesitated. Though not a solitary man by nature, he was almost innured to solitude. Luce and the others had accepted him only grudgingly because it took a black man to run down and kill another black man in an all-black neighborhood. Having been fingered as the hit man of several black mobsters trying to muscle in on his employer, he had had to avoid the company of his brothers.

Cook went to the closet to select some suits for his trip in order to gain more time. His voluntary exile might be of longer duration than he was willing to admit, but the stolid Kelley was such rotten company. He had often seen him brighten up a room by leaving it.

"Well, yes or no?" the young but sepulchral Kelley prompted.

"Okay. But that hot food'll play hell with your Irish gut."

"That, baby, is the least of *my* worries."

Four hours later the voice over the public address system in a plush VIP room at JKF announced, "Last call for Aeronaves Flight 783 to Mexico City. All passengers please board." A diminutive, high-breasted hostess in a smartly tailored blue uniform, who earlier had expedited all travel arrangements for her sole first-class passengers Cook and Kelley, beckoned to the hammers to follow her toward their waiting plane. The warm smile she flashed the two men might have graced an ad for a halitosis remedy.

As the trailing hammers passed a bank of telephones, Cook spotted Fine pretending to speak into a dead receiver. He did a little tango shuffle and sang out gaily, "Adios muchachos, companeros de mi vida, barra cuerida. . . ."

Somewhat chagrinned, Fine stepped out of his bubble to observe the hammers being escorted to the departure lounge. When they were through the doors he turned around suddenly and bumped into two college girls smirking at a camera-laden man in a straw planter's hat and checkered trousers who was hurrying from the ticket counter to catch up with the other passengers on the flight to Mexico. Fine found it a minor irony of the times that an innocent looking tourist evoked ridicule while two swaggering, cold-blooded murderers elicited service and respect. He fervently hoped Cook and Kelley would suffer from severe jet lag when they disembarked.

But both hammers, as befitted their occupation,

were seasoned travelers. After filet mignons washed down by complimentary champagne, they slept peacefully for most of the flight and arrived fresh and relaxed at the taxi stand outside the Mexico City Airport. Cook, who spoke flawless Spanish, negotiated a price with the driver to take them south over the mountains through Taxco and Cuernavaca to their final destination on the Pacific: Acapulco.

The tourist in the checkered trousers, who had been plagued by an earache from the pressure throughout most of the trip, took the taxi which pulled up after the hammers departed.

It was late afternoon when their taxi speeded through the hillside shantytown outside Acapulco and began its perilous descent along the road winding down to the sun-drenched coastal resort. While Kelley snored loudly in his seat, Cook rolled down the window to breathe in the fresh, sparkling ocean air.

The taxi pulled up to a white-washed villa nestled on a rocky promontory above the azure bay. Cook paid off the driver and told him to keep the change.

"You shouldn't do that," Kelley reproached Cook. "They'll think we're made of money."

The hammers carried their suitcases up the flagstone path to the villa. Kelley gave the two-story stucco residence an appraising glance. "It must have cost you a fortune."

"I earned it," Cook said, unlocking the carved oak door with an outsized wrought-iron key.

After their luggage was unpacked, Cook asked his traveling companion, "How about a swim?"

"I'm starving."

"The maid'll be here later. She'll make dinner for us then. It's dangerous to swim on a full gut."

Kelley sniffed at his armpit. "You go ahead. I'll take a shower."

Cook snatched up a towel and his swimming briefs. He was beginning to think he had made a serious error in taking along to Mexico such a confirmed child of the city pavements as Kelley.

The sight of the clean, white beach caressed by waves, made Cook forget his misgivings about including Kelley in his plans. For a while he watched the great rollers diminish into milky fans on the pressed sand. Then he raced into the surf, dove into the water, and surfaced like a porpoise. He stood in the calm sea up to his narrow waist, threw out his muscular arms, and tossed his shaven head back ecstatically. Immersed in sheer sensual pleasure, he never saw the tourist in the checkered trousers who had been observing him from above the beach, turn and make his way back to the villa.

In an upstairs bathroom in the villa, Kelley reclined lazily in a sunken, tile bathtub tunelessly singing while a shower sprayed his pale hairless chest.

The mirrored door opened into the steamy room. Kelley turned his head around. His freckled face registered a heart-stopping shock and he exuded fear like a bodily secretion. He tried to scramble up from the slippery tub but the killer chopped him in the throat with the edge of his hand and crushed his larnyx. Kelley was mercifully unconscious as the steely fingers encased in white surgical gloves closed around his neck and forced his head beneath the water.

Ten minutes later Cook, wearing a bathrobe he had carried with him into a Madison Square Garden ring for his unsuccessful attempt to win the middleweight crown, entered the kitchen in search of some fruit juice. As he opened the double-door refrigerator, he felt the drops of lukewarm water on the crown of his head and jerked his face up at the dripping ceiling. Slamming the doors he raced upstairs to the bathroom and yanked on the doorknob.

Three feet of dammed-up water poured out, forcing Cook backwards. As he struggled for his balance on the soaking floor Kelley's naked body floated toward him.

Cook stared at the dead man's drowned face then whirled toward the stairway. He had reached the head of the steps when he felt the clammy hand upon his shoulder. Before he could shrug it off a knife was buried to its hilt beneath his shoulder blade.

The hammer instinctively rose on the balls of his feet and bobbed and weaved. Then he tottered backward and slithered and bumped down the stairs on his back, until he reached the bottom.

The killer bestrode the body of Cook like a colossus. He felt a curious disappointment which he attributed to an overanticipation of the event. After all his detailed planning he had dispatched his victims without effort. He stared down at the twisted face. He had expected so much more of him. At the last moment Cook had been seized by panic. Fear like a jungle beater had made him bolt to his death. The killer stepped over the corpse and left the villa.

Minutes later two Mexican policemen making their rounds of the posh residential neighborhood inhabited almost entirely by wealthy foreigners, noticed a figure moving in the villa's garden. They leaped from their car, sprinted over the lawn, and pounced on the tourist in the checkered trousers emerging from some hibiscus bushes near the kitchen.

"Que pasa aqui, Senor?" one demanded.

The tourist rose to his feet, pulled out his wallet, and flipped it open. The two policemen exchanged puzzled looks and leaned forward to inspect the suspect's identification.

The quiet was suddenly shattered by an ear-piercing scream as Cook's maid, who had just arrived at the villa, discovered her employer's body sprawled at the foot of the stairs. The Mexicans looked wide-eyed across the garden to the house and then at their prisoner's flushed face.

"Oh, shit," muttered Detective Sam Weller, slapping the side of his head with the heel of his palm so hard his planter's hat fell off.

CHAPTER TWENTY-FOUR

The initial symmetry of the bulletin board had been further disturbed. Doing the honors again, Davis shifted the photographs of Cook and Kelley to the side of the dead, just below the Zimmermann brothers. Only Cassell, Strauss, Julian, and the hammers Croft and The Professor, remained among the living.

Slade, slouched in his chair, looked at the photos like a fan at the ballpark studying the scoreboard. He took a puff on one of the cigars Weller had distributed that morning in honor of his third daughter's birth, and to prove to his wife he was no male chauvinist.

Fine marched into the Special Squad bullpen, went directly to the bulletin board, and removed the photograph of Bill Strauss. Davis's eyes widened in surprise. Slade looked questioningly at Fine.

"No, kiddies," Fine said, wagging his balding head. "The Ice Man hasn't struck again. Strauss died in his bed this morning. Heart attack. It must have been the aggravation."

"We'd better get over to the hotel The Professor is holed up in," Slade said to Davis. "Or we'll be playing more musical photos."

The Professor, lying on the bed in his underwear in the dingy hotel room, had aged considerably since

Slade had last seen him on his release from the jail in Saranac Lake. His puffy face was covered with a three-day growth of stubble and his horn-rimmed glasses lay on the drink-stained night table. He did not bother to look at the two detectives standing over his bed.

"You've got to be out of your mind to stay here," Slade told him.

The Professor turned away on his hip and stared at the peeling wallpaper. "I don't want my wife and kids to see me die." He coughed hollowly. "They think I work in the post office. Can you imagine? They've never ever checked. People just don't care these days."

"You could get the hell out of town," Davis advised him.

The Professor snorted bitterly and spun around laboriously to face the two detectives. "Where do you suggest? Acapulco maybe? I'm telling you, the guy's got a book on me too. There's no stopping him. Look how fucking successful you guys have been. I've been in this business twenty-five years and I know what I'm talking about. The hunter has all the advantages over the hunted. Time, information, money, you name it. The guy you're after has to live meanwhile, and to live is to finally goof. Do me a big favor and get out of here and leave me alone."

The Professor rose wearily and shuffled across the threadbare carpet in his bare feet to the pitted clothes bureau. He poured himself a glass of brandy from one of the two bottles on its top, took his drink over to an armchair against the wall, and slumped down into it. He took a big gulp of brandy then rubbed away the droplets that ran down the corners of his mouth into the matted stubble on his chin. "Ain't no way to live, ain't no way to die," he murmured.

An hour later Slade returned to the Special Squad bullpen. Fine, alone in the room, looked up sharply from a report he had been reading. "Where's Davis?" he asked.

"I left him at The Professor's fleabag. That room was getting on my nerves."

"Let's go back."

"Why? Joe can handle it."

Fine stood, unable to conceal his anxiety. He searched carefully for his words before he spoke, "I've told you before, John, I've always had strange vibes from Davis. Don't ask me why now. We've been through that before. I'm sorry I didn't clear it with you, but I started checking on Davis after the Zimmermanns ate strychnine."

"What the hell for?"

Fine glanced around nervously to reassure himself that no one had entered the bullpen after Slade. "Because he had to piss just as the Zimmermanns' food was coming. Because on his way to the toilet he bumped into the waitress and fell against the service hatch. Because that broken window in the bathroom was a little too convenient."

"Come off it, Howie. The restaurant was jammed with people and there was lots of time for any one of them to spike that food."

"You know me better than that, John. That's not all. I dug out his personnel file. He'd spent a lot of time in Vietnam early on in the war. When I asked the Pentagon about it they clammed up. Top Secret, they said, information about the subject of the inquiry classified. Now what does that smell like to you?

Intelligence? One of those special units where everybody's a real pro with a garrote and a knife and every other instrument of death you can think of, including explosives and poisons? Give a psychopath that kind of training, make him a cop, and who the hell knows what he'll do out of a twisted devotion to law and order?"

Slade frowned. "That's not enough either. There's 29,000 police officers in this town. Some of them were Commandos, CIA, Green Beret, all the rest. As far as mental health in the force goes, it's no better, probably worse, than any other job. But that doesn't make Joe Davis the Ice Man."

"John, you know it had to be someone who could pinpoint the hammers' movements. We've been talking insiders, outsiders, screwballs, you name it. We've been looking everywhere except in our own back yard. Well we've got a lot of info in our files on those guys. And Davis read them. He's the kind of guy, you remember, who likes to do his homework. Real gungho."

"You realize what you're saying, Howie?"

"Sure I do. And I don't like it. But I can't go against my instincts. I roll it around in my head and the more I think about it, the more I keep coming up with too many coincidences. When Cook and Kelley got it in Mexico, he just happened to have that weekend off. The day we had the bloodbath up in the mountains, he went home sick. *Five minutes after the troopers called!*"

Slade's jaw went slack. He started for the door. "Oh, Jesus, I didn't know that," he groaned. "That bastard hasn't been sick a day in all the time I've known him."

Slade drove with his siren on through the rush-hour

traffic and he and Fine arrived at the hotel entrance thirteen minutes later.

Davis had left his post and was nowhere to be seen outside.

The two detectives jumped out, abandoning their car in the middle of the street, and ran up the two flights of stairs and down the moldy corridor to The Professor's room. Slade found the door unlocked and barged into the room. "Drop it, Joe," he shouted.

Detective Joe Davis, his gun in his hand, stood over The Professor who was slumped in his armchair before the window. The dead hammer's head rested on his chest. His undershirt was stained crimson from a heart wound.

The black police officer looked with astonishment at Slade and Fine. He stared down at his own gun with a peculiar expression. Then dangling it on his finger by the trigger guard, he pulled his arm back and tossed the weapon in the air to Slade. "The Professor was dead when I came in to see why his phone was ringing so long," he said. "If my gun's been fired in the last week, I'll eat it."

Slade sniffed the cold barrel of Davis's gun. Looking up he noticed the neat round hole in the hotel room window and walked toward it, avoiding Davis's reproachful stare. He bent to calculate the angle along which the bullet had passed to hit The Professor in the chest, then squinted upward through the hole. Only Forensic, he decided, could tell him from which of the three visible rooftops the sniper had fired.

"It's all my goof," Fine said haltingly to Davis. "I apologize."

Slade stepped to The Professor's body. He looked puzzled as he observed the position of the armchair. It had, he recollected, been against the wall when he had left the room an hour ago. "I'll be damned," he said. "The Professor pushed the chair up to the window to make it easier for the guy."

"Professional courtesy," said Davis balefully.

CHAPTER TWENTY-FIVE

A tall, leggy brunette with a chorus girl's face and matching figure squeezed her fare and tip through the slot in the bulletproof glass separating the driver and his passenger. She got out of the cab, checked her watch, and sauntered into the lobby of a top-security luxury apartment house on Park Avenue. The green Oldsmobile that had been following her cab for the last twenty minutes, pulled over and found a parking spot on the other side of the street.

The armed security guard stationed at a desk near the elevator smiled lewdly at the approaching tall brunette. By his telephone was a console with four screens showing the other guards on duty and himself, at the building's four entrances onto the street and through the basement parking area.

The brunette dropped her calling card on the desk, mentioned the name of the gentleman expecting her, and studied her lacquered fingernails. The security guard continued observing her closely as he rang the designated occupant of the twelfth-story apartment. "This is Milt in the front lobby," he said respectfully when he was connected. "Visitor for you, sir. She says her name is Laurette Berger. Like in hamburger. She says you know she's coming. Should I ask for more identification?"

Milt's head snapped and his expression grew puzzled at the reply. "A birthmark on her what?" he demanded, then frowned with concentration. His homely face brightened. He leaned across his desk and studied Laurette's crotch. "I'd sure like to see that birthmark," he said into the phone, "but I don't think she's going to show it to me."

Milt offered Laurette the phone. She wiped off the mouthpiece before speaking into it, "I'll be right up, funny man." She leaned forward across the desk to hang up, caught Milt ogling her breasts above her neckline, and straightened up quickly.

"Top-floor penthouse," Milt informed her. "Twelve A. There's only two doors on that floor. One says A, the other B. Like a Chinese menu. A and B."

Laurette rummaged through her pocketbook, found a loose ten dollar bill, and tossed it on the security guard's desk. He looked up wonderingly. "That's for your tuition at night school," she told him. "Maybe they can teach you the other twenty-four letters."

Laurette strolled by the scowling security guard. A young black messenger, seated on a bench and awaiting a reply to a note he had brought for another occupant of the building, grinned at the brunette's sally.

Standing outside the door of the penthouse apartment marked 12A, Laurette rang the chiming bell, waited, then made a funny face into the peephole. The door swung open. Jimmy Croft, a bandage around the lower half of his face, let her in. In the vestibule Laurette examined the hammer's lips protruding through the hole cut out for his mouth. "You look different," she said. "Had a haircut?"

Croft's lips compressed into what, Laurette debated with herself, might or might not have been a smile. He took the girl's wrap and tossed it over a chair. It slid to the parquet floor. When he left it lying there and moved inside, Laurette glanced at her discarded garment, shrugged, and followed her host into the sunken living room.

Croft took a bottle from his wall bar and poured two stiff bourbons. Laurette gazed around the enormous room leading out to an equally large wrap-around terrace. The expensive furniture was conventionally modern. Laurette guessed that every piece was bought at the same time. The walls were covered with framed Remington prints and color blowups of western montain, desert, and canyon scenes from the Sierra Club. The decorations she remembered seeing at Croft's brownstone in Brooklyn Heights. Putting on a Texas drawl, she said, "So, this is where you've been keeping yourself, cowboy. Quite a spread."

The hammer handed her a drink. "Yup. Carved it out of a wilderness."

"Some folks are good with their hands."

"It's a gift of God."

"What have you been doing with yourself?"

"This and that."

Croft stepped close to Laurette. She lightly brushed her fingers on the bandages around his face, and asked, "You're sure you're up to, uh . . ."

"It's my mouth, not yours," Croft said, unzipping the brunette's dress and yanking on it sharply so that it fell around her ankles.

The naked Laurette kicked her clothes away. "You're so romantic."

Croft looked her body over unhurriedly. "Turn around."

"Why? You got a branding iron?"

Croft spun her around roughly. Laurette stood there a few minutes and turned to face him. He stroked her shoulder and said, "I've had a lot on my mind lately. I feel like a party tonight."

Laurette nodded. She had the satisfaction of knowing that she had received as close to an apology as anything Croft had ever given. "Whoopee," she whispered.

An hour later Laurette came out of the elevator into the lobby. The security guard Milt glanced at his watch and called, "Where you running off to? My relief comes on in fifteen minutes and I'm free to go."

Laurette regarded him with disdain and moved on past him.

"I'm serious," Milt said. "I got the hots for you. I'd love to stick it to you."

"Stick it in an icebox and slam the door," she replied without breaking stride and continued outside to hail a taxi.

Five minutes went by before a cab arrived. During that time Laurette brushed off two amorous motorists who generously offered her lifts. She never noticed the green Oldsmobile parked across the street nor the slouching killer inside who waited until she had pulled away before putting on his pair of white surgical gloves.

Back inside the lobby Milt combed his hair in the reflection of the console screen. He was adding on the finishing touches of a pompadour when a motorcycle policeman with goggles on charged into the lobby. "What the hell is up?" Milt demanded.

"We got a report that there's a guy up on the roof," he answered, rushing past the security guard's desk to the elevator. "Above the penthouses," he added, impatiently jabbing the button.

Two more patrolmen ran in and joined the motorcycle policeman at the elevator. The excited Milt switched on the intercom system of his console. "Ray, Terry, Manny, this is Milt here," he called to them. "Stay put and keep your eyes on my gate. I'm going up. There's a prowler on the roof."

Milt dashed after the motorcycle policeman and the two patrolmen entering the elevator. The door was just closing as he arrived but he stuck his hand in to force it open so he could go with the others.

At his desk at the side entrance the security guard named Ray saw on his console the arrival of two more patrolmen at Milt's vacated station. "I guess they'll be wanting us to stick around when the relief comes on," he said discontentedly to his coworkers Terry and Manny. "You think we'll get paid for it?"

While the three security guards downstairs speculated on the possibility of extra remuneration, a second motorcycle policeman appeared briefly on their screens as he ran to the elevators. "That makes six cops for one prowler," Manny shouted. "That's some fucking overstaffed police force we've got."

The first two patrolmen to reach the building took a last look around the empty roof of the apartment house, then hurried back down the service stairs to the twelfth floor. They saw the motorcycle policeman who had come up on the elevator with them banging on the door of Croft's apartment, 12A, while Milt watched anxiously. At the other end of the corridor the door to 12B suddenly opened and the two other patrolmen emerged. One of them yelled, "Nothing in 12B."

"Still no answer from this one," the motorcycle policeman at 12A hollered back. "Son-of-a-bitch must be deaf."

The elderly tenant of 12B appeared at his doorway in his dressing gown. He recognized Milt among the men in the corridor and yelled, "Three thousand a month! Absolute safety and security!" He slammed his door in disgust.

The four patrolmen, the motorcycle policeman, and Milt gathered around the door of 12A and exchanged baffled looks. "You got a passkey?" the motorcycle policeman asked the security guard.

"No such thing in this building," Milt replied proudly.

The motorcycle policeman drew his revolver, pressed it against the lock, and ordered the others, "Stand away from the door."

The second motorcycle policeman to arrive was climbing the service stairs between the tenth and eleventh floors when he heard the muffled shot of a revolver, followed a moment later by the blast of a shotgun. He paused, removed his heavy motorcycle gloves, and flexed his fingers still encased within the rubber ones.

The killer felt a surge of elation. It was all going precisely according to plan.

Inside apartment 12A, Croft, crouched behind a sofa, kept his double-barrel shotgun trained on the five police officers and Milt who had burst into his living room.

"Keep your hands up, damnit," Croft told them.

The six men reluctantly did what they were told.

"You're making a terrible mistake, sir," Milt said ingratiatingly. "They're only doing their jobs. I know most of these officers personally."

Croft, clad only in a pair of jeans he had hurriedly pulled on when he heard the banging at his door, considered Milt's explanation. He lowered his shotgun and said, "Well, there's nobody in here but me. So everybody out now."

The six men hesitantly let their upraised hands fall to their sides. The motorcycle policeman picked up his gun from the floor. Two of the patrolmen muttered profanities but filed out of the apartment with the rest.

Milt and the policemen, growing more conscious of their narrow escape from death as the shock wore off, maintained a stony silence during the elevator's descent to the lobby. The doors slid open. Milt said diffidently, "Sorry about that, fellas. Everybody's a little jumpy these days."

"Forget it," replied the motorcycle policeman. "I'd just like to get my hands on the bastard that sent in that phony alarm. He nearly got us killed by that crazy mother up there."

Twelve flights up, Croft, his shotgun cradled in the crook of his arm, poured himself a bourbon with his free hand then inspected the part of the wall near the door. It was pitted with pellets from the blast he had fired above the intruders's heads. The tight, round cluster of holes two inches deep was just what he had expected and he patted his shotgun approvingly. "I'm going to put a cleaning rod right through you," he said softly to it, walking to his desk and opening a drawer in which he kept his shotgun cleaning kit.

It was while Croft was screwing the two parts of the

aluminum rod together that he looked toward the entrance of his apartment and became aware of the hole in the door left by the blasted-away lock. His face darkened. It dawned on him that the net result of all the commotion about the nonexistent prowler was that his door could no longer be locked.

Hurriedly switching off the lights, Croft backed out onto his terrace, knelt behind a pillar, and aimed his shotgun at the damaged front door. He knew someone would be coming through it. The only question that remained was when.

On the roof the killer peered over the ledge down onto Croft's terrace and wondered if at last Fortuna, the Roman goddess of chance, had deserted him. No matter how far forward he leaned he could see no more than the leg of Croft kneeling motionless below. Croft would stay in that position for hours if need be, he told himself, as still and as patient as the hunter he was.

Holstering his silencer the killer crept along the roof until he was just beyond the wall running down and flush with the terrace. He took out the thin twenty-foot rope he had brought with him, tied it around a ventilator, and tested the knot for strength. Satisfied it would support his weight he shut his eyes. He ordered his mind to disregard his fear of heights. At no time was it to receive a suppressed desire to fly which is at the heart of all acrophobia. Then, like a mountain climber on a sheer rock face, he began to lower himself down the side of the building until his feet were level with the terrace's ledge.

For over a minute the killer rested suspended, calmy watching the street twelve stories below. A man and his dog out for a walk shrunk to two dots as they passed directly below him, and expanded again as they proceeded on. When they had disappeared around a corner he swung his body into the wall and worked his way toward the terrace. His left foot found the ledge.

Croft alone among the hammers, a man who had shot his first buck before his thirteenth birthday, could have heard the scraping of a crepe sole on concrete. He whirled around just as the killer sprung at him and grabbed his shotgun.

The two men grappled in the half light of the moon. Croft, breathing heavily, forced the killer back against the terrace ledge and bent him halfway over it. Using the leverage he had achieved, the hammer tried to force his shotgun down across the killer's throat like a man straining to close a trunk lid.

The killer, summoning up a manic strength, pushed back on the weapon until he stood erect. He shoved Croft away momentarily but the two struggling men became entwined once more. Wrestling for position and possession of the shotgun, they rolled along the terrace.

Croft struck upward with his fist and knocked the killer's goggles off as he jerked his head away from the full force of the blow. The hammer had a glimpse of the killer's triumphant face before he felt the sole of his opponent's foot pressed against his own stomach.

The killer rolled backward onto the floor of the terrace pulling Croft with him, and in one fluid motion kicked the screaming hammer high over the ledge behind them and into the dark void below.

CHAPTER TWENTY-SIX

It was deputy Commissioner Talbot's turn to do the honors. He transferred Croft's photograph to the ever-mounting collection of dead men and turned to the glum-looking Slade and Fine beside him. "Don't take it so hard," he said, patting them on the shoulders encouragingly. "You did your best."

"Yeah," said Slade. "We managed to keep score."

Talbot, aware that further commiseration was both pointless and unappreciated, looked back at the bulletin board and the two remaining survivors, Cassell and Julian. "The word is they hate each other's guts," he said reflectively. "Ought to be interesting."

"It's sure getting to look like one of them imported an all-star hitter," Fine agreed. "Or we've got a Super Freak on our hands."

Talbot and Slade nodded slowly. Fine suddenly smiled. "What's so funny?" Slade asked.

"Look at it this way," replied Fine, holding up two fingers. "One way or another, it can't go on much longer."

Uptown in the paneled library of a condominium overlooking the United Nations Building, Eddie Cassell and Alex Merritt of the National Committee came to a similar conclusion while discussing the impasse brought about by the depletion of the Big Four's highest-ranking men.

"I tell you, Julian is plain scared," Merritt said emphatically. "He's sent that kid of his to Switzerland and he's barricaded himself in his house. He won't take a step out."

"Now that Jimmy Croft's dead, he can't suspect me," Cassell argued. "He's got to come out."

Merritt shook his crew-cut head. "No way."

"Listen, you tell him we've got to get together. All the punks that used to work for Luce and Strauss are setting up on their own. There's new guys coming in every day and cutting themselves in. Nobody's paying us dues. It's chaos."

"Eddie, Julian is a very, very rich man. As long as there's a one-man Murder Incorporated running around loose, Julian won't budge."

"He will if the National Committee tell him to. If he doesn't, he knows he's finished and he ain't never coming out. You call a meeting. He can't refuse. At least to talk to me."

Cassell held up his beefy hand to prevent Merritt from protesting further, then rose and began to pace around the room. "Look, this is the way you put it to him. You say that him and me will meet first in a place *you* pick. No one will know where until you stop the car. The two of us will square things between us. Afterwards, you say you'll bring in those bighead punks and me and Julian will read them the riot act."

"Eddie, he doesn't trust you."

Cassell smiled wolfishly. "He'll trust you."

Merritt pondered Cassell's plan. Finally he asked resignedly, "When?"

"Make it for tonight."

"That doesn't leave much time."

"It's time enough."

Merritt picked up his phone and punched out Julian's number on the board.

At ten o'clock that evening Merritt drove his Lincoln down the ramp of the West Side Highway and turned toward the Bronx. Seated in front beside him were the two agreed upon bodyguards provided by Cassell and Julian. Their employers, as far away from each other as possible, reclined in the vast recesses of the upholstered rear. Merritt, in his rear-view mirror, could see Julian's face. There was a nervous tic under his left eye. Merritt began to worry that at any moment Julian might change his mind and call off the meeting.

The Lincoln pulled over to a curb and parked. Julian stared out of the tinted window at the dark deserted building. It had been a multiple dwelling before its conversion into offices. Julian had a faint recollection it had been used for Tommy Luce's vending-machine operation. Cassell reached for his door handle. Merritt said, "I'll be back in an hour with the others."

"Drive on," Julian ordered. "I don't like this spot. Pick another."

Merritt was about to argue but Cassell told him, "If Matthew wants another place it's fine with me."

Looking at Julian coldly, Merritt threw up his hands, then spun around and drove off.

A half hour later the Lincoln arrived at a warehouse in the upper Bronx. Julian nodded his approval of the new site and Merritt got out of the car. He moved swiftly toward the front door of the furniture-storage warehouse to unlock it. Cassell, Julian, and the two bodyguards followed.

Merritt swung the door open then regarded the two chieftains in turn. Julian and his bodyguard, as if by a prearranged signal, squared off to face Cassell and his. The chieftains unbuttoned their jackets and held them spread apart. Merritt stepped between the two groups and removed the guns of Cassell and Julian. Cassell moved past the four men to enter the warehouse.

"Wait a minute," Julian said.

Cassell stopped and looked back over his shoulder at Julian. "Something wrong, Matthew?"

"I'd like my guy to check you out, Eddie."

Cassell pursed his lips. He turned around to submit to a search. Julian's bodyguard stepped forward and began thoroughly to frisk the large powerful man. At a curt nod from Cassell his own bodyguard went up to Julian.

Julian raised his hands. Cassel's bodyguard patted him under the ribs just long enough to block Julian's view while Julian's bodyguard slipped a .25 automatic into Cassell's jacket pocket.

The preliminaries over Cassell and Julian entered the warehouse, leaving their bodyguards posted at the door. The two chieftains, side by side, proceeded down a long corridor toward an office with a glass door. Their matched footsteps echoed loudly. A series of naked light bulbs illuminated the seemingly endless walkway. The two men's faces were like death masks in the harsh glow. They listened to each other's deep breathing.

"We should have had this out a long time ago, Matthew, and cleared the air."

"Now's as good a time as ever, Eddie."

They were halfway down the corridor when Cassell slowly slipped his hand into the edge of his pocket on Julian's blind side. A few steps further he withdrew the .25 automatic.

The two men reached the office door. Julian, looking straight ahead, said, "The meeting was your idea. You go in first."

"Anything you say," Cassell murmured and brought his gun around in front of him toward Julian's ribs.

Julian turned at the exact moment a startled expression crossed Cassell's face. The burly chieftain's jaw went flaccid and a faraway look came into his eyes. His leonine head snapped back and he pitched forward, two bullet holes in his back. His .25 automatic clattered across the floor.

Julian looked back over his shoulder. The killer stood in the shadows at the far end of the corridor. The only part of him that was visible was his right arm and shoulder. Julian made out the white-gloved hand holding a silencer. It was pointed at him.

Kneeling, Julian picked up the weapon Cassell had dropped and cradled it in his palm as if testing its weight. Then he rose and, carrying the .25 automatic at his side, advanced steadily along the corridor toward the killer.

The killer lowered his silencer. As Julian drew abreast of him the man in the shadows nodded almost imperceptibly in a gesture that could have been taken as a salute. Julian continued past and walked out of the warehouse.

The bodyguards were gone.

Merritt, alone in his Lincoln, saw Julian striding resolutely toward him with the .25 automatic in his hand. Gripping the steering wheel tightly he waited motionless until Julian had entered from the other side, then looked up sharply.

Julian pointed the gun at Merritt's chest and pulled the trigger. The gun's firing pin clicked on the empty chamber.

Merritt started up the engine and eased the Lincoln away from the curb. After they had gone a few blocks, he said, "To tell you the truth, Matthew, the National never thought you'd pull the whole thing off."

Julian and Merritt drove south along the West Side Highway, cut through Central Park, and headed for the brilliantly lit Fifth Avenue. The wide, store-lined thoroughfare seemed to open before them invitingly. Julian sighed contentedly, then stiffened as if embarrassed by his momentary lapse into relaxation. "Now we can really get down to business," he said.

PART II

Fifteen Months Later

CHAPTER TWENTY-SEVEN

When it turns bone-chilling cold in October, New Yorkers have a legitimate grievance. A great city ripped by so many social ills of its own making does not need nature's premature icy gusts to render it unbearable.

Bundled-up citizens on their way to work that Monday morning struggled forward into the lashing winds which howled through their streets. They were dispirited by both the unseasoned weather and the commencement of another working week. It was little wonder that they would not raise their bowed heads to notice billboards erected by the Citizens' Committee to Elect Alan Coombs Governor, or read the impressive words below his pictures:

HE SAYS WHAT HE MEANS!
HE MEANS WHAT HE SAYS!

Besides, election year had rolled around again. The city was plastered with signs and posters of candidates for every conceivable public office. Admittedly, few had as slick a photograph as the one of the shirt-sleeved Coombs or as stirring a slogan, but it was not enough to make a chilled New Yorker lift a numbed face to the cloud-filled sky.

Slade, padding around the shiny kitchen of his new apartment in the east 80s, found the pitcher of cream for his coffee. After taking a sip he flipped through the dials of an alarm-clock radio which Sylvia and Howie Fine had given him as a housewarming gift three months ago.

"There is today in this state an Unholy Alliance between organized crime, corrupt government, and crooked business interests," came Coombs' impassioned voice across the airwaves. "I ask you by your votes to give me the power to smash that Unholy Alliance."

The applause that followed the last ringing phrase was cut off abruptly and the news commentator intoned, "With these words Alan Coombs on Sunday night launched into the hardest-hitting speech of his whirlwind campaign for Governor. . . ."

Slade switched off the radio. Climbing off the stool, he carried his empty cup to the sink where he carefully rinsed it out and set it in the dish drain to dry. Then he went into a tastefully furnished living room, still immaculate from a two-hour visit by a male cleaning service the previous week. Slade saw that the two young men sent by the service had even polished the frames of the several photographs of his sons. He took up the ones the boys had sent him only last month from their private school which he could now afford. With mixed emotions he picked out the faces of the serious-looking James and the smiling Warren among the members of the Hudson Academy junior football team. The contrast between his sons' expressions was indicative of their prowess at sports: James succeeded only by intense determination and extra effort; Warren was a gifted, natural athlete. The thought crossed his mind that everyone had always said Warren was his mother's son while James favored his father. Putting the photographs down he checked his desk calendar to determine when the next visiting day was.

He dressed leisurely in his bedroom. Returning to the living room he slid open a drawer of his desk, took out his revolver, and slipped it into a discreet, new hip holster. Then he pulled on the jacket of a modish flannet suit, adjusted his dignified tie, threw a Burberry trenchcoat over his arm, and went out the door.

A moment later a disgruntled Slade reentered his apartment. He picked up the attaché case that he was constantly forgetting and left again for work.

At the elevators in the lobby of Police Headquarters he met Talbot waiting with other departmental personnel for the car to arrive. "Morning, John," said Talbot.

"Morning, Frank."

In the crowded, rising elevator car, a sleepy blond file clerk glanced up through puffy eyes, brightened, and said to the recently appointed Commissioner, "Good morning, Mr. Talbot."

"Hi," Talbot replied politely, then edged around the girl toward Slade. "How you coming on your budget figures?" he asked.

"My girl'll type them up this morning."

The elevator doors sprung open. Everyone got out, Talbot and his aides going off one way down the corridor, Slade another. He reached his office. On the door was his old name and new title:

JOHN SLADE
COMMUNITY RELATIONS

An attractive secretary rose from her desk and smiled at him as he entered. She took his trenchcoat, shaped it over a hanger, and hung it up in the clothes closet. "Early skiing this year," she said, retaking her seat.

He nodded vaguely at the girl's reference to the weather and headed for his office. As he opened the door his assistant, Sam Weller, came out of the adjoining office. He handed Slade a cigar in celebration of the birth of his fourth daughter. "It's the last you're getting from me," he told his superior. "I'm getting teed off."

After searching for a suitable reply, Slade said, "Well, at least you weren't off in Mexico when she was born."

"That's a thought," Weller replied. "Anyway I'm just on my way out. I'll be down at City Hall all morning."

"Okay by me," said Slade, then went inside and closed the door behind him.

The office was stuffy after the weekend of continous heat and no airing out, so he opened the window wide. He sat down at his impressive desk littered with paper work, loosened his tie, sighed, and dug into the pile of morning mail. Ten minutes later his secretary brought him in his usual jelly doughnut and his morning coffee in a colorful ceramic mug.

He turned on his dictaphone machine and slipped into the routine of another day. He was already bored.

CHAPTER TWENTY-EIGHT

"When the hell is Hank coming?" the strung-out junkie asked irritably. He paced around the East Harlem apartment that the group was using as a "shooting gallery," oblivious to the few pieces of tattered furniture dragged upstairs from neighboring garbage areas, the green paint peeling from the smelly grease-stained walls, and the tub in the kitchen choked with soiled diapers. All he was conscious of was the girl in the bedroom crooning a lullaby. It made his flesh drawl.

Stepping over the two addicts peacefully asleep on the grimy floor, the strung-out junkie walked jerkily to a wooden crate that served as a table. He picked up a transistor the handsome youth on the sofa had shoplifted that morning. Switching it on, he held it to his ear, heard nothing, and shook it angrily. "This mother fucker doesn't work."

"Easy, baby, there's no battery," the handsome youth said. "You got to pay extra for that."

"When the hell is Hank coming?" the strung-out junkie asked again, this time more loudly.

Joe Davis, dozing in a gutted, stuffed chair, stirred. He raised his head from between his legs and moaned his protest at the noise. "What the fuck is the beef all about?" he demanded.

The strung-out junkie and the handsome youth glanced over vacantly at the filthy, disheveled black with the bloodshot, runny eyes. There was a rumor that a year ago he had been busted from the police force for stealing $100,000 worth of confiscated heroin, but neither addict gave much credence to it. They forgot about Davis the instant they turned away to resume their conversation.

"Goddamnit, man, I asked you a question," the strung-out junkie said to the handsome youth.

Before the handsome youth could recall exactly what the question had been, an angelic-looking eighteen-year-old girl came out of the bedroom. An infant in a shoulder sling sucked loudly at her breast beneath her rolled-up T-shirt. Mother and child strolled through the living room to the kitchen. She tossed more diapers into the tub, ran the hot water, and searched around for some detergent.

On contact with the steamy water ammonia gas rose from the urine-soaked fabrics floating in the tub and the odor wafted through the apartment. The strung-out junkie was about to voice a complaint when there was a knock at the door. He moved to it hurriedly and called through it, "Hank?"

"Hank's sick. I'm doing his rounds."

The junkie looked apprehensively at the handsome youth who shrugged back his own indecision.

"Last chance, baby. That door don't open now, I'm splitting."

The door was unlocked and a swarthy, stoop-shouldered pusher entered. He received a beatific smile of welcome from the young mother. "Would you like a cup of hot coffee?" she asked him.

The pusher shook his head and sauntered past her

into the living room. He put down her offer of hospitality to a mental disorder.

The mother popped her child off her nipple, burped it with surprising efficiency, and set it down half asleep in a magnificent carriage stolen by the handsome youth in Central Park. Then she reached up into a cupboard above the tub for the shooting apparatus, carried it to the handsome youth, and went to the stove to warm a jar of baby-food bananas.

The pusher took two packets of horse from the band of his hat and dangled them before the two addicts. The strung-out junkie proffered some crumpled bills.

"You're light ten bucks. Price has gone up," the pusher said matter-of-factly.

The junkie made a desperate grab for one of the packets, but the pusher jerked it out of his reach. Grinning, the pusher shoved the junkie back against a wall and swaggered up to him. "You want your medicine, you be nice to doctor."

The handsome youth signaled to the girl in the kitchen and she moved languidly toward the three men in the doorway. Reaching into the pocket of her jeans, she extracted a neatly folded bankroll, peeled off the required amount, and handed it to the handsome youth. He passed it along uncounted to the pusher, who gave him one of the packets in return.

"You cocksucker," cried the junkie to the handsome youth in a whining voice that was nevertheless filled with genuine pain. "I ain't got an old lady turning tricks for me with old farts who like to suck milk out of her titties."

The insult only made the young mother sigh. She counted off two $5 bills to make up for the junkie's

shortage. The odds were one in four, she knew, that
he might be the father of her child, and that fact carried
a certain obligation to him on her part. She gave the
money to the pusher and drifted back into the kitchen
as he studied her buttocks with interest. He had been
considering of late that peddling flesh might be a
more attractive occupation than trafficking in dope.

"Let's go, man," the junkie said, stretching out his
trembling hand.

The pusher tossed him the other packet and shook
his head in mock sorrow at the way his customer
hurried away to grab the needle from the handsome
youth. There was no doubt in his mind that as a pimp
he would at least deal with a better class of purchasers.

The junkie prepared his fix. The pusher turned to
go. Joe Davis bounded from his chair, raced across the
living room, and smashed the junkie's hypodermic out
of his hand onto the floor. While the others gaped in
amazement the pusher broke for the door. His hand
was on the knob when Davis collared him, carried him
bodily to the tub, and held his head under the sudsy
water.

The handsome youth and the junkie leaped on
Davis's back to pull him off, but the powerful black
easily shook them off. Then he jerked the pusher's
soaking head out of the water. "Who sent you?" he
screamed.

The pusher maintained a defiant silence. Davis
shoved his head under water again. This time he kept
it submerged for almost a minute before finally yanking it up. "Give, damn you, give," he warned.

Coughing and sputtering the pusher shook his head.
Davis smashed the heels of his palms into the pusher's

ears in a vicious clapping motion. The stricken man sunk to the floor with ruptured eardrums.

The junkie rushed at Davis again and took a stiff-arm in the face for his efforts. Davis snatched up the loaded needle from the floor and sat down hard on the pusher's chest.

"Hey, that's mine, you crazy bastard," the strung-out junkie wailed hysterically as Davis waved the needle under the pusher's nose.

"Who gave you this shit, high and mighty man?" Davis demanded. "It's your last chance."

The pusher's eyes brimmed with pain and terror. "Give me a break, man."

Davis stuck the point of the hypodermic needle inside the pusher's nostril. "I'm going to make you a member of the club."

The pusher's eyeballs rolled upward in their sockets as he jerked his head back. Davis moved the needle forward and pricked the flesh of his captive's bloodless lips.

"He's downstairs waiting," the pusher cried. He sucked on his lip where the needle had penetrated and spat furiously. "Right outside the building."

"What's he wearing?"

"Overcoat. Yellow."

The pusher began to sob convulsively. His body shook. Davis stabbed downward with the needle toward the pusher's arm. The point struck the floor a fraction of an inch from its target. The pusher fainted. Davis jumped to his feet, pulled off the pusher's shoes and trousers, and threw them out of a window. The infant woke and bawled piteously as Davis ran out of the apartment and down the stairs.

At the ground floor he saw the back of a man in a

yellow mohair overcoat leaning against the front entrance and watching the snowflakes fluttering in the wind outside. He grabbed the man by the shoulder and spun him around. Recognizing the bewildered face, he hit it as hard as he could.

CHAPTER TWENTY-NINE

"John Slade's office," his secretary said into the telephone.

The voice with the heavy German accent on the other end of the line wished her a good morning and afterwards requested, "Mistehr Slade, please. Zis es Gunter, mit ah umlaut over zee ooh, Freisler, at zee Vest Chermann Embassy."

The secretary rang Slade on the intercom. When she was through she told him, "Detective Fine's on the phone."

He picked up his receiver. "Haven't you got anyone else to play with?"

"Funny you should mention that. I've got an old playmate of yours right here. Why don't you come down from the executive suite and see some life in the raw again?"

Welcoming the distraction from his paperwork, Slade hung up, walked casually past his secretary's desk to the corridor, then hurried for the elevator.

Inside the interrogation room of the Special Squad bullpen, Davis chucked the prisoner's chin and turned him around for Slade's inspection. He recognized him immediately as Sonny, Sailor Sapinski's former henchman. The color of his left cheek ranged from deep purple around the closed eye to pale pink above his upper lip. His mohair coat was blood-splattered.

"Big Boy's a hit man now," Davis said. "Takes out junkies for nickels and dimes." The black detective picked up the needle he had taken from the junkie. "Full of poison. A fink named Hank spotted one of his customers having a beer with a narc. He got so nervous he told his supplier and he called in Sonny to slip him some dirty shit."

"I don't know fuck-all about any dirty shit," Sonny insisted. "I was just getting out of a snow storm."

The prisoner looked around at the detectives for their reactions to his story. He seemed to notice Slade for the first time. His hand darted out and gripped the fabric of Slade's trouser leg. "Nice threads. Didn't get these at Robert Hall."

Slade brushed Sonny's hand away.

"Hey, come on, I remember you," Sonny purred. "You must have come up in the world."

Davis squeezed Sonny's chin between his thumb and forefinger, turned his head around to himself, and said, "I can tie you into three DOAs, including that fifteen-year-old on Avenue C. Did you know she only popped half? She was saving the rest for later. It took her three days and four nights to die."

Jerking his head away Sonny massaged his swollen chin where Davis had gripped it. "Fucking cops," he snarled. "I know all you guys." Whirling around toward Slade he added scornfully, "Especially you, big shot. Sailor got in his boat to get away from you. Into the sunset like a big-assed bird."

Slade listened woodenly. Fine deeply regretted he had invited him to the interrogation. Sonny had touched some nerve, there was no doubt of that. He had found a spot where touching hurt, for there was fury behind Slade's unmoving face. Suddenly Sonny yanked on an imaginary gallows rope around his neck, let his one opened eye sail up into his skull, and stuck out his tongue through his battered lips.

His ghastly face became wreathed in a smile at Slade's discomfort. "Such smart cops," he cackled.

At lunch that afternoon in a Chinese restaurant near Police Headquarters, Slade picked at his food with his chopsticks while Fine consumed his with gusto. "If you're not going to finish those butterfly shrimps," Fine said, reaching across the table to Slade's plate and spearing two of them, "I will."

Slade splashed his chopsticks into his bowl of cold, uneaten won-ton soup. Fine, glancing up and seeing how rattled his friend still was, said, "If scum like Sonny made me lose my appetite I'd starve to death."

Fine chewed the shrimps he had appropriated and used his tongue afterwards to work out a shred of ginger from between his teeth. He cocked his head at Slade. "Oh for Christ's sake, John are you starting that whole *mishagoss* again?"

A waiter tried to remove Slade's untouched meal but Fine snatched the plates from his hand and set them back down next to him. Slade slid his teacup toward Fine for a refill, took a sip, and said, "Look Howie, police business is like any other business. You're supposed to show a profit at the end of the year—or at least hold your own. Well we sure as hell didn't. We went bust."

"It happens all the time. With Chrysler and NYPD. How many unsolved murders are there in the files? Thousands? Buried and forgotten for all time. Though we don't admit that. We have our little euphemisms like 'inactive file,' 'open file,' or 'pending' to hide our lack of success. You're deluding yourself if you think otherwise. We goof continually. You want to show a profit. Open the books. Every year it's the same thing, a long string of minor bankruptcies."

"Minor!" Slade exclaimed. "Julian's guy looted the store with us watching. He made us look like assholes."

A pained expression settled on Fine's face. It was his own damn fault, he admitted to himself, to have allowed Slade to steer the conversation back to the murder of the hammers and Luce and Cassell. He should have let his friend stew until the frustration of his defeat at Julian's hands had run its course once more. "Ah, John," he pleaded, "we've been through this before so many times. It's all over. Julian won. He raked in the pot. He called in the Ice Man and got rid of all the uglies, even his own. So there'd be nobody left heavy enough to buck him. When it was all over he sent the Ice Man home with love and kisses. The town quieted down again. Everybody's happy. Everybody, that is, but you."

"You're goddamn right I'm not," Slade exploded.

Several of the other diners looked at the two detectives nervously. Slade tried to stare them down but gave up and turned back to Fine. What was the use, he asked himself. He could not make Fine understand how he, as a failure, despised the easy acceptance of failure. He signaled the waiter for the check.

Fine shrugged wearily. "I just don't get you, John. You came off the street for a big job upstairs, and everybody knows they're grooming you for a bigger one."

"Waiter, the check please," Slade said loudly. To be rewarded for failure was even worse than casual acceptance of it.

"You just can't leave it alone, can you, John? You're like a little kid who picks his scabs so they won't heal."

Slade was still brooding as he and Fine walked back to Police Headquarters after lunch. The morning's light snow flurries had turned to an icy rain. They halted at a corner for a light and Fine noticed a Coombs for Governor poster in a cigar-store window. "The bookies have him even money now," he said.

"Onward and upward," Slade said aloud. And to himself: Another screwup reaping rewards.

"A nebbish with an image," observed Fine, relieved to be discussing the inanities of politics instead of Julian and the annihilation of his opposition.

The streetlight turned green. The two detectives started across. Fine said, "As Will Rogers used to say, 'Politics is all apple sauce.'"

"What did he mean by that?"

"Beats the shit out of me."

Reaching the opposite sidewalk they proceeded cautiously along the treacherous, slippery city streets.

CHAPTER THIRTY

Slade ran smack into the middle of the fracas. As he came into the reception area of his office after his lunch with Fine, Weller was patiently explaining to a chic, handsome rather than pretty, woman in her late 30s, "I'm really sorry, Mrs. North. I can't help you. I'm no longer with Missing Persons."

The secretary rose to show Mrs. North the door. She said to the woman frostily, "I did try to make that clear to you, madam."

Mrs. North looked imploringly at Weller. "I want to speak to *you*. I don't know who else to turn to."

The secretary employed the crusher from her arsenal of bureaucratic fob-offs. "If you go *back* to the third floor there'll be someone *there* to help you."

Tears welled up in Mrs. North's pale blue eyes. Weller, uncomfortable, put his arm hesitantly around her shoulder to comfort her. Slade regarded his assistant and the stranger quizzically. Weller hastily removed his arm from her. "Come into my office," he told her. "We can talk in there."

Avoiding Slade's eyes Weller showed Mrs. North into his office.

"What's her problem?" Slade asked his secretary.

"I don't know. She insisted she had to see Sam."

"What about?"

The secretary shrugged. Her expression was sour as if she had made five typing errors in an important letter at the office closing hour. Slade wandered into his own office. Through the adjoining door to Weller's office that was left ajar, he saw Mrs. North taking a seat on the sofa. She noticed him and signaled his presence to Weller, who came forward and shut it softly. Slade stared at the closed door a moment then picked up a sheet of paper. On it were his calculations on the budget he had promised Talbot for that afternoon. It would not be finished on time. It depressed him that he had glibly lied that it would be.

A half hour later both doors of Slade's office opened at once, jolting him out of his reverie. From one came his secretary bearing a mug of coffee; from the other Weller carrying a folder. The two men talked about this and that until the secretary left. Then Slade asked, "What was all that about?"

Weller flopped down heavily on the chair in front of his desk. "Voices from the past," he said. "Her husband went missing a little over a year ago. I got very involved."

Slade raised his bushy eyebrows. "With her *case*," Weller assured him quickly. "Although I did have a lot of sympathy for her. We couldn't come up with anything. And we couldn't find any reason for his leaving."

"Maybe he couldn't stand his wife."

Weller made a face somewhere between a pout and a frown. "I considered that possibility and rejected it. Anyway, when we came up dry she hired a private investigator." Weller waved the folder. "The guy spent eight months and a lot of her money running down leads. Mostly *stuups* that Mr. North played around with at one time or another."

Weller riffled through some different-sized photos attached to the report in the folder. Slade caught a glimpse of one of them and was taken aback.

"But no trace of the husband," Weller resumed, not noticing Slade's surprised reaction. "All of a sudden last week the private investigator calls Mrs. North and tells her he's dropping the case."

"Can I see that report, Sam?"

"Sure."

Slade turned the pages of the report Weller handed him until he found the photo of the bikini-clad girl with the shimmering blond hair cascading down onto her bare suntanned shoulders. He had not been mistaken. It was Ginny Jackman. He realized that Weller was speaking again. ". . . the private investigator just quit cold. Mrs. North thinks it's all very suspicious. Her financial advisors said she was paying the private investigator above the mark, so why the hell was he turning down good money. To get her out of the office I had to promise her I'd look into it."

"Mind if I hang on to the report awhile?"

Weller dropped his gaze to Ginny's photograph. He studied her critically. "You know her?"

"Faces from the past."

"Are you going to let me in on it."

"Sure, Sam. Later."

Weller could find no further excuse for lingering and went back into his own office. When he was alone Slade reached into the bottom drawer of his desk and extracted a thick file. He opened it and found a series of police photos of Ginny reenacting her discovery of Pete Bremner's body in Bungalow 11 of the Four

Winds Motel. Slade clasped his hands, formed a steeple with his forefingers, and tapped his lips with it as he examined the photos spread on his desk. They neither told him nor suggested anything. He took up the private investigator's report. There was a label on its cover with a neatly centered title:

INVESTIGATION INTO THE
DISAPPEARANCE OF OTIS J. NORTH.

and below, embossed and staggered,

WALLACE WALGREEN
PRIVATE INVESTIGATOR

Slade flipped the cover over to the first page. There was a photograph of a man identified as Otis Jay North. It showed a ruggedly handsome man in his 40s with whitish-blond hair, gleaming even teeth, and a glacial smile.

When Slade's secretary entered the office an hour later to say goodnight she found her boss swiveled around toward the window. He was staring dully at the mackerel clouds turning to pink in the cold, clear October sunset.

CHAPTER THIRTY-ONE

Slade waited impatiently. After several minutes the panel in the door of the West 11th Street brownstone slid back, revealing a pane of security glass. Through the wire mesh he could discern the outline of a face.

"Good evening, sir," came the gruff, English-accented voice he presumed belonged to the butler.

"Deputy Inspector Slade. I phoned earlier."

The panel slid shut and the door opened. The butler, a wizened figure with a candy-striped waistcoat beneath his livery, studied him solemnly, then swept him into the vestibule like a pile of dust. "Will you follow me, please?" he asked, leading Slade through a corridor toward a high-ceilinged living room looking onto the garden behind the house. It was cluttered with heavy antique pieces of oak and walnut which had the look of furniture that had been in the same family for a long time. Mrs. North, seated on a large sofa, glanced up timidly. She indicated a nearby chair for him with a graceful wave of her hand. "Please be seated, Mr. Slade."

Slade sat down carefully on the edge of the chair. Mrs. North said with a trace of embarrassment, "I apologize for the scene I made in your office today. I'm afraid I'm suffering from nerves."

He noted the pale, slender woman's slurred speech, glazed eyes, and slowness of motion that could have been caused by either pills or gin. "That's all right," he said, slipping the private investigator's report out of his inside jacket pocket and leaning forward toward the woman who had commissioned it.

Mrs. North flushed slightly. He opened the report brusquely and showed her the photograph of Ginny Jackman. "I'm interested in your husband's connection with this girl."

Mrs. North grimaced at the photo and said sullenly, "Oh, her."

"You knew about her and your husband?"

"Not until I received Mr. Walgreen's report. But I knew there had to be someone like her. Otis liked them hard."

"Hard?"

"Hard," Mrs. North repeated vigorously. She curled her legs up under her like a child and allowed herself a self-deprecating smile. "I suppose we all have our sexual weaknesses. When I was at school Otis was every girl's dream man. When he asked me to marry him I thought I was the luckiest girl in the world."

Slade searched in vain for signs of self-pity in Mrs. North's tone that would match her words.

"Difficult to believe, isn't it, Mr. Slade, that in those days all a man needed was to be handsome? A look at today's leading men in the cinema shows you how much styles have changed."

Mrs. North's attempt at lightness only intensified her soft defenselessness. Slade held the report slightly aloft to bring the discussion back to the present. "The private investigator searched for your husband. He couldn't find him and quit. That's not unusual. Yet you're suspicious. Why?"

Mrs. North nibbled on her lower lip as she framed her reply. "I think he found Otis. And Otis scared him off."

Slade settled back into his chair and shook his head dubiously.

"My husband had a reason for not wanting to be found," Mrs. North stated firmly. "I'm the beneficiary of several considerable trusts. I foolishly persuaded the trustees to let Otis manage some of the funds. Soon after his disappearance we discovered large shortages in the accounts."

Mrs. North paused and looked over her guest's shoulder. Slade looked behind him. A teenage girl stood in the doorway of the living room. Physically she resembled her father but her worried, apprehensive expression derived from her mother. "I'll be along in a moment, darling," Mrs. North told her daughter.

The girl did not bother to acknowledge her mother's polite dismissal. She stared suspiciously at Slade a moment and left the room as soundlessly as she had entered. Mrs. North continued, "Otis never had any money of his own. I thought by letting him handle mine I could hold on to him."

"I know your private investigator, Mrs. North," Slade argued. "Walgreen's an old acquaintance of mine. He doesn't scare easily."

Mrs. North shrugged off his protest. When she spoke again her voice had a distant quality. "You don't know my husband. He can be very frightening."

Slade glanced at the photograph of Otis J. North smiling his wintry smile. He was disposed to debate the point.

"Looks can be deceiving," Mrs. North said, anticipating his objection. "Nothing about Otis was ever what it seemed."

While Slade mulled over her remark, Mrs. North mixed herself a snifter of brandy and Benedictine at the trolley bar. "Would you care for something?" she asked.

He shook his head. "What was he like, Mrs. North?"

She swirled the amber-colored liquid around the sides of her glass. "He could be charming. Or he could be cruel. He had the hunter's instinct for finding a person's weakness. He was a born destroyer."

"A lot of men destroy their marriages."

She went rigid. "I didn't mean that," she said angrily, moving toward the sliding doors of a room off the one in which they were and motioning him to follow.

He hesitated. It was only after Mrs. North slid open the doors and disappeared into the darkened room that he got to his feet and went in after her.

At the far end of the oppressively overheated study Slade saw a pair of eyes glowing eerily in the darkness. Mrs. North clicked on the light switch, startling him, and he saw that the glowing eyes belonged to the mounted head of a bighorn Mountain goat balefully staring into space.

He looked around the room at the other trophy heads then noticed the host of photographs of Otis J. North in various hunting poses. His gaze rested on one in particular: the woman's missing husband squinting through the telescopic sight of a rifle pointed directly at the safari photographer's camera. "Killing became an obsession," she said in a hushed voice.

Slade glanced at her inquiringly as she hunched her

shoulders and drew her arms across her chest. "One night," she recounted as if beginning a story to a child, "a couple of months before Otis left, we woke up and heard someone downstairs breaking into the house. I picked up the phone by the bed to call the police. Otis stopped me. He took a pistol from the bedside table, told me to stay absolutely still where I was, and sneaked downstairs. A few minutes later I heard a shot. Then Otis came back. He said I could call the police and tell them my husband just shot a burglar. I'll never forget the look on his face. So cold. So composed. So at peace with himself."

She drained the remains of her drink, pressing the edge of the glass hard against her thin lips as if to hold them still. Slade looked back at the photograph of her husband sighting down the scope of his rifle. Then he glanced at her and saw that tears were coursing down her cheeks and streaking her makeup.

"I'm sure," she said, "Otis stalked and killed that burglar just as though he was one of the animals in this room."

CHAPTER THIRTY-TWO

The thumping noise hurt Slade's ears. Huddled inside his trenchcoat in the frigid old-fashioned office on Lower Broadway, he watched Private Investigator Wallace Walgreen bang furiously on the steam radiator with his size thirteen shoe. He was a massive, rotund man halfway through his 50s. His eyes seemed to be pushed toward his temples by the puffiness of his jowls.

"Radiator's stone cold," Walgreen grumbled in a curiously high-pitched voice. He knocked on the radiator some more. "And the janitor's stone deaf."

Walgreen glided across the tattered carpet toward his heavy, cluttered desk, holding his arms stiffly at his sides. His movements reminded Slade of the graceful way some fat men dance. Scattering papers to create a place for his hands, Walgreen parked himself behind his desk, looked morosely at Slade, and said, "Nothing works anymore."

Slade shrugged with indifference. Walgreen puffed out a few times like a whale to observe the frost on his breath, then said, "When you first came in here in all your new sartorial splendor I hardly recognized you. For a moment I thought you were one of those fat-cat lawyers from upstairs. Nice to see someone's making it."

"You must be doing okay, Fats. Not too many PIs can afford to turn down a client like Mrs. North."

Walgreen looked up suspiciously although he had guessed beforehand that the reason for Slade's visit was hardly social. He fumbled for a hip flask in his top drawer and slid it across the desk. Slade pushed it back unopened.

"I saw those expenses you stuck her with, Fats. You'd need an extra asshole to eat that much."

Walgreen unscrewed the cap of the flask, took a snort, and said offhandedly, "When you're looking for a guy like North you tend to visit the better class of joint."

"You visited fifteen states, three European capitals, and Barbados in January."

"Guys on the lam tend to go south."

"You had yourself a nice little joyride on Mrs. North's money. All first class."

Walgreen took another belt from the flask, put his hands behind his fleshy neck, and studied the ceiling.

"I remember when you were honest, Fats. Down to the last nickel phone call."

Walgreen leaned ponderously across the desk. "We were all rubes in those days," he said conspiratorialy. "Then everybody became a wise guy. Except you, John. You always were one." He grinned at his own joke. "Anyway you didn't come up to this igloo to discuss our lost youth."

"Why'd you drop Mrs. North?"

"I didn't want her business. Nothing to do with her race, creed, color, or sex, so it ain't yet against the law."

The clanking noise of the radiator made both men start. Walgreen nodded to it and said, "Aha, Sleeping Beauty hath awakened down in the cellar."

"Fats, why'd you drop Mrs. North?"

"I had my reasons, John. They're staying mine. And I don't give a hoot about my license being renewed. The way things are going I'd just as soon trade it in for food stamps."

"You won't need food stamps in jail. I'll see you do six months for those padded bills."

Walgreen's slanted eyes widened in insolent surprise but his voice was small when he asked, "You wouldn't?"

"How long have you known me, Fats?"

"Fifteen, sixteen years." Walgreen frowned at an unpleasant thought and added, "You would."

"You're right."

Walgreen finished the last of the flask and asked, "Would it help if I told you that my wife needed an operation for the Big C?"

"It would. If you had a wife."

Walgreen smiled faintly but the jauntiness was gone. The odor of stale bourbon hung in the air between the two men after the frosty breath of each had vanished. The PI rubbed his hands together as he spoke, "When I took the lady's case I figured it for a simple trackdown. The hubby leaves his office one night and does a skedaddle. I check out the various ladies he'd been laying and I find this big blond Ginny something-or-other left town around the same time he did. *Cherchez la femme.* Find her, find him. So I circulate their particulars amongst my confreres across this great nation of ours. They come up with leads, most of which I personally check out. But no trace of the big blond. Or North. I got to figure North prepared his Houdini well in advance or he got some help. I come back to Fun City and start to nose around here. And then I begin to get that creepy feeling down the back of my neck. Like somebody's watching me."

"You spot the tail?"

Walgreen shifted uneasily in his chair. His blotchy face shuddered. "I never saw a soul. But the feeling never left me. Anyhow I started checking out people who knew North and I discovered that of late he had become palsy-walsy with one Matthew Julian, a gentleman with whom I'm sure you're familiar."

Twiddling his thumbs Walgreen waited. A jagged bead of sweat traced his hairline. To make the PI continue Slade rapped his knuckles on the desk like a player signaling the dealer for another card.

"Julian wanted to screw society debutantes," Walgreen went on woodenly. "North got them for him. Sweet young things who swoon at the sight of a gangster's pecker."

Walgreen hoisted the flask, remembered it was empty, and tossed it down on the desk. "I dig a little deeper into the relationship between North and Julian and one day I get a visit from a couple of heavyweights. Real life-takers. They didn't quite give me a heart attack, but I tell you, John, all the symptoms were there. They told me to let it alone. I think about their well-intentioned advice. I come to the conclusion that if North's got powerful friends who say let it alone, I better do just that."

Slade shot Walgreen a reproving look. The out-sized private investigator averted his eyes and said out of the side of his mouth, "Look, John, I'm not much to behold, but I'm all I got in this world."

Slade rose abruptly. Walgreen's sweaty face and the stench of booze, were unbearable. He walked rapidly to the frosted-glass door. He heard Walgreen call squeakily, "John," and turned around to face his desolate friend.

"John, when you get to my stage of life, there are some streets you just don't go down anymore."

CHAPTER THIRTY-THREE

Slade brooded over the name. Otis J. North. Like the correct answer in a crossword puzzle it fit exactly and allowed the person to fill in other blanks related to it. North knew Ginny. Did she unwittingly set up Pete Bremner for him in a Riverdale motel? Perhaps. North knew Julian. If Julian gave him the orders to eliminate his rivals, had North the ability to carry them out? Yes, Slade was certain of that.

His check of North's college and service records showed the missing man was more than the handsome, empty-headed bully his wife had described. Among his achievements were: New England AAU decathalon champion at Yale in 1950; U.S. Marine First Lieutenant, marksman, battlefield commission, and holder of the Silver Star from Korea; Fulbright Scholar and accomplished linguist; small-boat sailor and big-game hunter par excellence, holder of the record for the largest bonefish ever caught according to the International Game Fish Association.

From Julian, too, North could have received much of the information and all of the funds required to kill the hammers and the other chieftains. Julian's wealth was vast and it was no secret that the organizations within the Big Four had kept close tabs on each other's personnel, for intelligence of that nature was useful if not absolutely necessary in the event of any falling out between them.

Slade had made a start on the puzzle but could not go further. There were still too many gaps in his knowledge. It occurred to him that the relationship between Julian and North, for example, might be more complex than merely one between a master and his willing servant. Indeed the possibilities in that respect were endless. The bonds were as curious between men who share women as between those who share power. And North's wife had warned him that nothing about her husband was what it seemed. Whatever tie existed between the two men, Julian had felt compelled to scare off Walgreen from delving into it too deeply.

Grasping the stein of half-and-half between his hands, Slade spun around in his chair and watched the game of cribbage being played between the wall-eyed merchant marine and the bar's owner, a lively young Scotsman who had parlayed ambition, stamina, and the capital of American relatives into a goldmine of a saloon on Hudson Street, appropriately renamed Andrew Carnegie West.

The merchant marine lost and paid off the bar owner with a twenty-dollar bill. The grinning Scotsman in a pert brogue offered Slade the loser's vacated chair. He declined the opportunity to increase the immigrant's growing fortune, turned away, and resumed his melancholy speculations on Julian and North while awaiting the arrival of Fine and Davis.

Walgreen's information that North had served as a procurer raised as many questions as it answered. Relationships like that between Julian and North are

born of a long familiarity, but Slade could find no
evidence that the two men's paths had crossed or that
they shared other social or financial interests. The inability to link Julian and North together in a solid
fashion nagged at him like some piece of meat embed-
ded in a distant tooth which the tongue finds, shifts,
but cannot dislodge.

His head began to ache. He used the condensation
from his stein of beer to trace a maze like the one he'd
glimpsed on Julian's lawn that afternoon of his visit to
Angel. As he put down new lines on the table's surface, old ones disappeared. The shifting pattern was as
elusive as the solution to the mystery he wrestled with.

He recalled that Angel, Cellini, Luce, and the Zimmermann brothers had died before his eyes and only
minutes had separated him from witnessing the death
of The Professor in his shabby hotel room. Being so
close to the events it was as if he were in the very heart
of the shifting maze he drew with his moistened finger, unable to step back or rise above it to view the
intricate design.

His want of perspective was accompanied also by a
lack of detachment, an even greater handicap in his
search for answers. The bungled attempt to arrest Sapinski and his futile mission to Angel had been personal failures. He had complained to Fine at lunch in
the Chinese restaurant that their inability to prevent
Julian's coup was a black mark on their professional-
ism, but the truth was that his resentment went far
deeper than that. Julian had made a fool of him personally. And there was even the possibility he had
been used by him.

Over the last fifteen months, of all the self-
accusations Slade had leveled at himself, that one

stung most. He could not blind himself to the simple fact that he had made it easier for the killer to run down his prey. All the killer had had to do, time and time again, was to follow Slade and his detectives. What was it Croft had said to him and Fine that night in the country and western bar? "You stink of death. You draw the flies like garbage." He hated the killer, but he hated Julian even more. Julian had anticipated his every response. In his mind's eye he could see the chieftain smiling enigmatically upon his balcony as Angel whispered in his ear. Was Julian even then contemptuously regarding Slade as an ineffectual fool? No wonder Julian had not ordered his death at the lodge, for make no mistake, Slade told himself bitterly, the cross hairs of the marksman-killer's scope must have rested on his heart. Spare Slade. We can still use him. Or had Julian considered Slade not worth killing?

Fine and Davis threaded their way through the mixed lunchtime crowd of longshoremen, students, office workers, and the local unemployed, and sat down. "You can scratch San Francisco," Fine announced. "An English professor from the University of Kansas and a big-boobed baton twirler with a thirst for poetry. Nothing on North and Ginny from anywhere else."

"What about the feds?" Slade asked Davis unhopefully.

"Negative. No one answering their descriptions. And by the way, they weren't thrilled about checking it unofficially."

"What do they care?"

"They want to know why we're looking for someone so hard who hasn't been charged. They're nervous."

"They're nosy, you mean."

"A bit of both. I had to tell them it might be connected with Matthew Julian, so they're probably thinking it's a new rackets investigation."

"And that's always good press," Fine interjected. "The feds sure as hell could use some of that now."

"North is all I'm interested in," Slade said.

"Good, but from now on they want Talbot's signature on aid requests," Davis told him.

Slade shook his head dismissively. "Let's keep him out of it for now, Joe. Just tell them they owe you a personal favor."

"I'll try."

A waiter in a butcher's apron took the three men's orders for sandwiches and beers. When they arrived Slade stirred his foam with a swizzle stick to build up the head.

"I figure we've used all our contacts," said Fine in between mouthfuls of roastbeef. "You got any other ideas, John?"

Slade stared at the creamy froth atop his beer. Without looking up he replied, "It's not a matter of new ideas, Howie. It's the old story. You guys have got to get back to everybody, including the feds, and tell them to look harder."

CHAPTER THIRTY-FOUR

After lunch the three police officers left Andrew Carnegie West, walked to the subway, and parted there. Slade and Fine headed downtown for Police Headquarters, while Davis took the crosstown bus to Astor Place to catch an eastside IRT train north for Bloomingdale's. It was Davis's thirty-fifth birthday and he had decided to take the afternoon off.

Davis's wife, Corrine, a successful fashion model, met her husband in the men's hat department of the store. A dessicated clerk handed Davis a Borsalino and ushered him over to the mirror. Davis stared warily at the wide-brimmed hat in his hand.

"You promised you'd try it," Corrine reminded him. "I think it's groovy."

"Then you wear it."

"Honey, come on."

"The name is Joe Davis, not Marcello Mastroianni."

"Ain't nobody going to confuse you for him."

Davis glowered at the smirking clerk, then tried on the Borsalino. Corrine smiled approvingly. Davis scowled into the mirror, removed the hat abruptly, and handed it back to the clerk. As his wife sighed theatrically Davis instructed the elderly salesman to find something more conservative.

"You're some sport," Corrine said.

"You can give me a Borsalino for *your* birthday. I'll wear it as a present to you."

The clerk returned with a porkpie. Davis adjusted it and studied his solemn reflection. Suddenly he glanced upward toward the corner of the mirror to catch a flash of blond hair disappearing from the frame. He wheeled around the startled clerk and saw the back of the statuesque, long-haired girl as she entered the elevator. Once inside she turned. Before the doors closed he was positive he recognized Ginny Jackman.

"Joe," Corrine yelled in dismay, but her husband was too far away to hear.

Davis arrived at the elevators. The indicators for all three showed they were descending. He looked around frantically, spotted the escalator, and ploughed roughly through a crowd of shoppers to reach it.

The escalator was rising. "Goddamn," Davis cried. Retracing his steps he found the down escalator, dashed to it, and ran down the moving steps three at a time to reach the ground floor. A stout woman loaded with packages yelled at Davis crossly for trodding on her toes as she searched between the counters piled high with merchandise. An apprehensive floorwalker, trying to decide whether or not to draw his gun, advanced on the black detective.

"Something wrong?" the floorwalker asked Davis. The instructor at the security agency's one-month training course had impressed upon him the need of remaining calm with kooks.

Davis craned his neck to look over the floorwalker's head, saw Ginny going outside through a side exit, and shoved the floorwalker out of his way. He raced outside to the street. There was no sign of her. Furious, Davis hurried back into the department store and ordered the bewildered floorwalker to take him to the manager's office.

It was almost an hour later when Davis, having sent his wife home, walked out of the department store alone toward the parked police car and climbed into the back. Slade and Fine shifted around for his report.

"She used a charge account," Davis said. "In the name of Mr. Sidney Stillman. The store received his authorization for her charge two weeks ago. Sutton Place address."

Fine shook his head knowingly. "It's an up-and-coming neighborhood they tell me."

Davis ignored his colleague's remark. "I checked with the super of the building by phone," he went on. "Stillman installed her last month. He's a wealthy shoe manufacturer from Boston. Has his factories in Brockton. Comes to New York every few weeks on business and spends his spare time with her. An elder cocker."

"*Alter* cocker, not *elder*," corrected Fine.

CHAPTER THIRTY-FIVE

Slade worried that Ginny Jackman would catch her death of cold as she strolled alongside him on the East River Promenade in the chill November night. Her raincoat was slung loosely over her shoulders and she wore only boots, blue jeans cut down to shorts, and a Snoopy T-shirt over bare breasts. Her white poodle, romping along behind, shivered beneath his Stewart-plaid dog coat.

"You picked a bad time to call, John. Mr. Stillman's upstairs doing his isometrics."

He shot Ginny a side-long glance. He was pleased that the intervening year and four months had not made her any more reverent. Catching his admiring look, Ginny added with a wry smile, "Mr. Stillman's a youthful sixty-four. He says that isometrics tone up his muscles. Of course he's got one that could use toning up. What brings you around, John?"

"Otis J. North."

Ginny stopped in her tracks and looked at him strangely. "That's ancient history," she said. "How'd you find out about him and me?"

"His wife made inquiries after he disappeared. Now I'm looking for him."

"How the hell would I know where he is?" she asked with genuine surprise.

"When you left me you didn't go with him?"

"Left you? Come off it, John, you threw me out. You have no claim on me. What the hell do you care who I . . ."

"Hey, Ginny," he interrupted savagely, "this is an official visit."

Ginny pulled a long face and began to stroll again. "Fire away," she said tonelessly when he caught up.

"Did you go off with North?" he asked. It amazed him how raw and sullen he sounded.

"Go off with North? No way. After you called it quits I hung around for a while, and then I split town. On my own. I found a string of fast traveling companions. Miami, Malibu, Vegas, Honolulu. A lot of hotel wallpaper. But each time with a different guy. None of them North, I swear to you."

"Okay," said Slade. He knew there was no point in pursuing Ginny about her leaving with North. She had said she hadn't and that would suffice. He knew that while she might fail to tell him the whole story about something, she would not lie in any material way. "So after those guys?" he asked.

"So after those guys, as you so charmingly put it, Mr. Stillman." The thought of her sprightly lover seemed to restore her good humor. "You know, it's time I settled down. I'll be twenty-two next month. I got to start thinking about my future."

Before he could continue his questioning a young man walking his Doberman stopped in front of them to let his dog sniff at Ginny's. He smiled at the girl and received a smile in return. Slade intimidated the young man by staring him straight in the eyes. Tugging at his dog he moved off down the Promenade.

"Did North know about you and Pete Bremner?" he asked when they continued their walk.

Ginny did not reply.

"Did he know?" he asked more insistently.

Again Ginny halted. She slid into the sleeves of her raincoat and edged toward the railing overlooking the river. From the piers across the water came the faint whirring of a crane unloading cargo. "Is it important that I tell you, John? It was a long time ago, at least in *my* time scale."

"I have to have the answer, Ginny," he replied, standing close to her. "It matters a lot."

Ginny turned to face him. The hand on her hip and her tilted head gave her a defiant stance which contrasted oddly with her troubled expression. "Yes. He knew. He used to come to the motel after Pete left. To see if he could top his act I suppose." When Slade looked away Ginny shrugged and added, "What can I say? You know I'm very physical."

"Was North due the day Bremner got killed?" he inquired softly, still looking beyond her at the river.

A wind rose whipping Ginny's raincoat. The sounds of the city seemed to recede. "He was due," she said, "but he didn't show up. After what happened to Pete, how could he?"

Slade watched the moonlight dance on the great oily patches on the water's surface. They resembled purple islands floating in the blackness. "Did North ever mention Matthew Julian?"

Ginny's whole body went rigid. He searched her face but clouds scudded across the moon and he could hardly make out her features. "Hey what's all this about?" Ginny asked vehemently. "I thought we were talking about a missing person."

"You knew they were friendly?"

"Why are you asking?"

Slade did not feel like giving reasons for his inquiries. He preferred to let the silence do its work, no matter how painful it was to both Ginny and himself. Finally Ginny said plaintively, "According to North they were."

"You never saw them together?"

"No."

"But North said they were friends?"

"He admired Julian." Ginny's voice dropped to a whisper. "He was fascinated by his power."

Ginny abruptly started down the Promenade. Slade took a deep breath and hurried to catch up with her. She slowed her pace and they walked along together.

"Ever see North after Bremner was shot?"

Ginny flinched. After a long pause she answered, "I saw him just once. The night Pete was killed. He called me up. I didn't want to see him but he kept insisting."

"And?"

Ginny shook her head as if to bring the memory into clearer focus. Her hair shimmered in the returning moonlight. "That night he was really weird. I'd never seen him like that before. He kept going on and on about how he finally had the key to open all the doors. He said that if he played it right and didn't goof, he'd grab fate by the nuts and make him scream. It was spooky." Her eyes had a haunted look and she touched his shoulder in a curiously abstracted way. "It was the way he said it, John," she continued. "It made my blood run cold."

They were at the end of the Promenade. Slade said, "I'll walk you back to your door."

Ginny slipped her arm through his. She clutched him fiercely. "We can go somewhere else if you want."

"Some other time."

The pressure of her body on his ebbed. "Okay."

At the door to the apartment house where Ginny lived, he gently withdrew his arm from Ginny's. "Would you do me a favor?" he asked.

"Try me."

"Get Stillman to take you out of town for a few weeks. Or go yourself. That might be even better."

"For whom?"

"For you."

"Okay," said Ginny once more. She gathered up her poodle in her arms and ran into the lobby without looking back at him.

CHAPTER THIRTY-SIX

The incessant ringing would not stop. It took Talbot several seconds more to realize that it was not his alarm clock summoning him from sleep. He stretched a bare arm out of the covers toward the night table and lifted the phone. Mumbling a gruff hello he laid the receiver on the pillow near his ear and listened. The connection was poor. Through the screech and crackle he heard his name repeated several times.

"Who's calling?" Talbot groaned.

"Alan Coombs here. Is that you, Frank?"

Talbot was instantly wide awake. "It's me. Is everything all right?"

"Fine, fine. Except we're snowed in up here in lovely downtown Albany. I'm sorry I woke you but I just wanted to get you before you left for work. I forgot to tell you last night that there's going to be a girl in your office this morning from *The New York Times*. She's doing a profile on me for the magazine section and wants to chat with you about my stint as Commissioner."

"Why me?"

" 'Cause I can't blow my own horn, sweetheart. Anyway she's a sensational looker. Could you see she gets everything she needs? Professionally I mean. What you do on your time is your business. Maybe you could lay on a tour or take her out to lunch somewhere. She's a Mexican food freak."

"I'll see to it. Don't worry."

"That's great, old buddy. How's everything else?"

"Perfect."

Talbot waited anxiously until Coombs said, "This campaigning is driving me nuts, Frank."

"It'll be over soon."

"I suppose so. Peace."

"Peace. See you later."

When Talbot heard Coombs hang up he reached out to replace the receiver in its cradle. "Who was that, Frank?" Coombs' wife Anne asked sleepily.

"Alan."

"Oh," she said carelessly through a yawn. "What'd he want at this hour?"

"Nothing important. I think he just felt like talking."

Anne Coombs extended her arms and shuddered pleasurably. The covers fell away from her upper body, still firm and shapely at thirty-seven from sports and unstinting care. She scratched under one pear-shaped breast and rubbed her flat stomach with a circular motion like one looking forward to a sumptuous meal. When she had stretched once more she rolled over on his hip and kissed Talbot's throat with her dry lips. "I'm still thirsty from last night. That grass was yummy."

Talbot's hand sought the small of Anne Coombs' long back as she began to press her body insistently against his. Within him guilt briefly warred with his rising desire. The phone call from Alan Coombs still troubled him. It bordered on the obscene to casually

converse with a man while you shared a warm bed
with his wife. More painful still it highlighted the be-
trayal of his mentor's trust. No amount of devoted
service on Talbot's part could fully compensate
Coombs for that treachery.

Anne Coombs' breath quickened. Talbot, weaken-
ing, stroked her smooth buttocks. "If you want it that
way," she said, "I'll have to get up and find my hand-
bag."

Talbot kneaded the fleshy globes indecisively, then
opted for the more conventional sexual expressions of
love. Anne Coombs smiled through half-parted lips
and bit him hard on the shoulder. Talbot marveled at
the lovely woman's unbridled sensuality. As always it
robbed him of all resolve.

Three years had passed since the Coombses had
come to town from Washington for Alan to take up
his new appointment. Talbot had been introduced to
Anne Coombs at a reception for her husband and gone
to bed with her a week later at her instigation. Ironi-
cally the first day of the adulterous relationship had
coincided with Talbot being unexpectedly picked by
Coombs, over a dozen more experienced lieutenants,
to be his deputy.

Three years. In all that time the lovers had found a
scant thirty or so opportunities to renew the joining of
their bodies. And as with all delights infrequently sa-
vored, their occasional meetings had served to
heighten the intensity of each and whet their appetites
for the next.

Coombs on the phone had called him "old buddy."
The familiar appellation reverberated in Talbot's
mind. It reminded him how inextricably bound were
their careers, their personal lives, their futures. And

how he had let the older man promote his professional interests in order not to lose the stolen chances for sleeping with Alan's wife. More than the act of infidelity that breach of faith shamed him to the core.

Talbot gasped as Anne Coombs' mouth enveloped his erection. The contrast between her fine Virginia breeding, polished by an Eastern education, and her almost primitive wantoness left Talbot once more perplexed. In spite of all the lustiness of their previous lovemaking he still expected from her the modesty and restraint he associated with her origins.

Alan Coombs vanished from Talbot's thoughts. The bedroom, bathed in soft morning light, became for both a remote island forgotten by the world. Talbot gently tugged Anne Coombs up into his arms, spun over on top of her, and knelt between her thighs. She raised her bent legs and rested the backs of her ankles on his shoulders. He edged forward on his knees. She cried out as he entered her.

They moved with a clumsy force for a while before settling into a graceful rhythm that slowed and quickened with their needs, until there were at last no needs left unfulfilled.

Talbot arrived at his office in Police Headquarters well after ten o'clock and sat down at his desk. His sense of well-being was momentarily punctured by the remembrance of the man who had occupied his chair before him and who, over the strenuous objection of political powers within the city administration wishing to put in one of their own men, had insured that his deputy would succeed him upon his resignation.

One of Talbot's aides, a perpetually worried-looking young lawyer with muttonchop whiskers, handed his superior a letter. Talbot saw immediately that its top had been neatly sliced apart with a letter opener. "I opened it, saw it was marked *Confidential*, and stuffed it back in the envelope unread," the aide explained nervously.

"It says *Confidential* on the envelope."

"On the front it does. It was in your mail pile face down and I just opened it without turning it over."

Talbot nodded but his face clearly showed his displeasure. He read the contents of the enclosed memo, then looked up to find his aide regarding him expectantly. "I'll handle this myself," Talbot said evenly, making a mental note to have his aide transferred to another department.

The Commissioner busied himself with his other correspondence until his aide had left his office. Then he again picked up the letter marked *Confidential*, reread it carefully and, controlling his mounting anger, had his secretary call John Slade. "Tell him to get up here on the double," Talbot ordered savagely.

CHAPTER THIRTY-SEVEN

"Why?" Talbot exploded at Slade. "I'll tell you why. Because it's going behind my back, damnit, that's why." He waved the *Confidential* he had received that morning from the FBI. "You know damn well I'm supposed to sign all requests for Federal-agency assistance."

Slade shrugged unhappily. "Frank, I didn't bother you because I had nothing at that stage. Just a hunch. It's still not much more."

"Who the hell is this guy North?"

Slade sat back in his chair before Talbot's desk and let out a long low groan. Then starting with Mrs. North's appearance in Weller's office and ending with last night's interview of Ginny Jackman, he told the Commissioner everything he had learned thus far and still suspected.

Talbot listened patiently without interruption or interrogation. After a lengthy silence at the conclusion of Slade's report he shook his head slowly. "John," he said tersely, "you are opening up one hell of a can of worms."

Slade asked in puzzlement, "How do you mean, Frank?"

Talbot entwined the fingers of his hands and put

his elbows on the desk. Leaning forward to promote an air of confidentiality, he said, "The whole thing with the Big Four and the hammers wasn't exactly one of the department's most spectacular achievements in crime detection. Fortunately a lot of time has gone by since then."

"And you'd like to leave it buried, Frank?"

"I didn't say that, John."

"But it's an embarrassment to you?"

"Not to me, John." A hard edge crept into his voice. "I wasn't Commissioner then. Alan was."

"I can't sit on an investigation for Alan's sake."

"Good Christ, John, will you stop putting words in my mouth. What the hell do you take me for? That son-of-a-bitch ran me down when he missed putting a bullet through me. I want his ass in the worst way. And Julian's."

Slade had tired of their sparring. He had a good idea now of what Talbot wanted from him, but having jumped to two wrong conclusions in as many minutes he asked simply, "Okay, Frank, what am I supposed to do?"

Talbot sought the precise phrase to convey his request. He knew it would be, no matter how he expressed it, open to more than one interpretation. "I'd like you to be discreet," he said at last.

Slade made his characteristic steeple gesture with his clenched hands. Talbot pushed back his chair and walked toward the window. He stared out at the buildings, their outlines starkly etched in the intense, shadowless winter light. Glancing away he saw on the wall his college diploma from the University of Arizona and his law degree from Syracuse, then he turned back to Slade. "You've already got Fine and Davis in-

volved," Talbot said to him. "Let's keep it to that."
He looked toward the closed door leading to the reception room. The reporter from *The New York Times*,
"a Mexican food freak" he suddenly remembered
Coombs calling her, was undoubtedly out there waiting to interview him for her profile on the candidate.
"Above all I don't want the press involved until
there's something to give them besides a raking up of
old coals."

Slade considered Talbot's appeal unenthusiastically.
He would have preferred no restrictions whatsoever
and unlimited manpower available, but he was not
unmindful of the pressures, real and imagined, that
Talbot felt. He could appreciate that the new Commissioner owed a debt to his predecessor. He could
even sympathize with Coombs' predicament. As an
anti-rackets candidate, Alan did not need to have the
voters reminded of his department's glaring failure to
apprehend a multiple murderer who had made possible Julian's rise to supreme power. After all, Alan had
been in charge at the time. A candidate's record in
fighting crime differed from his record in fighting,
say, inflation. In crime fighting, you were judged on
your results. In inflation fighting, you could always
pass the buck here and abroad. "All right," Slade said
at last. "I don't see any harm in that."

Talbot smiled thinly. "Of course, John, if you could
make an arrest with an iron-tight case against North
before the election, well, that would be something else.
We don't mind looking good."

"It would vindicate Alan's judgment in picking
you," Slade could not resist pointing out.

"Something like that, John. It'd look good for all of
us."

All of us. Talbot had not hesitated to lay his cards out on the table. Slade recalled Fine's remark that he was being groomed for a big job. He wondered uneasily if Talbot were secretly pleased that everyone on his way up was forced to make certain modest adjustments in the courting of success. He hurried out of the office before Commissioner Talbot could thank him for his cooperation.

CHAPTER THIRTY-EIGHT

A howling gust of wind whipped through the trees surrounding the Four Winds Motel. Fallen leaves stained the bottom of the pool. A cabana door, carelessly left unlocked, banged with startling distinctness. Slade, the collar of his trenchcoat turned up against the wind, sat hunched and alone at one of the poolside tables surveying the desolate scene. He had bolted Talbot's office that morning obsessed with the compromise he had made, but on further reflection he wondered why. When all was said he had reached a dead end in his search for Otis J. North, anyway. No more men than Fine and Davis were required for the continuing investigation: between them they had already exhausted every lead. As for the press getting hold of the story prematurely, what interest did they have? There was no progress to report. And they could give him no aid in tracking down the missing man.

"Where do we go from here?" Fine had asked Slade in the latter's office before noon.

"Back to the beginning," he had replied shortly, and together the two men had left Police Headquarters and driven north to Riverdale. Along the way Fine had confessed he was glad their investigation was finally in the open. Given the current economic situation and his forty-one years, he had pointed out, it was not an opportune time to seek new employment. He had added that as a hedge against financial reverses he was halfway through the first draft of a police novel loosely based on the murders of the hammers.

"Can you make any money with a book on cops and robbers?" Slade had asked.

"Joseph Wambaugh sure as hell does," Fine had replied, citing him instead of Ed McBain because Wambaugh had been a cop.

Slade stared across the pool to the door of the bungalow in which Pete Bremner was shot to death almost a year and a half ago. Suddenly the door opened and a young couple without luggage emerged. They looked furtively at him, questioningly at each other, got in their car, and drove out of the driveway. At least some things stay the same, thought Slade, as Fine appeared behind him. His friend blew his nose with noisy vigor, drew up a chair, and fumbled with a chapstick.

"Try this one on, Nanook," said Fine when he had smeared his lips with balm. "North pops the prowler and something clicks in his head. He's got a whole new role in life, a new métier if you like. He decides to knock off Bremner as a test case then tells his pal Julian what he did. And offers to do the same to the other contenders."

"I don't see the 'test case' bit."

"And I don't see Julian sending him out untried. It would have come back to him if North bungled it."

Slade's eyes began to smart in the icy wind and he rubbed them with the heels of his palms. "Yeah," he said, "then what?"

"Julian thinks it over and sees his opportunity to make a big move. North's perfect. A complete outsider with proven professional ability, good enough with Julian directing him to take out all the hammers."

"Catching one hammer with his pants down wouldn't prove you'd be good enough to get the others when they're out watching. Any way you look at it, Julian would have been taking an awful risk going with North."

"I agree, but for all of it, it was the *least* risky. Where was he ever going to find an outside hitter? If he tried to go that route, it had to come out eventually. You just couldn't keep it from guys like Cassell and Luce. No, Julian had to get a guy who was brand new."

"North pimped for Julian."

"And who'd believe a pimp could hit hammers?"

Slade nodded uncertainly. He picked up the briefcase lying at his feet, removed the photo of North looking through the telescopic sight of his rifle, and studied it closely for perhaps the hundredth time. Fine peered over at the head shot. "Super Freak," he said.

Slade stood up abruptly and beat his arms across his chest for warmth. "Let's get back to the car, Howie. I'm freezing my nuts off."

The two men strolled by the pool, poisonous gray in the overcast day, and reached the driveway. "Well what do you think?" Fine demanded.

"About what?"

"About what I was talking about back there," Fine replied, disappointed at Slade's indifference to his theory.

"You could be right."

"And that's all you've got to say?"

"What more can I say? We'll know if you're right after we find North."

"*If* we find him after all this time."

"I figure he'll find me if I don't find him."

Fine jerked his head up to stare at Slade, then instinctively glanced over his shoulder.

"We're not going to spot him that easy," Slade said with a grim smile. "If that's what you're worried about. Walgreen's a genius at intercepting tails and he didn't see hide nor hair of him."

Fine looked thoughtful.

"You don't have to get involved, Howie. I mean that. You know what that guy did. And what he can do. You're worried about making a living. This is a matter of staying alive."

"I'm scared but not that scared, John. I just hate not knowing when the trouble's coming though."

"Nope, there won't be any warnings. Julian's not going to threaten me like Walgreen. He'll just send North out when I'm close. Or when he thinks I'm getting close."

Fine swallowed his protest, opened the car door, and slid behind the wheel. He thought about what Slade had said. Whether or not they found Otis J. North, the prospects in either case were not appealing.

CHAPTER THIRTY-NINE

Slade reached the hunting lodge in the Adirondack Mountains shortly after noon the following Sunday. He had spent the greater part of Friday and Saturday revisiting the scenes of the other hammers's deaths: the dentist's office across the street from Carnegie Hall where Minnick was stabbed; the elevator in the Brooklyn apartment house where Irving died from the poison gas; the Yorkville German restaurant selected by the Zimmermanns for their last supper; the seedy hotel room on 23d street which served as The Professor's next to last resting place; the terrace of the Fifth Avenue security apartment house from which Croft had been hurled to his death; even Sapinski's sailing sloop sold by his estate and now in dry dock in a Bronx basin. At each place he had made a painstaking mental reconstruction of the murder in hope of finding a crucial detail overlooked or some relationship between the crimes not apparent at the time. He had left each murder scene as frustrated as he had been more than sixteen months ago.

He left his rented car in the walled courtyard and walked slowly toward the lodge. He halted at the sight of tire tracks and knelt to examine them. There were dry, untrammeled leaves within the set of parallel marks and he decided they could not be fresh. Going on, he climbed the weathered stairs to the porch. He leaned on the railing and let his gaze sweep the surrounding hills. Only a dull remnant of autumn's colors remained in the maples and oaks. The rest of the almost bare trees blended with the raw-umber tinted earth. He moved toward the door.

For several seconds he studied the broken padlock from where he stood a few feet away. Then he took hold of it hesitantly and turned it over. There were no rust signs where it had been sawn through. Bits of filing lay on the scuffed doorframe beneath the lock. He estimated the forced entry had occurred within the last few days.

He removed the padlock and slipped it into his pocket. He pushed on the door. The upper hinge gave with a sharp rasping noise and the door dipped down almost forty-five degrees from its perpendicular. Drawing his gun and a flashlight, he inched around it into the main hall.

It took more than a minute for his eyes to grow accustomed to the semidarkness. The window panes were frosted over, allowing thin wedges of milky light from the slanting rays of the sun to filter through. The floorboards creaked as he advanced. The toes of his right foot struck something that clattered metallically across the room. He waited, his heart hammering in his throat, before switching on his flashlight and letting its beam play about the floor. The circle of light surrounded a beer can which had come to rest right side up.

He swept the walls with his flashlight, found the fireplace, and went toward it. Even before he was within ten feet he smelt the charred wood on the grate. He doused his flashlight, saw there were no smoldering embers, pressed the switch back on, and continued his search.

The tension Slade felt popped like a balloon as his beam of light found a car blanket with a used condom resting on one of the folds. He decided both items had been left behind by lovers either sexually inexperienced, impecunious, or both. He headed down a corridor leading off the room.

A groaning door behind him brought him up short. He edged back along the wall, raised his foot, and was just about to kick in the door when it blew open. Peering in he saw a gleaming toilet bowl overflowing onto the soaking floor.

He went through the rest of the lodge's rooms rapidly, found nothing, and stepped out onto the porch again. He breathed deeply, warily descended the stairs, and retraced his steps through the courtyard. There was no point, he told himself, in cautiously scanning the hills around him. He had been an easy target for a marksman since he had left the cover of his car to travel to and from the lodge.

He reached in through the window of his rented car and leaned on its horn for several seconds. The blast resounded through the countryside sending a partridge flapping furiously from nearby cover.

It took almost two minutes for Fine's car to reach the courtyard. He drew abreast of Slade, stuck his head out the window, and asked anxiously, "We got company?"

"I wouldn't be tooting the horn if we did," Slade said irritably. "What about you?"

"I got here two hours ago. I've been down on the

road since then. I watched you go up. Then it was as quite as a grave. Nobody came in after you."

"How about the road the sniper used?"

"I had a look at it on the way up. It's almost washed away. It'd take a tank to get up it. There's no one around and that's it."

Slade frowned. "Which means we're not getting warm and they know it. Come on, let's look around outside."

"Anything you say, John." Fine's incipient peptic ulcer ached from the anxiety of trying to flush a possible tail by having Slade act as bait, but he climbed out of his car and followed uncomplainingly.

Slade led the way up to the hill from which the sniper had killed Luce and Cellini before pinning down him and Talbot long enough to make his getaway. Looking back he could see the roof of the lodge just visible above a ridge.

From the crest of the hill they scrambled down toward the area where Angel's car had been blown apart by the buried land mine. The crater in the road had been filled in with dirt but enough had sunk in the intervening months for the two detectives to see the outline of the enormous hole.

Slade pivoted slowly and studied the hills beyond the country road. There was a disturbing sameness to what he saw: color, shape, and distance blurred into an indistinguishable mass, like a landscape in runny paint.

Slade pointed to the unvarying hills. "Now where did we all come down from?" he asked Fine.

Fine's brow wrinkled. "Jesus, John, it's hard to say. Talbot was right there I think," he said, jabbing his finger toward a ridge. He swung his hand some twenty degrees right and added, "Yeakel's yo-yos were right there. No, can't be. I take that back. They were closer to us, over behind that mound, out of sight from here."

"How about us?"

"I can't see where we were from here. We'll have to go back up."

Slade nodded in agreement. "We'll save that for later," he said.

Falling in step unintentionally, they marched back up the dirt road from the filled-in crater to the lodge. They were at the gate of the walled courtyard when Fine, glancing back over his shoulder, suddenly brightened. "You can see where the troopers were now. I think we were just over there. Wasn't that the big tree you climbed?"

"I'd say so, Howie. It was the biggest one up there and I could see into the courtyard."

"You saw more than I did, that's for sure."

"Yeah. Some people have all the luck."

Slade had had the better view all right, but what exactly had he seen, he asked himself. He tapped his forehead with his knuckles to jog his memory. It was important, he realized, that the events summoned from the past be clear and detailed and, more important still, in the chronological order in which they'd occurred.

First Cassell, his bully boys, and the man who could not be identified getting into the Fleetwood. Yes, that had happened before the rest. They had driven away past Julian's lounging bodyguards.

Afterwards Angel had appeared. Examining his car for bombs while the hammer Cook looked on. Driving away. That came next. Luce and Strauss were getting into a car.

Then Julian leaving. No, not quite. *Starting* to go. His car had stopped and he went back for a word with Luce and Strauss before proceeding.

For some reason the last detail stuck in Slade's mind. He shook his head uncomprehendingly.

"What's up, John?" Fine asked. Slade's perplexity was as disturbing as his previous long silence.

"I was just thinking. When I was up in the tree I saw Julian get out of his car to talk with Luce and Strauss."

"So?"

"The meeting was over. They must've discussed everything they came to discuss. What the hell was so important that Julian stopped his car to go back?"

"While Angel kept going?"

"Yeah."

"Simple."

Slade looked at Fine inquiringly.

"Julian was stalling, that's all. He didn't want to get too close to Angel on that winding dirt road and get hit with the fallout. A piece of flying shrapnel could have killed him too."

Slade, looking strangely subdued, pondered over Fine's explanation. "Sure, that makes sense."

The two men strolled down the dirt road. Slade glanced at his watch and saw it was going on five o'clock. They skirted the outline of the crater and continued to make their winding descent. "We'd better hurry," Fine said. "It'll be too dark to see anything soon."

Slade stopped dead in his tracks. He whirled around suddenly toward the hill where the sniper had concealed himself. Fine's eyes widened in alarm. "Now what's wrong?" he asked, panic creeping into his voice.

When he did not reply, Fine's hand involuntarily sought his gun at his hip. "You see anything or don't you, John?"

Slade waved his hand dismissively at the hill to reassure Fine he had neither seen nor heard a sniper. He blinked several times and said almost reverentially, "Something just dawned on me."

CHAPTER FORTY

Exploding flashbulbs made Slade turn his head away as he entered Alan Coombs' suite at the Carlyle Hotel. The cocktail party was in full swing. More than a hundred guests—contributors, political power brokers, patronage seekers, beautiful people, and other assorted campaign riffraff—partook of the freeloading and chatted happily. Slade regretted he had allowed Talbot to talk him into coming.

He handed his coat to a breathless campaign worker pressed into service as a hatcheck girl. Looking out over bobbing heads he caught sight of the candidate entertaining a small group of men in evening dress with a story. He heard a press photographer call out above the din, "Could we have one with the Senator, Mr. Coombs?"

Coombs plucked the Senator out of his audience, turned him toward the camera, and put his arm around his shoulder. Anne Coombs quickly joined the office holder and the office seeker to make a threesome. They all smiled brittle smiles as the cameras clicked and the pose was recorded for posterity.

Slade spotted Talbot arguing with the PR man Dugan and headed toward them. As he passed a draped reception desk, a square-set man with a chipped face seated there glanced at a panel in front of him and saw the lights flashing crazily. He hurtled around the side of the desk, blocked Slade's path, and leaned into him to smother any possible movements. Two other men, lean and athletic, swiftly materialized at each side of the man who had intercepted him.

The encirclement and neutralization of Slade had happened so fast and so smoothly that only Talbot noticed it. He pushed through a knot of guests and hurried over. "It's all right," he told the men around Slade.

The three gave signs they had heard Talbot but they did not visibly relax. Slade sensed their potential for violent action without compunction, but he held his ground and his tongue. "Rod Trumbull," Talbot said, indicating the big man from the desk. Next he introduced the two who had come to his assistance, "Stan Humphries, Orin Schroeder. I'd like all you jokers to meet Deputy Inspector John Slade."

Slade folded his arms and inclined his head to each man in turn. Trumbull rubbed his palms together and grinned. Though his muscles were overladen with fat, his energy and strength were still apparent. He tapped the bulge made by Slade's holster beneath the waist of his jacket. "Sorry about that," he said, "but you rang all the bells."

Slade glanced back at the metal-detector box beneath the draped reception desk and nodded unsmilingly. "You should have set that machine up outside in the hallway," he said. "I could've pulled a gun in here and knocked Alan's head off."

"No you're wrong," Trumbull said amiably. "You would've been dead as a doornail before you fired."

He laughed a split second too late to take the hard edge off his remark.

Talbot said so long for both himself and Slade and escorted the new arrival into the party. Even before Slade could inquire about the three men at the door, Talbot was explaining, "Alan hired them last week." He lowered his voice and added, "Alan has received threats. The campaign's hotting up. He's making a hell of a lot of powerful enemies."

Slade darted a look back at Trumbull, Humphries, and Schroeder. They were still watching him. The corners of their mouths turned up in tight smiles. Talbot, who had caught Slade's backward glance, continued, "They've worked for Coombs before when he was in the government. They go way back together as a matter of fact. They're highly efficient according to Alan."

"You offer Alan our protection?"

Talbot smiled wryly at the question. "I did but he said he'd feel more secure with his own."

Slade watched Humphries and Schroeder glide past him and Talbot to circulate vigilantly among the crowd. He took a final look at Trumbull sitting poised like a circus bear on the edge of the desk. He sat immobile; only his eyes moved as he scrutinized a party of late arrivals.

Alan Coombs spotted Talbot and Slade forcing their way through a crowd toward him. He took his wife Anne's arm and steered her in front of him to meet the two police officers halfway.

"Hi, John," Coombs said. "Glad you could make it. My wife Anne. John Slade." Talbot required no introduction.

Anne Coombs reached across her husband and

firmly shook Slade's hand. "I've heard a lot about you from Alan and Frank," she said.

Slade smiled. He had a grudging admiration for people who could lie outrageously while looking him straight in the eyes. Anne Coombs exchanged some set-piece pleasantries with Talbot, then saw a short, curly-headed guest holding forth animatedly to a rapt young woman at the other end of the room. Sighing at Slade as if parting from him would cause her sorrow, she said, "Excuse me while I try to build some Coombs bridges to the Literary Establishment."

The abandoned men watched Anne Coombs make the writer's acquaintance. Coombs chuckled softly when the literary figure raised his fists on guard as if to defend himself against the candidate's wife's blandishments. "If she gets his vote," Coombs observed, "she's performed an act beyond the call of duty."

"It's nice to have those dudes on your side," Talbot reminded him.

"Maybe," said Coombs. "How many legions has the Pope? How many votes can a best-selling author deliver? The answer might be the same in both cases."

Coombs, Talbot, and Slade helped themselves to drinks from a passing waiter's tray. The candidate noticed a portly newspaper publisher he faintly knew trying to attract his attention, told his guests to enjoy themselves in his absence, and moved off briskly in the direction of the molder of public opinion.

"How about dinner afterwards?" Talbot suddenly asked Slade. "Just the two of us. There are some things I'd kind of like to discuss with you, John."

"I'm meeting someone, Frank. How about first thing in the morning in your office? Or lunch tomorrow?"

Talbot's voice was tinged with disappointment as he replied, "Either'll be fine." He looked to Slade as if he wanted to say something more, but all he did was pat him on the shoulder and walk off to say hello to someone Slade had never seen before.

Left alone, Slade coolly surveyed the cramped festivities, then edged between two arguing guests to get at the buffet table. He was reaching for a piece of celery filled with Roquefort cheese when Dugan came up next to him. "You're supposed to mix, not stuff your face," he told him loudly.

Slade shook an admonishing celery stalk at his friend. Dugan grinned through a mouthful of cocktail sausages. "You're rubbing elbows with a lot of very important people, John. Circulate. Make connections. It grieves me to see you throwing away a heaven-sent opportunity to advance yourself among this glittering array of our city's most distingué citizens."

Slade bit his celery stalk in half. He saw Coombs across the room guffaw at the newspaper publisher's joke. "The polls have our friend four points ahead of the incumbent," he said casually to Dugan.

"The People's Choice," replied Dugan, pronouncing the last work as if it were spelt "Cherse." He stuck a toothpick into a dish, deftly speared a pair of Swedish meatballs, and glanced at a chesty woman wearing a see-through dress. "The one in the middle must be her head," he said.

Trumbull, patrolling past Slade and Dugan while Schroeder manned his desk, overheard the PR man's remark and laughed uproariously. He slammed his ham-like fist into his palm like a baseball catcher and said, "I've got to write that one down."

Slade and Dugan watched Trumbull making his

232   THE ICE MAN

rounds for a while, then sampled several other canapes. Dugan twisted his small mouth into a grimace. "I liked it better," he said, suddenly serious, "when all a politician had to do was give out a bucket of beer and a Christmas turkey. Things have changed, my bucko."

Slade looked around at the prosperous, expensively-clothed men and women voraciously drinking and eating with an almost manic intensity. "Is that a fact?" he asked.

"I wouldn't kid you, John."

A waiter took Slade's and Dugan's empty glasses and offered them another. The PR man accepted; the detective refused. As Dugan threw back his head and drained his sixth drink in the last hour, Slade observed a young couple at a window pull aside the curtains to gaze out at the skyline. The man and woman looked admiringly at the scene below for a moment and then returned to the party. Trumbull unobtrusively stepped forward to the window and nonchalantly drew the curtains shut again.

Slade saw that Dugan had noticed Trumbull's precautionary action. A look of revulsion swept his face. "Politics used to be just a dirty business," he said. "Now it's also scary."

Trying to josh Dugan out of his doldrums, Slade said, "You don't take politics seriously, do you, Mike?"

"Not since I ran Henry Wallace's campaign in New York and had a nervous breakdown afterwards," Dugan replied.

They exchanged winks. Slade helped himself to another morsel from the buffet table. Dugan wagged his head disparagingly and said, "If you must eat, John, at least stay away from the mayonnaise. It gets on your fingers and you can't shake hands."

Neglecting to thank Dugan for his last piece of unsolicited advice, Slade wandered away from the PR man and mingled with the other guests. The girl in the see-through dress, who recalled from a conversation with Anne Coombs that Slade was something-or-other in the city administration, stepped up to him and told him that while she was in favor of equal, integrated education she thought busing was psychologically harmful to the children. "So what do we do?" she asked.

"Bus the teachers?" he suggested. Seeing Talbot standing alone in a corner, he made his escape before the strikingly proportioned girl could ask his opinion about New York City's financial crisis.

He had almost reached the Commissioner when he realized that Talbot was following Anne Coombs about with his eyes. Startled by his discovery he abruptly changed direction and walked toward the window. Looking back he saw Talbot in casual conversation with an intense young woman who kept a lighted cigarette in her mouth when she spoke. He wondered if he had really seen what he thought he had.

Drawing back the window curtain he gazed out over the city. From the height at which he stood, the layer upon layer of buildings seemed to step down to the horizon like wooden models in a children's toy display.

Through an involuntary association, Slade thought of Mrs. North. That afternoon he had visited her for a second time in order to obtain some vital information about her husband. The image he had carried away of her sitting in lonely and silent splendor in her house made him sad, and he pitied her. Slade had been so right about Otis J. North: nothing about him was ever what it seemed.

CHAPTER FORTY-ONE

Fine, carrying a briefcase he had borrowed from his eldest son, made a face at his watch as he came out of the medical building on East 19th Street and made his way toward Second Avenue. A filing error by a receptionist more than two years ago had caused a two-hour delay in his schedule.

Still, all's well that ends well, Fine lectured himself philosophically as he walked purposefully along. He stayed close to the buildings to shield himself from the icy winds rolling in from the northeast.

Fine turned the corner and saw the muzzle of the gun a split second before the flash. Shot point blank between the eyes, he fell back dead on the pavement.

The killer reached down to the crumpled corpse at his feet, snatched up the briefcase in his rubber-gloved hand, and moved off down the street toward his parked green Oldsmobile. He walked neither too quickly nor too slowly. Both, he knew from experience, were likely to attract attention. Getting in his car he started up the motor and drove away a few seconds before a young Puerto Rican couple huddled together for both love and warmth came on Fine's body sprawled on the pavement. The pool of blood around his agonized face made him look like a haloed martyr in an Italian Renaissance painting.

The boy and girl stood dumbfounded for a moment, then turned on their heels and ran away as swiftly as they could without letting go of each other's hand.

Two hours later, Davis, standing on an elevated subway platform in the East Bronx, waited for his train downtown. His nostrils were moist from the cold. He was dressed in shabby clothes for another undercover assignment. Nearby a ragged wino on a bench drank slowly from a bottle wrapped in a paper bag.

Davis heard the approaching train and stepped forward to watch it rumble into the station. When he was a foot from the edge of the platform, the wino, dropping his paper bag, sprang at his back with cat-like speed and grace.

The force of the violent shove propelled Davis into the path of the oncoming train. His body on impact spattered outward like an exploding projectile. The train screeched to a halt. Sparks cascaded along the length of the platform.

The killer, resuming the stance and gait of the wino, staggered down the stairs from the platform to the station. He was followed a minute later by the train driver who ignored what he took for a shuffling drunk going out the door and rushed to the attendant in the booth. "Call an ambulance," the train driver told the man in the booth. "Some spade fell in front of the train."

CHAPTER FORTY-TWO

The elevator doors in the Carlyle Hotel lobby opened noiselessly. Slade waited until several other guests from the party got out ahead of him before going over to the reservation desk and banging on the bell for the clerk. When he arrived Slade showed him his identification and said, "I left my name here at the desk earlier this evening. Any calls for me?"

The clerk searched through a stack of messages near the switchboard. "Nothing for John Slade."

"From a Detective Howie Fine," Slade prompted.

The clerk checked the names of the calls instead of their intended recipients. "I'm afraid not, sir."

Troubled and perplexed he left the reservation desk. He told himself that Fine had probably gone back to Police Headquarters, but when he called from a pay phone in the hotel lobby he was informed the detective had not shown up nor were there any messages for him. He decided to go back to his office on the off chance Fine was en route there.

He walked west from the Carlyle Hotel to Fifth Avenue. Then he headed north along Central Park to 78th Street where he had parked his car. There was a cold mist rising through the leafless branches of the plane trees growing next to the wall that separated

Central Park from the sidewalk. He tried not to dwell on the possible reasons why Fine had not called him at the hotel as he had been carefully instructed to do.

He unlocked his car and had nearly opened the door wide enough to climb in when the bullet thudded into the front fender. Diving to the street he placed his head under the vehicle and looked back in the direction the shot had come from. A shadow thrown against the broadloom brickwork of an empty street outran its footsteps and disappeared around a corner. Scrambling up to his feet he chased after the retreating figure. Events ran too quickly for him to fasten on them singly after the initial shock of the ambush, but one thought ran over and over through his mind: *The miss had been deliberate.*

And so there was little need to exhaust himself. He slowed down to an easy jogging pace. As he followed along, he also realized that the gunman had not chosen the street they were on at random. A part of his mind took in the boarded-up stores and empty apartment houses marked for demolition in the deserted neighborhood. Another part reckoned he was chasing a decoy and not the killer.

He halted. The sounds of the running decoy had ceased. He strained his ears and eyes for the slightest noise or movement. A bullet from a silencer whizzed by his ear with an ineffably delicate sound, and he scurried back from the curb to the cover of a recessed doorway in a store-front. For a long while he stood there panting. It was the fatigue of excitement not of exhaustion, and it grew like a living thing in his back and hamstrings.

He checked the .38 in his hand. The thought struck

him that he could not remember when he had first drawn it from its holster.

Minutes passed, measured and distinct.

The killer's decoy, a slender youth no more than twenty Slade guessed, broke into the open from his hiding place three stores further along and sprinted across the street toward a darkened alleyway. Slade calmly watched him go. Had he stepped forward from the storefront, he could have easily shot the young man dead in the middle of the street. But the killer, for reasons Slade could only guess at, wanted him alive and he would not be lured out of cover. His eyes darted up and down the street in search of Julian's messenger of death. The shot from his silencer, which had forced him into the storefront, was proof of just how close he must be.

Out of the corner of his left eye Slade saw something move with whip-like suddenness in an abandoned wrecked car. He held his breath while he raised his .38 toward the derelict vehicle. A tabby cat jumped noislessly down from the car window, glared at him as it arched its back, then scurried away.

Slade felt the rush of wind on his neck, and he knew with crushing certainty that he had failed. When he had been driven deliberately to cover in the recessed door, he had remained there so long that killer had had time to enter the store from the rear, or even the top. His first mistake. But not nearly so serious as his second. It was that which nullified everything, his flash of intuition at the lodge, his careful stalking of the decoy. He had neglected to check if the boarded-up door of the store was locked. Instead he had assumed that boarded-up doors of deserted stores were nailed shut. Which is usually true but not always. The nails can be removed. As they were by the killer before Slade arrived.

Out of instinct he tried to scrunch up his neck and raise his hands, but he was too late. The blow to the back of his head spilled him from the storefront onto the sidewalk. His .38 popped from his hand. He tried to rise but the ground beneath him gave way. He slid forward on his stomach groping for his gun.

The killer stepped on his hand.

His fingers pinned to the ground, Slade got to a kneeling position. His head, too heavy for his body, slumped against his chest. The killer jerked his head back up and kneed him in the face. He flew backwards and rolled headlong down a basement stairwell onto a trio of garbage cans.

Lying across the clammy, cold metal lids, Slade heard the killer's footsteps grow louder as he descended without haste after his prey. He could feel the back of his head tingle where the killer's eyes were fixed upon it. He fought for breath. The killer's savage kick had broken his nose and there was blood in his mouth.

"Other people know!" he shouted desperately, and turned over painfully onto his back. He shook his head to clear it, then looked up into the impassive face of Marty Angel.

CHAPTER FORTY-THREE

"Fine and Davis are dead," Angel said flatly. "And I took North's dental records off of Fine."

It was as if Slade's insides had turned to slime. "That's not enough," he said wearily. "You've got North's records. I've got yours. They won't match the teeth they found in your Mercedes."

"You're bluffing," Angel said.

"From when you were on the force."

Angel blinked once.

"I got them when I lifted the coroner's report," Slade went on, breathing laboriously. "You can forget about getting hold of that too."

Slade pulled himself up with effort to a sitting position. He clasped his hands together so he could not give Angel the satisfaction of seeing him touch his throbbing head. Then he saw it, just to the left and behind Angel: his gun lying tantalizingly close to the pavement edge of the stairwell. He commanded himself not to look at it again and stared hard at Angel instead.

The hair was dyed and a skillful plastic surgeon had made an artful start to giving Angel a new appearance. His lustrous, anthracite eyes, however, would require death itself to change them. He stood perfectly balanced over Slade, his legs slightly apart, his silencer swinging in never changing arcs like an inaudible metronome.

"You'll never be able to come back," Slade suddenly yelled at him, but his moment of triumph was dampened by the memory of Fine and Davis who would also not return. "No plastic surgery, no new identity, nothing is going to work. They'll never stop looking for you. Not with what I can give them. It's all buried somewhere safe, along with your records. Everything I figured out. All written down, nice and clear, easy for anybody to understand."

Slade saw a flicker of light in the depths of Angel's eyes. He relaxed, realizing that Angel had to determine exactly how far Slade's figuring had taken him. He was confident he could take his time.

"The blood bath at the lodge had us all suckered," Slade began. "It was good, very good. Only one thing seemed odd. A detail. But it kept bothering me. Bothered me everytime I got to thinking about you on that dirt road winding in and out of the hills while Julian hung back to talk with Luce and Strauss. It seemed obvious that Julian just wanted to stall so he couldn't be looking up your ass when the mine exploded. It was because it seemed obvious that I couldn't get it out of my mind. Because all along, whenever Julian appeared to be doing the obvious, he wasn't." He blew blood out of his nostrils and continued, "Then it hit me. Suppose it wasn't himself Julian was stalling, but Luce and Strauss. Suppose he was keeping them, not him, from going down the road too soon. Because there was something happening down there he couldn't let them see. Like you. Stopping your car in a bend of the road out of sight. Pulling a corpse out of your trunk. Sticking it behind the wheel. A corpse by the name of Otis J. North. The rich-boy pimp to Matthew Julian."

"He came in handy," Angel said matter-of-factly. "And he deserved it too."

"Why? What'd he do?" Slade asked sardonically. "See you hit Bremner that day at the motel when you got careless, and think that that would entitle him to sit at the big table with Julian? Maybe cut himself in on the deal?"

"What's the difference?" Angel asked guardedly and Slade knew for sure that both he and Angel had been surprised that Ginny had been carrying on an affair with both Bremner and North. "North put his nose in where it didn't belong. Like you."

Slade's face was expressionless. He picked up the thread of his story and said, "I calculated you were out of sight for twenty, twenty-five seconds. Enough time to do the switch, then push your car down the road so we'd see it blow. With everybody watching the fire it was no sweat getting up that hill to bump Luce and your protegé Cellini as a bonus. A beautiful touch to a beautiful touch, that. We all had to believe the killer had been up on the hill the whole time. It kept us from thinking switch. All very neat. Up to that point everybody suspected you of those first four hits, including me. But suddenly you were dead. It took the heat off Julian. And made it easier for you to take out the rest of the vermin, because the last man on earth anybody was looking for was Marty Angel."

Angel stroked his chin. Slade's eyes inadvertently strayed to his gun lying on the ledge. He rose to his feet. Angel lifted the barrel of his silencer to his chest.

"You worked it all out," Slade went on. "Down to

the last detail. You couldn't be seen from the lodge. And we couldn't see you from where we were staked out."

Slade hesitated. He watched Angel lean forward expectantly, saw his expression grow avid. At that moment, for the first time since revisiting the lodge, the detective was certain that what he had suspected but hoped was not true had actually happened. "Of course," he added offhandedly, "there was one guy who could have seen you. From the hill on the other side of us. Where he'd placed himself to watch and make sure we couldn't. Frank Talbot." He shook his head in disgust. "Talbot made sure it all went right. The orchestra leader. Kept it all humming nicely by charging up the hill like a hero. Saved me from getting run over. Oh, it fooled me good. And it locked Talbot into Julian for all time. You got your money's worth from Frank that day, though. And every other day he fed you what you had to know. Where Sapinski had got to. The Mexican destination of Kelley and Cook. The Professor's hotel room."

Angel shrugged as if Talbot's effectiveness was beside the point. It struck Slade that Angel, Julian's faithful, self-effacing servant, could not totally submerge his ego and resented sharing the glory of his multiple murders with Talbot. With no forewarning Angel said, "We're going to have to have those records. Otherwise they're death certificates. For you. And for those two kids of yours, James and Warren I believe, at that fancy Hudson Academy."

"Those records'll cost you more than that."

Angel inclined his head a fraction like someone slightly deaf.

"Everybody's got theirs," Slade said venomously. "Now I want mine."

Angel smiled coldly. "So you finally spread your legs."

"You ought to understand. It's good business. I want out. And you and Julian are going to buy me out. One million dollars. Traveling expenses. It's easy for me to believe that to you guys that's chicken feed."

"Your bargaining position isn't that good."

"The hell it isn't. I got the records. They'll surface if I don't. And they won't be addressed to Talbot. One million. That's my price. Everybody can chip in. All you guys worked very hard. You've got a lot to lose. I still say a million's cheap."

Angel wavered. He glanced from Slade to the silencer in his hand, then up again.

"What are you waiting for?" Slade asked savagely. "You got my message. Run it along to Julian. Don't tell me you're thinking of getting your rocks off again tonight?"

Angel, without taking his eyes off Slade's face, reached back over his shoulder, casually took the gun from the ledge behind him, and slipped it into his pocket. "You'd have saved me a lot of time and bother by going for that. We'll be getting back to you."

Slade rubbed the back of his aching head as he watched Angel unhurriedly climb the stairs to the street and walk off into the darkness without so much as a glance behind. His shadowy form dwindled and merged into the night.

CHAPTER FORTY-FOUR

The FM disc jockey on WNYC talked about the almost forgotten blues singer Bertha Chippie Hill and her neglected rendition of "Trouble in Mind," the saddest jazz song ever written. He finished by reminding his audience that a desire for immortality was something we all outgrow, then announced the time was coming up to four o'clock in the morning.

Slade got up from the couch in the living room of his apartment and turned off the radio. He had been home for four hours. The phone had been ringing as he came in but he had not picked it up. He had reasoned that Julian and Angel could not have reached a decision and formulated their plans so quickly. He had suspected the caller was Sylvia Fine or Corrine Davis, and he had been unable to bear the thought of speaking with his friends' widows.

His temples were throbbing and he padded along to the bathroom for some aspirins. He glanced at his reflection in the mirror as he washed down the tablets. His face was the color of slate and there were deep furrows coursing down the sides of his swollen nose. He returned to the couch, telling himself he must rest. No matter what Julian's answer was, tomorrow would be a long day.

Lying in the darkness he tried desperately to think, but his mind was a swirl of mist. His heavy lids began to droop and soon afterwards he dozed.

Slade was not sure whether he had actually awakened from his familiar nightmare until the dark shapes in the living room formed themselves into well-recognized objects. Only then was he certain he was truly conscious. And alive. The survivor of all forms of death. From the beginning and against all odds.

Eleven children out of 800 and Slade had been among the fortunate. Seven hundred and eighty-nine children burned to death, drowned, or frozen in the wintry north Atlantic and he and ten others alone had escaped.

It had been a curiously modern catastrophe. Conceived in fear, carried out with high humanitarian ideals, and disclaimed and forgotten as soon as it had become a cropper and suffered its inglorious end.

In 1940 on the night of September 7th, London, his birthplace, had been set ablaze for the first time as wave after wave of the thousand aircraft of *Luftflotte* 2 dropped explosives and incendiaries on the civilian population. Göring and Kesselring gleefully had watched the airships set out for London from the chalky cliffs at Cap Blanc Nez between Calais and Wissant.

The fires raging in the east end of London had served as guiding beacons for the attack the following night that lasted from 8:00 P.M. to 5:00 A.M. On that morning Göring had telephoned his wife in Berlin telling her triumphantly, "London is in flames."

British War Office officials, in an effort to forestall panic and inspire confidence, had hit upon a plan a week after the first raids to evacuate the children of the east end of London and ship them across the Atlantic to Canada.

It was a crackpot scheme which belonged to a bygone age when the deaths of children in war had meaning. The ocean was cluttered with U-boats, argued the few who opposed the evacuation plan, and what was wrong, they asked, with relocating the children in remote rural areas in Scotland and Wales? But the bureaucratic wheel, once set in motion, had been difficult to halt.

Eight hundred children were to be accepted. The application for the seven-year-old John Thomas Slade had been the 112th received. The official knew with a glad heart, when only half way into the letter, that here was the perfect candidate. Slade's regular army father had died on the beaches of Dunkirk. His distraught mother, saddled with John and his infant brother, had already been bombed out of her east end house.

On October 11, 1940, the ship *City of Benares,* carrying a full crew and 800 children, left Southampton on its errand of mercy. Slade had carried away a memory of that day: standing at a ship rail between a host of other tearful children and waving farewell to a crowd of indistinguishable faces on the mist-shrouded dock.

Two weeks later within sight of Newfoundland, a German U-boat returning from a successful hunting trip in the Caribbean had used its last two torpedoes to blow the *City of Benares* out of the water. Only 328 children had gotten off the ship in lifeboats and 239 of those were to die from the deck guns of the surfaced U-boat. Had they known the sea was full of children, he often wondered? A terrible Atlantic storm screaming south from the Arctic Circle had claimed another sixty-three lives before the few pitiful survivors were sighted and picked up by a British destroyer. But once aboard the rescue ship the dying continued. Fifteen more of the children succumbed to their thirty-six-hour exposure to freezing rains and towering seas, despite the naval doctor's intensive efforts.

And so eleven out of 800 boys and girls under the age of twelve reached the safety of the New World alive. They had fled the ravages of war. A Children's Crusade in reverse but with equally horrific results.

The evacuation plan was quickly abandoned by the wartime British government after Winston Churchill himself ordered its cancellation. Newspapers, fearful of the loss of morale that would occur if all the facts of the tragedy were fully reported, contented themselves out of a love of country with a brief mention about the *City of Benares'* fate but no acknowledgment of its human cargo.

Canadian authorities, deeply embarrassed by the plan's appalling failure, found to their great relief an orphanage to accept the English youths for the duration of the war. Young John Slade, however, was destined for a continuation of his journey. It was discovered that he had relatives near New York City and, two days before Christmas of that year, he was transported by bus from Montreal across the border to the United States.

He had spent the next four years of World War II at the Sheepshead Bay home of his Uncle Arnold and Aunt Alice. It was Aunt Alice, the younger sister of his mother, who alone in the white wood house while her American husband worked the swing shift at the Brookly Navy Yard, would comfort her nephew when he awoke screaming from his nightmare of his ocean ordeal.

But because the young never really expect to die, they treat survival lightly. By 1944 Slade's nightmare had become so infrequent that he no longer resisted sleep.

All that, too, had changed overnight.

Four years and three days after the sinking of the *City of Benares*, Aunt Alice had taken the eleven-year-old Slade aside after breakfast and told him that his mother and younger brother had perished when a buzz bomb scored a direct hit on a farmhouse near Farnham, forty miles southwest of London where she and her child had moved to avoid the raids on England's capital.

After that the nightmare had returned more often and with greater intensity than ever before. And his days had become as troubled as his nights. A moderately well-adjusted child considering everything, he had at first turned taciturn, then violent. School psychologists, youth workers, and finally juvenile court judges recorded his development from a boy who all too quickly resorted to his fists in any dispute to a teenage delinquent to a youthful offender.

The ring of his phone shook him out of his reverie. He shuffled across the living room like a sleepwalker to pick it up.

"Your offer's been accepted," Angel said. He set the time and place for their rendezvous: there could be no negotiation of those points. He hung up without issuing a warning or a threat. There was no need for either.

Slade dwelt on Angel's brief message to him. His instructions had been delivered imperiously and without the slightest doubt they would be obeyed. The question arose in his mind as to why Angel was so certain he would show up for their appointment. He would have had to take leave of his senses to discount the strong possibility of a double cross. Was it simply that Angel knew him better than anyone else in the world, better even than he knew himself?

Slade had confided everything to Angel in those early years of their friendship, even the subject matter of his persistent nightmare. One long night he recalled, he had sat with Angel in an unmarked car on a stakeout of an upper Manhattan floating crap game and described to him the history of his turbulent adolescence. "The only reason I didn't go to jail," he had told Angel with a wry smile at dawn, "was the neighborhood cop knew my aunt and uncle. He said he wouldn't hang the burglary of Lundy's on me if I'd just go off and join the army."

On another occasion, off duty in a 14th Street bar near closing time, Slade had continued the story of his life to the older Angel. "I was on a troop ship for Korea when the shooting stopped, so they sent us to Japan instead," he had said. "A week after I got there I was in the brig for slugging a sergeant."

"You're lucky you didn't get courtmartialed," Angel had replied. Slade had learned later that his friend had been in a Seoul hospital at the time recovering from a near fatal head wound.

"A shrink took pity on me," he had confessed, explaining how an Army psychiatrist, aware of his patient's childhood emotional upheavals, had quashed a trial, then spent several sessions with him on the traumatic origins of his social discontent. "He told me I was striking out at others because I hated myself,"

Slade had added beerily. "What would you say, Marty?"

"You make too goddamn much of your upbringing," Angel had growled. "That's the trouble with examining your past. You can use it to justify anything in your present behavior. Just by picking out something from a million different experiences and discarding all the rest."

Angel's curt dismissal of Slade's cherished notions about himself had rankled deeply. "You don't believe that the past determines what you do in the present?" he had asked sharply.

"Not really," Angel had replied blandly. "It's simply a question of how you want to look at the past. Happy guys pick out the good things. Unhappy guys the rotten things."

"So we're one or the other, are we?"

"In a way. We either want to live. Or we want to die."

"According to your argument I want to die."

Angel had avoided answering the charge, he remembered with a start. Instead he had signaled the bartender for another round and the evening conversation between the two men had ended unresolved.

Slade watched the dark sky of night fade into dawn through the window of his living room.

He knew that Angel had classified him in the bar two decades ago as a seeker after death. And he was right. As a youth he was ashamed of the fact that he had lived. His nightmares persisted then, as now, not because of the sea-going terror but because his guilt-ridden subconscious could not alter the ending in which he survived. Growing older he had sought through a series of expiatory acts to end his life: the lure of violence in his teens; his army enlistment; and, ultimately, his joining the Police Force. Being a cop was the answer to a death seeker's prayer. To wear a gun at all times. To welcome the chances for its use. To wage eternal war against the enemy without peace or temporary lulls in the hostilities.

The irony was that the seeker after death was unsought by death. Others like Fine and Davis, who wanted to live, had died. And Slade, who wanted to die, lived on. Yes Angel expected him to show up for their rendezvous. For meeting Angel was a form of suicide either way he played it, a suicide of the soul or of the body according to whether he took a payoff or a bullet. If he sincerely wanted to die, he had only to appear.

And if he wanted to live?

Well then he would have to do the unexpected somehow, alter events, fail to conform to Angel's assessment of his character. He would have to kill Angel to demonstrate that he did not want to die. The proof of his desire would be in the outcome of their meeting that night.

He asked himself over and over again what he really wanted.

CHAPTER FORTY-FIVE

Talbot pressed the buzzer and gnawed at his knuckles while he waited in the corridor. A few moments later Rod Trumbull opened the door and stood there filling the frame. "Good morning, Frank," he said with the midwestern heartiness that irritated Talbot even more than usual that morning.

Talbot followed Trumbull into the Carlyle Hotel suite. The living room was still littered with the debris of last night's cocktail party, dirty glasses, plates of left-over food, and butt-filled ashtrays were spread over every available surface.

Alan and Anne Coombs, finishing their breakfast, glanced up from the table at Talbot's entrance. They were in their dressing gowns and had that raw, unfinished look of celebrants the morning after. Trumbull went discreetly to an adjoining room and shut the door behind him.

"Coffee, Frank?" Anne Coombs asked routinely. She had almost gasped when she first saw his haggard face.

Talbot shook his head a bit too emphatically and joined the Coombs at their table. When Coombs saw that Talbot's stress was not about to be brought under immediate control, he signaled surreptitiously to his wife to leave them alone.

"I've got to get dressed, gentlemen," she announced.

The two men ignored her departure. When the door to the bedroom closed Coombs looked questioningly at Talbot. "It's on for tonight," Talbot said softly and with distaste.

"They're going to pay?" Coombs asked surprised.

"All they said was the situation would be taken care of." Talbot fished around in a crumpled pack for his last cigarette. His hand trembled slightly as he lit it. "Damn it, Alan, they killed two officers last night," he added, not looking at Coombs.

Coombs sighed inwardly but made no reply to Talbot's outburst. He felt the best way to handle Talbot was to let him get it all out first.

"When we went into the deal," Talbot went on in a rush of words, "we told Julian, whatever happens, none of ours. That was part of the understanding. Everything's coming apart."

Coombs privately disagreed. He thought the only thing coming apart was Talbot.

"I don't give a shit about Julian's garbage," Talbot said. "He can do what he wants with them. But this, this. . . ." His voice trailed off despondently.

"I'm sorry about what happened last night, Frank," Coombs said into the silence between them. "They were our kind of people. But let's face it. Now it's our asses as well. Yours and mine."

Talbot shook his head dubiously then coughed slightly on his cigarette.

"If they tie you into Julian, they tie me in too," Coombs said calmly with the air of someone who had given the matter a lot of thought. "It's no secret I appointed you over considerable opposition. And they

won't have to be geniuses to figure out who's bankroll-
ing my campaign."

Talbot rose unsteadily. He walked to a trolley bar,
poured a stiff shot of whiskey into an unwashed glass,
and downed it to steady his nerves. Coombs frowned
primly at Talbot's back as he watched his guest refill
his glass to the top.

Coombs erased the expression of peevishness from
his face as Talbot returned to the table. "Frank, it
would solve all our problems if no one came out walking tonight. No Slade, no Angel. There'd be no loose
ends and we'd be free of Julian."

Drops of whiskey spilled over the rim of Talbot's
glass onto his shaking hand. He gaped at Coombs who
was lolling back relaxed in his chair, a faraway look in
his pale eyes.

"You know," Coombs whispered in a strange won-
dering tone, "that son-of-a-bitch Julian gave me a list
of people he says I'll have to appoint when I'm
elected."

Talbot steadied his hand before taking a sip of his
brimming drink. Coombs turned toward him with a
boyish smile. "We eliminate Angel," he said, "we
make it crystal clear to Julian that we're in control
from now on."

Coombs paused. He shook his head as if someone
other than himself had made the observation and he
was agreeing with it.

"After all," Coombs went on, "we helped Julian
build an efficient organization so it could work for us,
not the other way around."

Talbot tried to avert his eyes but Coombs' piercing
stare made it difficult.

"That was always our game plan, Frank. Now we have our opportunity. We should seize it."

Talbot gulped his drink.

"You know where the show goes on tonight, Frank?"

Talbot nodded slowly.

Coombs abruptly pushed back his chair and stood up. He walked rapidly to the adjoining door, opened it, and beckoned those within. Trumbull, Humphries, and Schroeder strolled casually into the room and stood at ease.

"Frank'll brief you about that operation we discussed," Coombs told the three men. "You can work out the details among yourselves."

Trumbull, Humphries, and Schroeder nodded agreeably as if asked to do nothing more arduous than help a stranded motorist change a tire. They left the room without having to be told.

Coombs scratched his uncombed head like someone trying to recall a minor point, then turned toward Talbot. "You'll have to go with them tonight, Frank," he said matter-of-factly.

Talbot sat bolt upright.

"It can't be done without you leading it, Frank," Coombs said pedantically. "That way the story'll be that you all went there with Slade to trap Angel."

Talbot set his glass down mechanically.

"Then in the shoot-out you got Angel, but unfortunately Slade was killed. In the line of duty."

"There'll have to be an investigation," Talbot protested excitedly.

"A *thorough* investigation," Coombs concurred. "And you'll put yourself personally in charge."

Talbot dully got up from his chair. His eyes were

full of anguish. Coombs went to him and patted him on the shoulder comfortingly. "It's got to be this way, Frank," he said, guiding him into the room in which Trumbull, Humphries, and Schroeder waited. Then Coombs returned to his own bedroom.

His wife Anne was in front of her vanity mirror brushing out her hair when he entered. She looked at the reflection of her husband as he came over and stood behind her.

"Frank looks terrible," Anne Coombs said.

"He's tired. You're fucking all the juice out of the poor bastard."

Anne Coombs continued stroking her hair. "You're crude," she said flatly.

"Aren't we all?" Coombs replied, massaging the muscles in her shoulders. He insinuated his hands into her dressing gown and idly fondled her breasts. "But let's not let it go further than this room."

Anne Coombs waited until her husband withdrew his hands, then began to make up her face. Coombs mimicked her intense concentration and withdrew from the bedroom to the untidy living room. Trumbull, Humphries, and Schroeder were waiting there for him.

"Frank's gone home to get ready," Trumbull informed him. "The operation's all checked out. We're set to go."

Coombs flopped into a chair and crossed his legs. "There's one more problem," he said. "A reliability problem."

Trumbull pursed his lips and bobbed his square head knowingly. "Sambo?"

Coombs nodded curtly.

"Can do," Trumbull said.

CHAPTER FORTY-SIX

Slade raised his head. Peering over the top of the long row of wooden doors which had been strung together to form a wall, he studied the half-block square construction site three storys below street level.

It had snowed throughout that Saturday morning. Now at the end of the afternoon there were streaks of ice in the scarred and trammeled earth of the excavation, like marbling on meat. At the foot of the ramp leading down from the street to the bottom of the site, there was a pinewood construction shack with a tarpaper roof. Smoke curled upward from a chimney pipe.

The door of the construction shack opened. Matthew Julian and his bodyguard came out followed by a construction supervisor in a hard hat. Hearing the hollow sounds of the three men's footsteps on the rickety porch, Julian's driver in the Daimler, parked in front of the shack, awoke with a start and sat stiffly at the wheel.

Slade kept his eyes riveted on the door of the shack while the supervisor exchanged a few last words with his employer Julian. No one else left the wooden building. Julian was traveling only with his bodyguard and driver that day. He smiled grimly thinking how secure Julian must be feeling to visit one of his

various legitimate business enterprises with but two
armed men to protect him.

The construction supervisor affably waved good-bye
to Julian and returned to the warmth of his shack.
The bodyguard moved ahead of Julian as the two
walked toward the Daimler and opened the rear door
for him to enter. When Julian was comfortably settled,
the bodyguard, beginning to feel the bitter cold after
his hour in the stove-warmed shack, hurried around
the back of the car to join the driver up front. He had
to signal irritably to the drowsy driver that he had
locked all four doors automatically after Julian. The
driver murmured an apology and reached over to the
dashboard to press the door-release button.

The bodyguard was halfway in the Daimler when
he heard the roar of another car engine. He spun
around and looked up in fear at the ramp. Slade's
rented Ford station wagon leaped into view over the
crest and hurtled down the inclined slope toward the
Daimler. The bodyguard started to scramble out but
the speeding car slammed the Daimler's open front
door into the bodyguard's chest. The crushed victim's
head snapped back against the top of the saloon with a
dull thud.

The big Ford station wagon careened off the Daimler. Slade braked hard. Julian's driver jumped out and
fired twice at the skidding car. Slade threw the station
wagon into reverse, shoved the gas pedal to the floor,
and catapulted backward. The driver tried to leap out
of the way, stumbled to one knee, and was screaming
in terror as the Ford ran him over and broke his hip.

Julian bolted from the Daimler and made a run for
the construction shack just as the supervisor, having
heard the commotion, stepped out onto the porch to

investigate. Slade wheeled his station wagon around the Daimler and accelerated toward the shack to out-flank Julian's retreat.

The Ford's front tires caught a patch of ice and it veered sharply at full throttle. Slade fought with the steering wheel. He had almost regained control of the car when it sideswiped the construction shack, caving in part of the wall and sending the supervisor diving inside the office as the porch collapsed beneath his feet.

Julian, cut off and close to panic, saw a toilet shed close by, raced toward it, and disappeared around the back. Again Slade wheeled the Ford around. He knew that Julian would be armed. Unwilling to take the risk of giving him a clear shot as his station wagon came around the hut in pursuit, he headed straight for the flimsy structure and demolished it.

The back wall behind which Julian was hiding blew out toward him, knocking him onto the muddy ground and spilling his revolver from his hand.

As the mud-spattered Julian struggled to his feet Slade hopped out of his car, drew his .45 automatic, and rushed him. Julian bent forward and covered his face with his forearms like a well-tagged boxer against the ropes. Slade thought better of hitting Julian about his head. In his rage he might crush his skull. Instead he darted in close, shoved the barrel of his .45 between Julian's legs, and brought it up with all his might into the crouching man's testicles.

Julian's hoarse cry died in his throat as vomit spewed from his lips. He doubled over, fell to his knees, and would have sunk to the ground had not Slade grabbed him by the collar. Julian offered no resistance as his captor dragged him through the icy mud toward the Ford and threw him into the front seat. It was not until he went to slam the door that Julian, his eyes blood-flecked, sprung violently at the slightly off-balance detective.

Slade measured the distance between himself and the lunging Julian, then coolly cracked him across the ear with the butt of his .45, knocking him unconscious. After stuffing his body back inside the station wagon, he got in behind the twisted wheel, glanced contemptuously at the crumpled figure beside him, and started up the stalled engine. The big Ford rocketed up the ramp from the depths of the construction site onto the deserted street.

CHAPTER FORTY-SEVEN

When Julian came to he found himself jackknifed over in the back seat of the station wagon, each wrist handcuffed to his opposite ankle. It was night but he had no idea of the time. Glancing out the window he realized Slade had parked the Ford in a deserted trucking depot on the waterfront. There were rows and rows of trailers, strangely unreal like the life models of dinosaurs in a museum closed for the night.

Julian managed to straighten up and look over the top of the front seat at Slade. "Why are you doing this?" he asked. "We're going to pay your price."

Slade paid no attention to Julian. He opened a wooden case the shape of a rifle stock and laid it on the seat next to him. Then he took out a 9mm Luger with an eight-inch barrel from within, snapped the case shut, and shoved a twenty-round magazine into the breech block.

"Did you hear what I said?" Julian shouted.

Slade glanced back with indifference at his prisoner as if noting him for the first time. He turned back to examine his versatile weapon, curiously calm. One of the deadliest handguns in the world, it combined the accuracy and range of a hunting rifle with the firing power of a submachine gun. His ex-wife's father, who had taken it off a dead Wehrmacht colonel at Anzio, presented it to him years ago as a birthday gift. He had been convinced his policeman son-in-law must share his passion for instruments of death. He stuffed four extra magazines into his pockets and slipped out his .45 from his belt. He turned around to observe Julian again as he slid the breech of the automatic back to put a round in the chamber, then let it snap forward with a loud click.

Slade had expected fear, bewilderment, or a combination of both from Julian. But his manacled prisoner had suddenly turned impassive. His eyes were as dull as pebbles. He was, Slade realized, figuring out future moves in his head like a skilled chess player. Growing aware that Slade was studying him Julian said calmly, "I accepted the deal. What's the matter? You want more money? That can be arranged. Guarantees? The arrangement is permanent as long as both of us keep our part. We don't move because you've made copies of the original documents by now. You don't use those copies because you've accepted our money and the hostages are still alive."

"What's more money mean?" Slade asked abruptly.

He could feel Julian's immense relief like a palpable object. He studied the shackled prisoner's assured and handsome face. He took an almost perverse delight in watching Julian's thoughtful expression as he sought an acceptable figure to quote to his captor. Too small an offer might mean instant death or at least more violence; too large could cast suspicion of the sincerity of the original deal. There were snares and pitfalls both in a hard bargain and abject surrender. "Why don't we say an extra quarter of a million?" Julian ventured.

Slade slammed his hand over Julian's mouth. When he took it away Julian's lips were sealed with a large square of adhesive tape. This time Slade noted with satisfaction that there was terror and perplexity in Julian's eyes.

A half hour later he sat in his idling car on West Street just south of 14th. He listened to the mournful blast of a tugboat's horn in the Hudson River just beyond, then shifted into drive and pressed lightly on the gas. The Ford glided quietly onto the pier leading out to the water. He turned right into the parking area in front of a New York Department of Sanitation Incinerator Building closed for the weekend.

Slade stared about the waterfront scene. A hunter's moon cast a silvery sheen over the deathly still pier and buildings. He saw no one. Getting out of his car he walked silently to the back door and opened it. Sticking his Luger against Julian's head he unlocked the handcuffs with his free hand. He dropped one set on the seat and used the remaining one to fasten Julian's arms behind his back. Then he pulled him out and, using him as a human shield, pushed him toward the Incinerator Building.

Across the street in a warehouse overlooking the garbage pier, Talbot, Trumbull, Humphries, and Schroeder exchanged puzzled glances among themselves.

"He's got Julian," Talbot whispered disbelievingly.

"And we've got a bonus," Trumbull replied gleefully. Thorns in Coombs' back were thorns in his.

CHAPTER FORTY-EIGHT

Angel grasped the edge of the narrow walkway along-side the northern wall of the Incinerator Building and swung himself up effortlessly onto its damp, slippery surface. In the slipway behind him his speedboat rode at anchor. He had selected the garbage disposal plant on the Hudson River because he would be able to approach and depart without being detected. Hugging the wall he moved forward in a low crouch to the front of the building. His head felt light. He had not experienced such a sense of being fully alive for many months. When he reached the corner of the building he peered around and saw Slade holding Julian in front of him and advancing cautiously toward the front door.

Angel's surprise gave way to admiration for Slade. Trust him to make it interesting, he thought, raising his silencer in pleasurable anticipation. He had told Julian last night that it was a mistake to underestimate Slade's resourcefulness. Now he would have to make amends by killing him.

Slade grabbed Julian and halted.

Angel eased the pressure on his gun's trigger. If Julian moved a fraction of an inch before he fired he would take the bullet intended for Slade.

Julian, breathing harshly through his nose, stared hard at the corner of the Incinerator Building. He had seen something move in the shadows and was trying to relocate it. He reasoned that it must be Angel where the mass of blackness was darker than the surrounding space. When the black mass shifted he was sure.

Slade felt Julian attempt to pull away and understood instantly that the maneuver was meant to give Angel a clear shot at him. He dove to the ground pulling Julian with him as a bullet from Angel's silencer plopped into a bulkhead behind them.

He let off a burst with his Luger driving Angel back out of range. He yanked Julian to his feet, then, spraying bullets to keep Angel from reappearing, he propelled his prisoner into the entrance of the Incinerator Building. He used the last few rounds to blast away the lock and violently pulled Julian before him into a reception area of the building. As they moved he pushed the lever of his Luger to eject the empty clip and shoved in a fresh one. He searched for a hiding place knowing Angel, at that very moment, would be working his way back the walkway to find another way to get inside. Forcing Julian down behind a locker, he knelt beside him and worked out his next move in the deadly battle now joined with Angel.

Angel found the window he had left open and crawled into the main storeroom of the building. From there he traveled silently through a pitch black corridor toward the reception area. A faint draught of air on his face told him that the glass door just ahead was ajar. He was certain he had closed it during his reconnaissance of the building earlier that afternoon. After a minute of deliberation he decided the wind, not Slade, had disturbed it, dropped onto his stomach, and crawled forward. At the door to the reception room he stopped a second time. Silence hung like an overcast sky in a remote wilderness.

Angel raised his head slightly and sniffed. Even without hypnosis he could smell deer on morning walks through the Ward Pound Ridge Reservation near his Westchester home. Through autosuggestion his olfactory sense was even keener. He picked out the odor of his fellow men.

There was a scraping noise as soft and fleeting as a sigh on the other side of a pile of crates in the reception area and Angel inched toward it. To come around the pile was foolhardy. Slade, he knew, would guard his flanks. Besides there was a fifty-fifty chance he might find Julian between himself and Slade on either encircling movement. To climb the crates also had its risks. One slip and his surprise attack was fatally exposed.

Angel rested and thought. Then he saw the catwalk ending just above the crates and retreated toward the stairs leading up to it. He pulled back without haste. The slightest sound could betray his position and invite a hail of bullets from what he took to be a burp gun wielded by Slade.

Mounting the stairs Angel crept along the catwalk until he was over the pile of crates. He lowered himself down upon them, testing each crate on top to make sure it was firmly in place, then slid forward to the edge. There he craned his neck and looked down ten feet to the floor below.

In the pale moonlight filtering through the window, Angel caught the metallic glint just beyond a storage bin at the base of the pile. He strained his eyes and saw the elongated shape of the barrel of Slade's Luger. It was pointed directly at the front door.

Angel cursed inwardly. Slade and Julian were just out of sight in front of the storage bin. He stretched out as far as he could but saw no more than the hands and forearms on the peculiar weapon. A snap shot was out of the question.

Holstering his silencer he withdrew a knife from his windbreaker. He slipped the blade out of the haft with his thumb. Studying the outline of the Luger's barrel as it extended beyond the storage bin, he worked out as exact a fix as possible on Slade's back. Then he gathered himself up like a cat and sprung outward.

Angel's leap was perfectly judged. He cleared the storage bin by inches, landed feet first behind the kneeling man, and slashed viciously across the exposed windpipe with his knife. The Luger rifle banged onto the floor. He jerked back his victim's head and froze at the sight.

Julian's eyes in death had rolled back in their sockets like those of a broken doll. Blood poured from a deep throat wound. His manacled hands were clasped together in an attitude of prayer.

Angel shoved Julian's almost severed head forward in fury and jumped back just as Slade stepped out of the shadows and blasted away with his .45 automatic. Wincing from shock rather than pain as a bullet grazed the back of his neck, he ducked behind the pile of crates and felt for his wound. When he removed his hand it was drenched with blood. Steeling himself he fired his silencer in Slade's direction to buy a moment's precious time to concentrate on his wound.

Slade gave Angel no respite. The blackness was stabbed with flames as he fired twice more. A moment later he heard Angel running along the corridor toward the storeroom. Pursuing him with caution he almost skidded in the wounded man's blood.

He pulled up at the door to the storeroom. He saw a trail of crimson blotches running toward a moonlit window and was overtaken by a wave of panic. Were Angel to escape he would exact a terrible vengeance on his sons. Slade was about to charge into the room when he shook himself mentally and forced himself to think clearly once more. There was no need to worry that Angel had fled. His murderous lust could not now be less than Slade's own.

He heard a soft dripping sound like a leaky faucet. He realized that Angel had gone to the window, somehow staunched the flow of blood from his wound, and doubled back somewhere to ambush his pursuer. Did the wound reopen? Were Angel's clothes so full of blood that drops fell from the saturated cloth? He located the spattering noise in a corner, whirled, and fired through a modesty panel of a desk.

The slug from Slade's .45 kicked into the seat of a chair inches from Angel's face and sent splinters digging into his chin. He raced for the door to the furnace room off to his right just as Slade fired again.

Sensing the kill, Slade went after Angel. There couldn't be enough blood left in Angel to keep a dog alive, he told himself.

Inside the room the glow from the banked furnaces fell like spokes onto the floor. Slade knelt and searched for Angel's blood trail. He heard a noise above on one of the catwalks which ran on all sides of the cavernous twenty-five-yard-long chamber. Although he could not see how the wounded Angel could have gotten there he fired upwards through the slats.

Crouched behind another furnace on the dusty floor of the room, Angel, his eyes full of madness, looked up sharply at the catwalk.

"*Get the both of them!*" screamed Trumbull.

There was a roar as Talbot and Coombs' three henchmen opened fire on Angel and Slade below.

Angel, in the center of the room and exposed to fire from all sides, was hit in the shoulder and knocked backward. Slade, only a few feet into the room, dove headlong behind a box full of shovels as bullets kicked up near his feet. Reloading he tried desperately to make some sense of the chaotic situation, but was hopelessly stymied. He fired at the flashes of light pouring down from the catwalk until his gun clicked empty. As he reached for another clip in his pocket, a ricocheting bullet exploded the .45 out of his hand and sent it bouncing along into a vast area of darkness.

He shook his stinging hand, started forward, then changed direction like a broken field runner. The last thing he saw before he made it to the rear of the furnace room was Angel struggling to his feet. Roaring at the top of his lungs he was firing blindly up at the catwalk.

A fusillade of shots knocked him down but he rose again, pulling on the trigger of his silencer, no longer realizing it was empty. More bullets thudded into Angel's body. His gun slipped from his grasp. He screamed at his body to hold him up but his flesh was beyond his call. His legs slid out from under him. He lay twitching on the floor as still more slugs pierced his senseless flesh.

A shred of life in Angel dimly perceived that the firing had ceased. He got to a kneeling position only because he would not die prone and looked up through his half blind eyes at the rubbery face of Rod Trumbull.

Trumbull pressed his gun against Angel's head and pulled the trigger. The shot made a noise like a baseball bat hitting an overripe pumpkin.

Talbot, awed by Angel's refusal to accept death until the final bullet exploded in his brain, came down the stairs of the catwalk and joined the pensive Trumbull. Together they regarded the riddled corpse. Angel's face, contorted in fury a few seconds earlier, was serenely still.

Picking up Angel's silencer Trumbull saw it was empty. He searched through the corpse's pockets until he found a spare clip. Reloading the silencer he pivoted wordlessly toward Talbot and fired twice. The black man grunted, clutched his chest, and toppled forward.

Unhurriedly Trumbull started for the fallen Commissioner but the sound of the heavy roar bay door of the furnace room sliding open made him spin around. He ran toward the back of the building shouting out the names of Humphries and Schroeder, and was gratified to see they were both already racing after the fleeing Slade. "Goddamn but we work well together," he congratulated himself aloud.

Trumbull returned to the corpse of Angel and wiped off his fingerprints from the silencer with which he had shot Talbot. He stuck the weapon into the dead man's hand and closed the fingers around it. Then he loped toward the front of the Incinerator Building to cut off Slade's possible escape route to the street.

CHAPTER FORTY-NINE

Humphries and Schroeder emerged from the open bay door of the furnace room and searched around the rear of the Incinerator Building for Slade. A mist, damp and acrid, rolled off the river at them like a wave.

The two men carried out an initial search with the speed and precision of a highly experienced team. Then Humphries hurried toward the north side of the building and advanced along the narrow walkway toward the front. Schroeder, noticing the garbage-loaded barge docked at the foot of the pier, remained behind to investigate.

Twenty yards long, the boat rode low in the water. Schroeder strolled along the pier edge peering intently into the hold full of treated refuse. He had just passed under a long garbage chute jutting out from the second story of the Incinerator Building when he sensed his danger and tried to jump back a moment too late.

Slade came out of the chute feet first kicking Schroeder in the chest and sending him flying into the barge. The garbage sucked the thrashing form under with a soft whooshing sound.

Schroeder rose from under the surface gasping. Blowing scum from his mouth and nose he tried to heave himself out of the slime but his wild flailing only caused him to be drawn under again. He struggled once more to the top of the oozing mass and saw Slade extending a pole toward him.

Slade pulled back the pole as Schroeder grabbed for it and smashed him with it on the shoulder. Before he could beat him further Schroeder managed to catch hold of the end. At first Slade tried to yank the pole away, but realizing he could never tear it from his opponent's grip, he braced it against his shoulder and drove him under instead. He held the pole under for almost a minute while the end in his hands vibrated violently. Then the pole went still like a fishing line that has lost its struggling catch.

He withdrew the pole at the same moment Humphries came back around the corner of the Incinerator Building. Throwing the pole at the startled man he sprang up onto the chute and scampered upward. Humphries, recovering, ran to the chute and fired up it at Slade. The bullets ricocheted inside the low metal walls with a pinging sound like pebbles shaken in a can. Slade scooped up handfuls of garbage and flung them back down at Humphries, momentarily blinding him. Then he gained the top of the chute and bounded into the Incinerator Building.

Running through the control room he passed panel after panel of luminous dials and switches. He flung open the first door he saw and found himself on the catwalk from which he and Angel had been fired upon.

Trumbull charged in through another door below and spotted Slade before he could duck down. The square-set man steadied his revolver on his forearm and fired at Slade above.

Slade spun around, started to run, then checked himself. Humphries was rushing in through the rear bay door. He and Trumbull fired in a noisy counterpoint at the crouching detective. Trapped in a cross fire Slade looked wildly around, spotted a window and rushed to it. Kicking out the glass he jumped twenty feet to the pier below.

There was a jolt that seemed to drive his backbone up into his skull as he hit the ground, rolled over to his feet, and started to run headlong toward the street.

He grew conscious of the sound of shattering glass followed by the report of a pistol. Like all events unordered by time or thought it made no sense. He looked up at the building and saw Trumbull leaning out of a broken window and firing down at him. A bullet tore the heel off his shoe and he veered away toward a disused, boarded-up wharf building opposite the garbage disposal plant.

Trumbull disappeared from the broken window as suddenly as he had appeared. A moment later he looked out of the one closer to Slade like a maniacal puppet in a Punch and Judy show. When he shattered the pane with the butt of his gun and snapped off a shot, Slade finally realized what his pursuer had been doing. He crouched along the wharf's wall hoping to minimize Trumbull's target.

When Trumbull leaned out of the next window directly opposite him the detective suddenly reversed direction and headed back toward the river. In his growing confusion he had lost track of Humphries. When he saw him some twenty yards away emerging from the Incinerator Building to cut off that avenue of retreat, he wondered for several seconds who he was and where he had seen him last.

Slade's exhausted body rebelled against further flight. He fell back against the wall of the wharf and watched Humphries slowly advance. A shower of tinkling glass across the way told him that Trumbull, too, had returned to torment him. The temptation to cease resisting was overwhelming. If Humphries had not fired and missed, Slade would have allowed himself to be killed without further struggle.

Shaken awake by the report from Humphries' gun he spun around and frantically ripped away the rotten planks covering a hole in the wall of the wharf. He did not feel the thick splinters burying themselves in the flesh of his palms nor his fingernails tearing away from his fingers. A bullet pounded into the wall near his ear just as he tore away the last board and squeezed inside the building.

Running through the gutted wharf he was perplexed by the odd alternation between dark and light. It was only when he stopped to gasp for air that he understood the hallucinatory sensation was caused by the moonlight streaming through the gaping holes in the corrugated iron roof and splashing the darkness with silver circles.

The rotting floor beneath his feet gave way and he fell heavily. He got to his feet and continued on until he hit another decayed patch of floorboards. This time he slipped through the splintering wood to his waist.

He struggled to wriggle out of the hole then froze as he heard the unmistakable sound of dried boards bending beneath the weight of an approaching person. He bent forward from the waist like a penitent at prayer and remained absolutely still. Some twenty yards away, deep inside the wharf, he saw Humphries advancing through the spotlights cast by the moon, inexorably narrowing the gap between them.

When Humphries was within five yards of him he stiffened suddenly as the sound of vibrating metal reverberated through the wharf. A flock of roosting starlings flew screaming through the gaping holes in the roof of the building.

Blinking the sweat out of his eyes Slade stared ahead. He heard the rumbling metallic noise again and realized that Humphries was treading on a sheet of fallen corrugated-iron roofing.

His bleeding hands snaked forward until he felt the edge of the metal sheet. He clutched it tightly like a drowning man and jerked it toward him.

Humphries' feet shot out from under him and he landed heavily on his back. By the time he regained his feet Slade had extricated himself from the hole in the floor and was whipping the corrugated iron sheet around in a wide slow arc. He caught the glint of reflected light and tried to duck, but a corner of the metal sheet dug into the small of his back. Though stunned he stayed upright and raised his gun.

The edge of the metal sheet on its backswing cut into the side of Humphries' neck like a sword. His gun flew out of his unfeeling hand.

Slade dove for the weapon as it slid across the floor, teetered on the edge of another hole in the rotting boards, then fell through to the water below an instant before his grasping fingers could reach it.

Lying there looking down at the swirling water through the hole in the floor, he heard Trumbull call out, "Humphries, where the hell are you?"

A great weariness settled on Slade. He regretted he had come so close to winning. It seemed unfair that

Coombs' men should mar his victory over Angel. Still, Julian and Angel had not survived him. There was no one to carry out the threats upon his sons. In a fundamental sense he had won after all. Untroubled he let himself down the hole into the frigid water and moaned with shock.

Trumbull, his back against the inner wall of the wharf, moved crabwise down the length of the building peering into the pools of light floating in the larger masses of darkness. His breathing was labored and he could hear the blood coursing through his veins. He tensed. There was the sound of a low gurgling cry which merged with the wind whistling through the scarred and decaying wharf. He saw something move in the shadows. Leveling his weapon at it he went hesitantly forward. The black shape slithered like protoplasm into an illuminated circle on the floor and he saw the agonized face of the dying Humphries.

Trumbull bolted. He ran out of the wharf and up the pier. He ran with his head down. He did not see the bedraggled Slade emerge from the entrance of the Incinerator Building with the Luger he had retrieved from the corpse of Julian. He ran until Slade's voice filtered through his almost paralyzed senses and he spun around, firing blindly at the embodiment of all his terror.

Slade brought the Luger slowly up to his waist and emptied the entire magazine into the madly cavorting Trumbull. Then he walked across the pier and stood over the dead man. Trumbull's large square frame seemed curiously shrunken in death. His left leg lay twisted up under his back and his close, cropped head shone like a bleached skull.

Suddenly Slade heard an engine starting up. He ran

to the street and saw the red Porsche come out of an alley. He closed his eyes against the blinding headlights and when he opened them the car had turned down the street away from him. Behind the wheel, eyes fixed straight ahead and arms stiff, sat Commissioner Frank Talbot.

CHAPTER FIFTY

Talbot fought to keep his eyes open like a traveler on a long night's journey in a stuffy train. The streets flashed by him on both sides and the steering wheel of his sports car vibrated in his hands. Though the rest of his body was cold, his chest burned intensely. He knew the heat was caused by the massive hemorrhaging beneath his rib cage.

The Commissioner left his Porsche at one of the entrances to Shea Stadium and, stiffly erect, his hand inside his coat like a madman with Napoleanic delusions, he walked inside. A policeman, recognizing him, raised his white billy in salute. The capacity crowd roared at the same moment. Talbot had the crazy notion that the policeman's stick, like an ochestra conductor's baton, had brought forth the swelling sound. It was only when Talbot glanced over at the pro football game going on on the brilliantly lit field to his left did he remember where he was and why he was there.

Talbot had just reached the midfield area when Slade spotted the Commissioner's abandoned car, jumped out from his battered station wagon, and charged into the stadium. By then Talbot's teeth were chattering loudly in his head as the numbing cold spread through his limbs. He paused to catch his

breath and continued along until he had reached the
fifty-yard line. For several downs he stood behind a
box of cheering fans. Then he entered the gate of the
box and pushed roughly forward. Row upon row
parted to let him through.

Moses and the Red Sea, Talbot thought giddily.

At last Talbot arrived at the front row. His shining
face was wracked with pain. He could not understand
why the couple in front of him was standing. It
dawned on him that they were on their feet to ap-
plaud a touchdown. He put his hands on their shoulders. Anne and Alan Coombs turned around to see the
grinning Talbot.

Alan Coombs tried to, but Talbot brought him down
from the rear. They stood up. They wrestled for a
moment. There was a muffled report of a gun.

Talbot lunged and locked his arms around the
slumped Coombs. They fell over the railing and floated
to the field below. Several huge, defensive linemen
rushed over from where they were sitting on the bench
and glanced with astonishment at the two men joined
together in death.

Waves of silence spread around the stadium.

Slade, reaching the twenty-five-yard line after the
hush had descended over the crowd, stopped short. He
looked behind him. A television camera swerved
around like a cannon to zoom in on the sideline for
more live coverage.

CHAPTER FIFTY-ONE

Alex Merritt, Sanford Melville, their wives, and a few selected guests crowded around the television set in the book-lined livingroom of Merritt's condominum overlooking the United Nations. The men wore formal evening clothes, the women stylish Parisian gowns. They had been at a richly laden dinner table when their host received a phone call informing him of the unusual developments at the Jets football game.

On the screen the blue of policemen on the green stadium field blocked off the blanketed bodies of Alan Coombs and Frank Talbot from the excited TV cameramen trying to get a shot of them for their viewers.

"Good God, the whole country's going crazy," said Melville's new wife, a beautiful girl with a small, fine figure who felt deeply about what she considered her country's declining role in world affairs.

Merritt nodded politely, then glanced over at her husband who had a disgruntled expression on his handsome face. He leaned across to the attorney and said softly for his ears only, "So what, Sandy? We don't get a new car to drive. We stick with last year's model that's all paid for. Times are tough all over."

CHAPTER FIFTY-TWO

Slade stepped aside to let some incoming policemen by as he walked out of the stadium into the parking lot. The cold air hurt his throat as he took one deep breath after another. Beginning to shiver slightly he approached a chestnut seller hunched over the coals of his brazier. The elderly vendor was huddled up in his army-surplus overcoat like a turtle in his shell. Slade handed him fifty cents and took a bag of nuts from the counter above the burning coals. He warmed his hands on his purchase.

"They're imported," the chestnut seller said.

Slade looked at him blankly.

"All chestnuts are," he explained with a toothless grin that caught the glow of his fire and made him look like a jack-o'-lantern. "America ain't got no chestnut trees no more. A blight wiped them all out in the 20s."

"Oh."

"That's the truth," the chestnut seller insisted gravely.

"I believe you."

The chestnut seller looked pleased at that. "Cold for this time of year," he said.

Slade nodded and walked away. The chestnut seller

yelled after him, "Them scientists say we're in for a new Ice Age." He shuddered at the thought. "As if we didn't have enough trouble in this town."

He found his car in the deserted parking lot. Standing there alone he looked like the last man left alive on earth after a catastrophic war.